T0026362

COWGIRL

Visit us at www.boldstrokesbooks.com

COWGIRL

by

Nance Sparks

2021

COWGIRL

© 2021 By Nance Sparks. All Rights Reserved.

ISBN 13: 978-1-63555-877-7

This Trade Paperback Original Is Published By
Bold Strokes Books, Inc.
P.O. Box 249
Valley Falls, NY 12185

First Edition: May 2021

THIS IS A WORK OF FICTION. NAMES, CHARACTERS, PLACES, AND INCIDENTS ARE THE PRODUCT OF THE AUTHOR'S IMAGINATION OR ARE USED FICTITIOUSLY. ANY RESEMBLANCE TO ACTUAL PERSONS, LIVING OR DEAD, BUSINESS ESTABLISHMENTS, EVENTS, OR LOCALES IS ENTIRELY COINCIDENTAL.

THIS BOOK, OR PARTS THEREOF, MAY NOT BE REPRODUCED IN ANY FORM WITHOUT PERMISSION.

Credits
Editors: Victoria Villasenor and Cindy Cresap
Production Design: Susan Ramundo
Cover Design By Tammy Seidick

Acknowledgments

I'd like to acknowledge all of the hardworking people at Bold Strokes Books who have helped me make my dream a reality. Thank you for taking a chance on me.

CHAPTER ONE

"Aunt Suzie, who lives on that farm across the way?" Carol asked, sitting cross-legged on the front porch swing. The porch looked out over vast green pastureland speckled with trees and edged by the dark Michigan woods on the farthest two sides. The haze of humidity had lifted with the noon sun revealing a large two-story farmhouse centered on the property Carol was curious about. The house seemed almost dwarfed by the even larger red barn looming off a bit in the distance.

"Well, I believe a woman lives there and works that place. Once upon a time, I could have told you her name, but it escapes me just now. She was the talk of the town a few years back," Aunt Suzie said, her words draped in a southern drawl.

"One lady runs that entire spread all by herself?" Carol replied, straining to take in the large working farm. "Does she hire help?"

"None that I've ever seen, and I don't think she even drives a car. She rides a big ol' brown horse everywhere to get what she needs. Sometimes, she hitches up a modified buckboard wagon and takes that to town." Susan chuckled before taking a sip of fresh lemonade.

"Did she always live there? I don't remember seeing anyone riding a horse around town when I used to come out to visit you and Uncle Frank. Who doesn't drive a car besides the Amish? Oh, wait, is she Amish? Man, that would've made a great paper for school, too bad I've already graduated!" Carol rambled on as her thoughts leapt forward.

"No, hon, she isn't Amish, or at least she certainly doesn't dress Amish. Besides, she works the land with a tractor too, so she's definitely not Amish. If I remember correctly, she used to live around here as a kid and then she went away to college, much like you did. She landed some big, fancy job down in Tennessee or Kentucky or something like that. She came back several years later when her sister took ill. I think the father had passed on the summer before or sometime around there. Anyway, the sister died shortly after. I swear, death haunts that land. I'll never understand why she came back at all. After that night, I bet she wished she'd stayed gone forever. There's always been a dark cloud hangin' over that farm."

"A dark cloud? What are you talking about?" Carol sat up taller to get a better look.

"There used to be a lot of drinkin' going on over there. The mother took a liking to the booze. Back then the place was really run-down, probably should have been condemned. Story goes that she and the mother got into a big fight the night of her sister's passin'. The mother ended up stabbed in the neck and bled out. The gal claimed the mother attacked her. Claims that she was tryin' to get away, but the mother's the one who's dead."

"She murdered her own mother?"

"Some say she did. Some say she didn't. Some say she was just trying to help and ended up maimed."

"If it was murder, then she would have been arrested. Was she arrested?"

"Nope. From what I heard, they interviewed her at the hospital and then dropped it. There was no proof one way or another."

"None of you ever went over there to help or to see if she was okay?"

"The place was slowly cleaned up, so we saw no need to interfere." Susan shrugged before taking the last swallow of her lemonade. Pieces of ice clanked against the glass as she lowered her arm back to her lap.

"What if she was telling the truth? Aren't you the least bit curious?"

"Rumors floating around town say that she's a bit off. I see no need in getting caught up in a mess like that."

"But what if she was really trying to get away?"

"What if she wasn't? What if she stabbed her mama right in the neck? Oh, sweet Carol, you're so much like your mother, God rest her soul, always wanting to see the best in people. Sometimes people just are who they are. Come on now, could we forget about that lady? Let's talk about you. What are your plans now that you've earned your master's degree?"

Carol sat back in the swing. She leaned her head back and closed her eyes. She'd rather talk about the lady across the street, or anything else, really. What were her plans? She'd moved out of her college apartment and sold the few tattered pieces of furniture she had to her name. Now, she found herself living out of a suitcase, searching for a job and a place to call home. Her few remaining possessions were neatly packed up in her car.

"I honestly don't know just yet. I always assumed I'd move back home and live somewhere close to Mom and Dad. Now that they're gone, there's really no reason to go back there. My friends from high school have all gone off in separate directions. So, I thought I'd come and visit you and Uncle Frank. Check out the area. See what might be here for me."

"Honey, you know our little town. You've spent a week or two here every summer for most of your childhood."

"I wouldn't call that knowing the town. I know where the ice cream parlor and the penny candy store are because Uncle Frank would take me there when he'd meet the fellas for coffee in the afternoon, but I was thinking of really checking out the area. Maybe I'll find a job here or in a neighboring town so I can be closer to you and Uncle Frank. I also have a friend from college who invited me to join her in Pennsylvania. I guess there's plenty of opportunities for me there. I emailed my résumé for a few positions before I left campus. We'll see what comes of it."

"Pennsylvania? But that's so far away."

"Maybe something will open around here so I can be closer to you two. I'd prefer that since you're the only family I have left."

"Well, we love having you here. Stay as long as you want. I'm so proud of you!" Susan reached over and squeezed her leg. "Your mom, well, both of your parents, would be proud too, God rest their souls. I wish they could have seen you getting your diploma!"

"Me too," Carol said somberly. "Me too, Aunt Suzie. I miss them something awful."

CHAPTER TWO

"Hey, you, cowgirl," Crystal, the teenage cashier, hollered. "Your horse is shittin' in the parking lot again. Ya know you're going to have to clean that up. We can't have people tracking horseshit all through the store. It's bad enough that you bring that flea ridden mutt in here."

All eyes seemed to turn toward Aren, who was wearing her favorite frayed Levi's, old worn western boots, and a faded flannel shirt with the sleeves rolled up to her elbows. A large Anatolian shepherd sat obediently at her side. Aren's weathered Stetson hat was pulled low on her forehead and sunglasses covered her eyes. She shook her head, realizing that she'd forgotten to set her gelding up with the dung bag again. She'd have to make a note for the loft door, "Don't forget about Wyatt's shit!"

"Did you hear me, cowgirl?" Crystal hollered out a bit louder.

"Yeah, yeah, I heard ya. The entire store heard ya. Do you have some cardboard or something? I don't have a shovel. Must've left it in my other saddle."

The other occupants in the small hardware store had stopped their shopping to watch the exchange. Some were smiling at Aren's sense of humor while others appeared a bit nervous.

"You are such a freak. I mean, who rides a horse into town anymore? This isn't the eighteen hundreds. There are motorized vehicles nowadays, ya know! Why don't you drive a car like everyone else?" Crystal asked, just as she often did, and in the same exasperated, all-knowing tone.

Aren gathered up the small assortment of hardware she'd needed to finish the repairs on the barn and headed for the counter. She loathed her trips into town. Luckily, this was her last stop today.

"Did you find everything all right?" Crystal hissed the required question and clearly didn't care about the answer.

"Yeah, and how about that piece of cardboard? That is, unless you've changed your mind about the shit." Aren glanced out the window at her trusty steed.

"That'll be twenty-eight dollars and thirteen cents." Crystal stuffed the items into a plastic sack, set the bag on top of a couple of pieces of cardboard, and held out her hand to accept the cash. "I'll bet you don't even have a checking account."

"Come on now, my money is green. Isn't that all that matters?" Aren handed her a twenty and a ten.

"What about a credit card or debit card? What are you going to do when people no longer accept cash?" she asked.

"When they make plastic our nation's currency, I'll deal with it. In the meantime, I'll just use cash. Thanks for the concern though." Aren tapped her leg. "Let's go, Bailey."

"Hey, Aren," Maggie Hatcher, the store owner, hollered. "Hold up a second, would ya?"

Maggie was in her late sixties, but Aren swore she hadn't aged in the twenty years that she'd known the woman. She stood tall for a woman all of five foot two inches and still looked good in a checkered sleeveless shirt and Wrangler jeans. Maggie kept her graying hair short and tucked behind her ears. The only thing Aren had noticed different over the years was the sparkle in Maggie's eyes had dimmed since the passing of her partner. Cancer had taken Ruby a year prior.

"What's up, Maggie?" Aren asked, eager to leave.

"I'm sorry about Crystal. I'll talk to her. New people have moved into town and don't know the whole story, just the exaggerated tall tales that never seem to go away. She likes making a fuss and being the center of attention."

"It shouldn't matter, Maggie. Explanations shouldn't be needed to be kind. Ya know what, just forget about it." Aren held up her hand. "It's not like she's the first or the last to go runnin' her mouth, and truth is, I'd like to forget about the old days. Maybe she could just try not to gossip."

"How are you holding up out there, anyway?" Maggie asked.

"The farm's great. It's never been the issue." Aren turned to leave, done with the conversation.

Several young boys were circling around Wyatt on their skateboards when Aren pushed open the glass doors. Bailey bristled with the sight and began to growl low in her throat. Wyatt stood statue still with a look of terror in his eyes. One particularly daring boy crouched down and zoomed beneath the large horse's belly on his board. Aren quickly pushed the door open and rushed toward her horse. She could see the gelding's nervousness growing. God damned kids, she thought. Wyatt would kick one, and they'd blame the horse rather than the stupid kid. Bailey trotted along at her side, continuing the deep low growl.

"Hey, get away from him! Didn't your folks teach you any manners? How about a little bit of kindness for one of God's creatures?" She stormed toward them, ready to pluck them off their skateboards.

"Fuck you, creepy hermit lady. Ma says you don't even believe in God!" one of the older boys called out before leading his friends away as they continued to laugh and jeer.

Aren walked up to her gelding's head and stroked the side of his face. She felt such sorrow each time she was around other people anymore. There just seemed to be so much hatred and judgment, so little understanding. "Easy, fella, come on now, let's get you home."

She stowed her purchases in the dusty leather saddlebag just as Crystal popped her head through the open glass door.

"Don't you forget to clean up that shit!"

Aren gritted her teeth and fought to ignore her. She decided that Maggie must have retreated to her office, having said nothing to the young woman. Shaking her head, Aren continued to buckle the clasp on the saddlebag, realizing that no amount of intelligent conversation would change their minds about her anyway. They'd never understand, and she didn't have to explain herself to anyone, even if it might have made things easier. She gathered up the two pieces of cardboard and worked the dung pile onto the larger piece, using the smaller one as a makeshift broom. The weight of the steamy wet dung was almost unmanageable on the flimsy cardboard, but Aren was able to get it balanced with both hands. She walked over to the garbage bin only to find it overflowing. Smiling mischievously, she headed back into the hardware store.

"What in the hell are you doing?" Crystal stepped back as Aren slid the dung covered cardboard onto the counter. The expressions of those standing around the counter contorted at the strong odor.

"The garbage bin was too full, but hey, the parking lot is now completely shit free." Aren managed to get the words out with a straight face. She tipped her hat to the young woman before turning on her heels, leaving the stuttering store clerk with her cardboard present. Aren didn't allow her smile to break free until she was untying Wyatt's reins from the anchored bench. It might have been petty, but she could only take so much before she had to give a little back.

CHAPTER THREE

Wyatt, a gentle four-year-old bay Percheron gelding who stood seventeen hands tall at the tip of the shoulders, was Aren's favorite horse on the property. She had been there for his birth, a tiny light in a very dark time of her life and felt especially close to him. It had taken her some time to stretch the muscles in her legs so that she was able to mount up on any of the draft horses without a step stool. Now, after riding almost daily for the past several years, she could expertly swing herself into the old leather saddle. She was glad that she'd only needed a few small supplies today. It saved her from hitching up the wagon this morning. But poor Bailey had to stay on the long leash until they were out of town instead of being able to copilot in the wagon's front seat. Once she was up in the saddle, Aren directed Wyatt out of the parking lot and began her long journey home.

She always took side streets in and out of town, trying to avoid traffic and the inevitable idiot who thought blowing the car horn directly behind a horse was a brilliant idea. As careful as she was on her journeys through town, she often seemed to encounter at least one horn-blowing fool, though so far today her luck was holding out. Small children reacting to the sight of a horse trotting down the street always made her smile. They'd run up to the edge of the yard and watch with bright, smiling eyes as the "big horsey" passed by.

Just outside the town limits, Aren pulled gently on Wyatt's reins bringing him to a stop. She slid down from the saddle and then released Bailey from her leash so the poor girl could tag along at her own pace. Aren stowed the leash in one of the saddlebags before fixing her left foot into the stirrup and swinging herself back into the saddle. Once again, they were on their way home turning west to cut through an old unused forest service road that eventually led to the back edge of her property. Wyatt's hooves created a relaxing musical rhythm on the hard-packed earth. Aren felt the tension in her shoulders drift away with the blend of soothing sounds. Birds chirped and fluttered above, squirrels chattered and scampered. She drew in a deep breath, then exhaled slowly. In these woods, she could completely relax. She knew what to expect. She felt in control of her surroundings. Aren closed her eyes and tilted her head back. From behind her eyelids, she could still see the faint flickering glare of sun filtering through the canopy of the treetops. In the dense woods, she had memories of happier times, memories of laughter. She felt at peace.

Aren squinted in the brilliant sunshine as they emerged from the dark, thick forest. She guided Wyatt onto a two-track path, lined on either side with pasture fencing, which led them through the property to the back of the barn. Wyatt's pace picked up a bit just beyond the perimeter gate.

"Easy there, fella. The faster you go, the longer we'll have to take to cool you down. Walk easy and the water is all but touching your lips." Aren soothed the large horse but could do nothing to stop Bailey from bolting ahead. She could feel Wyatt's muscles tense up in a yearning to keep pace with the dog, but he followed Aren's request and walked at an easy pace up to the barn.

Within minutes, Wyatt was tied off at the hitching rail, scraping his front hoof against the ground with impatience. His saddle had been removed, as had his bridle, the saddlebags and pad. Aren enjoyed the rides and took most of the distance at an easy walk. It was humidity more than hard work that caused him to sweat so much. She grabbed a currycomb and went to work on combing his wet fur before turning him out to get that much craved drink of water. Knowing him, he'd wade into the pond at least belly deep before dipping his head for a drink. He was goofy that way and his personality continued to tickle Aren's funny bone.

After evening chores, Aren made her way upstairs and tossed the saddle bag on the back of the dining room chair. She released a latch and pulled the large loft door inward. Light poured into the loft and a gentle breeze tickled her skin. She stood in the opening, taking in the brilliant blue sky. Heavy rain clouds loomed far off in the distance. Clouds coming in like this would make for a brilliant sunset. The evening was too beautiful to cook inside, and it seemed like a perfect night for a campfire.

"What do you think of potatoes and steak tonight, eh, Bailey girl?" Aren asked the dog while unwrapping a rib eye steak. Bailey barked twice, which Aren took as an agreement.

"Okay, I'll mix some in your food, but no potato for you. A girl's gotta watch her figure, ya know. You can have some of the cucumber and tomato salad if you want, but tomorrow you're back on your diet," Aren said, laughing as she set the steak on a plate. Bailey barked again and ran down the stairs. She never had company, and some days she longed for it. Longed for a conversation, but then, Bailey never talked back, made her feel bad, or asked questions she couldn't answer. It was for the best this way.

Aren diced up her potato adding a touch of salt and pepper along with a few other spices, then topped it with a tab of butter before sealing the aluminum foil pouch. Next, she cut up a tomato and a cucumber, adding a touch of olive oil to the mixture of vegetables in the bowl. The process of adding a touch of this spice and a dab of that always reminded her of the evenings she spent cooking with her foster mother as a teenager, learning the little touches that made things taste just right. The thought made her melancholy. She'd never have that chance again. Aren shook her head, letting the mental image drift away. She poured herself a large mason jar of cold tea from the refrigerator and gathered it all onto a tray before joining Bailey by the fire pit.

The fire pit sat about ten yards away from the entrance to the barn. She had a couple of logs set on the end for side tables next to her chair. She'd built the circular pit herself from a mix of concrete and rocks. She was proud of her work on it and quickly got it lit. Once the fire was established, Aren lowered the metal cooking grate onto the concrete ring, placing the potato packet off to the side to cook. Before long, she could smell the potatoes and knew it was time to lower the steak onto the heat. The meat instantly sizzled creating a smell that had long strands of drool running from the sides of Bailey's mouth. Aren inhaled deeply and smiled. It wasn't the life she'd once envisioned for herself, but at times like this, it was enough.

"Just a few more minutes girl," Aren said, flipping the steak one last time. "I'm going to run up and get the coffee pot. That steak had better be there when I get back!"

Campfire percolated coffee was one of Aren's favorites. Not much else tasted or smelled so good. Aren took the stairs two at a time and filled the old black percolator with water. She added grounds to the metal basket and assembled the parts before snapping the lid on tightly. Returning to the campfire, she found Bailey inching closer to the steaks.

"Careful not to burn your nose again." Bailey salivated and whined in reply.

Aren set the coffee pot on the hottest edge of the fire before scooping the steak off the flame. She cut a section off for Bailey, scraping the cubed fatty pieces into a bowl of dog food and then set it on the ground next to her chair. She fixed her plate with the fire-roasted potatoes and her salad. Just as she pierced a tomato chunk with her fork, Bailey began a deep-throated growl. The sky had darkened to a starless night. Heavy storm clouds were rolling in.

Chapter Four

Carol inhaled deeply. Two of her favorite scents teased her, campfire and coffee. She'd left her aunt and uncle's house about an hour earlier, craving an after dinner walk to help digest the heavily fried meal. She inhaled again, turning her head to find the source. She looked left and right but saw nothing. Then, just as she stepped past the dark, shadowy farmhouse on her left, she caught sight of an orange flicker off in the distance. Carol stopped mid stride in the center of the road. A silhouetted figure sat next to a campfire, talking to someone that Carol couldn't see. She waited for a reply, yet heard nothing. Carol squinted, trying to find a second person. She caught movement next to the silhouetted figure. What was that? A dog? Was that laughter she heard? *There's a dark cloud hangin' over that farm.* Carol could hear her aunt's voice in her head. She hadn't been able to shake the conversation with her aunt about this farm or its owner. Consumed with curiosity, she ducked between strands of barbed wire and made her way toward the fire light. She'd walked about half the distance when the silhouetted figure spun around.

"Who's out there? Make yourself known or I'll release the dog."

Carol froze in her tracks. She squeezed her eyes shut, chastising herself for trespassing onto this woman's property. What had she been thinking? She allowed her breath to escape and then drew in another before trusting her voice.

"My name is Carol Matthews. I'm here visiting my aunt who lives just across the way. I saw the fire while I was out taking a walk and thought I'd say hello."

"Would you come on up here to the light, Carol Matthews? I'd like to see who I'm talking to."

Carol's heart was pounding in her chest with such force she felt deafened by it. She put one foot in front of the other, cautiously making her way toward the stranger next to the fire. She looked around, taking in how large the shepherd type dog was, especially given that it was baring its teeth and growling at her. She felt every bit the fool for coming here. She froze, her breath catching, when the woman suddenly snapped her fingers and made a hand signal to the dog. Great, she would be mauled to death and no one knew where she was. Instinctively, her eyes squeezed shut, though she forced them to reopen when nothing happened. There was no movement, no dog lunging for her throat, nothing at all. Carol allowed the trapped air to escape when she saw the dog eating from a bowl on the ground.

The woman smiled at Carol, half of her face hidden in the shadows, half lit by the fire light.

"Hi, Carol. My name is Aren Jacobs and this is my dog, Bailey." Aren extended her hand in greeting.

Carol took one step forward, closing the distance needed to shake Aren's hand. She noticed, by touch more than sight, how rough and calloused her hands were.

"We're just sitting down to dinner. Would you like anything?" Aren motioned toward the plate of food.

"I've already eaten, thank you. I should go, allow you to eat in peace."

"Sit if you like, enjoy the fire. You're welcome to this chair if you prefer it over a log. I'm sorry I only have the one out. I don't get many visitors."

"Please don't give up your chair. A log is fine. I don't want to be any trouble."

"Well then, the log is all yours. Would you like a cup of coffee?"

Carol inhaled. She had to admit the coffee smelled wonderful, "I would love a cup, but I will only accept it after you've finished your meal. Please, eat. It was rude of me to intrude."

"Fair enough. So, you're visiting your aunt and uncle?" Aren picked up her fork. She scooped a few potato pieces onto the tines before popping them into her mouth.

Carol turned her attention to the flames dancing in the firepit. She heard the pop of the hot sap trapped in the log and then watched the released sparks as they floated up into the air. Suddenly, she realized she'd been asked a question. "Sorry, yes, visiting. I arrived a couple of days ago."

Aren nodded, chewing on another bite of her meal. She set down her fork. "The coffee is done. Why don't I get you a cup so I don't feel like I'm eating in front of you? The cups are just upstairs. It would only take a second."

"The coffee does smell amazing." Carol smiled.

Aren lifted herself from the chair. She was much taller than Carol had expected. She seemed so nice. Much too nice to be a murderer. The fire cracked and popped again, pulling Carol's attention back to the floating orange embers.

"Do you take anything in it?" Aren turned to ask.

"Yes, both cream and sugar, if it's no trouble. Thank you," Carol answered before she looked up. When their eyes met, Carol's breath caught in her throat. Aren's face was now completely lit by the fire light. Scars surrounded Aren's left eye, and the eye itself didn't look quite right either, though it was difficult to distinguish why in the dim light. Carol did her best to control her breathing and stifle her shock.

Aren nodded, turning back toward the barn. The large dog, Bailey, was right at her side. Her back was now illuminated by the firelight. Carol was working hard to gather her composure when she caught sight of a large wood handled knife secured on Aren's belt. *Who carries a knife around?* Carol's heart pounded. *What if she stabbed her mama right in the neck?* Carol heard her aunt's voice in her head again. She remained statue still, waiting for Aren to disappear into the barn before she bolted back to the fence line. She tripped on something in the grass and fell to her knees. She blinked a couple of times so her eyes could adjust to the darkness and then shot for the fence line. Carol ran all the way back to the safety of her aunt's house.

CHAPTER FIVE

At three o'clock in the morning, Aren forced herself out of bed, giving up on the hope of any decent sleep. Her dreams were relentlessly filled with demons from her childhood. Sitting on the edge of her bed, she wondered what had brought this round on. Surely talking with Maggie for that quick minute couldn't have been enough to trigger all of this. All she knew for sure were that her demons were screaming, demanding her attention.

Aren flipped on the lamp and stumbled into the kitchen hoping coffee would help. She picked up the coffee pot from the tray she'd carried up a few hours earlier and made her way over to the kitchen sink. Twenty minutes later, the Coleman stove was fired up and the coffee was cooking.

With a steaming mug in her hand, she walked to the loft door. In the evenings, she'd fasten large screen panels over the open doors which allowed a light breeze to flow in without the mosquitoes. Though the insects would still be out in full force, she removed one of the screen panels and sat on the ledge of the open doorway. The storm had intensified, throwing bolts of lightning across the sky followed almost instantly by loud claps of thunder. Lightning highlighted the huge raindrops falling over the landscape. Clad in only cotton shorts and a tank top, Aren was grateful for the deep overhang that kept her dry.

A downstairs light flipped on and then flipped back off a few minutes later in the house across the way. The house, she assumed, where Carol Matthews was staying with her family. Aren took another long sip of her steaming coffee and wondered what had spooked the young woman. Well, she guessed Carol was young. Her skin was fair and wrinkle free, at least by firelight. Aren thought of her own reflection and chuckled to herself as Bailey nudged her and curled up at her side.

"Not everyone weathers life quite as hard as I do, eh, girl. Look at me. I'd guess I was already in my mid-fifties instead of thirty-five, especially with these wicked scars!" Aren ruffled the dog's fur.

Suddenly, a blinding flash of light lit the landscape, simultaneous with a ground shuddering boom. The barn shook and rattled, almost jarring Aren from her perch. A loud series of cracks and pops pulled her attention back across the country road. She could faintly see an orange glow and smoke rising from the silhouette of a tall, old maple tree. Another bolt of lightning lit the sky, illuminating a frightening sight. The old maple tree had been split by the lightning, and half of the mammoth tree had crushed the house where she'd just guessed Carol Matthews was staying. The second story had splintered beneath the weight and momentum of the tree's collision. Boards stuck out at all angles through the tree's limbs and leaves like a monster from a nightmare.

Aren jumped up and ran for her jeans and boots. She stuck her knife into the back of her jeans out of habit more than need and ran for the stairs. At the base of the stairs, she grabbed a headlamp she used in the wintertime. She pulled the gadget onto her head and clicked on the lamp, then grabbed a large coil of rope before she bolted across the field and through the pounding rain.

Electrical pops and lumber creaks were all that she heard coming from the crumpled dwelling. Aren had never been inside the house and had no idea as to where to start looking for those who may be trapped.

"Can anybody hear me?" Aren yelled out, trying to be heard over the storm. She listened intently but couldn't hear anything.

"Hello, can anybody hear me?" she screamed again, stepping over debris to look into each window she passed.

"Over here. Please, please help me," a voice called out from the rubble.

"Keep talking so I can find you." Aren looked for a way to access the house. "Are you upstairs or down?"

"Downstairs, in the front, by the road, by the window." The voice was clear and scared.

Aren ran over to the sound of the voice. An arm reached out of a shattered window, and the frame creaked beneath the shifting weight above. Aren poked her face into the unstable opening and saw Carol buried under wood and drywall from the ceiling.

"Are you hurt?" Aren asked.

"My leg is stuck. I—I don't know what's got me pinned." Tears streaked the dirt on Carol's cheeks.

Aren twisted, taking in the mangled room. There wasn't any other way to help Carol beyond getting her through the window. Aren pulled her knife from the waistband of her jeans. She heard Carol gasp at the sight of the eight-inch knife but ignored it. She turned the knife around in her hand, clutching it by the sheath covered blade and poked the handle at the ragged shards of glass that stuck up from the frame, making them fall but careful not to send them toward Carol, who shielded her face anyway. Satisfied that she'd removed most of the larger pieces of glass, Aren grabbed a crumpled, wet pillow near the opening and laid it across the frame. She leaned in through the opening even farther, trying to see what was pinning Carol's leg. A beam from the ceiling had broken free on one end and hung diagonally across the room. Part of the beam crossed the bed with Carol's leg pinned beneath. If she could get in there and shift the bed just a bit, perhaps she could free Carol's leg without dropping the rest of the ceiling on them.

"Can you lean back a bit? I'm going to have to climb in there with you," Aren asked.

"I think so," Carol said, trying to push herself away from the opening.

Aren wiggled in through the window frame and carefully made her way to the edge of the bed. She looked more closely at the angle of Carol's leg. Deciding it was likely broken and she was going to have to pull Carol from the building, Aren tried to force the beam up using her shoulder, but it wouldn't budge. She felt around Carol's leg and realized how soft the mattress was. If she pushed down on the mattress, maybe Carol could pull her leg free. She explained her idea to Carol, who agreed to try. Aren wiped the rain from her face with her forearm and pressed down on the bed with all the force she could muster. Carol screamed out in pain. Wrapping her hand around Carol's ankle, Aren wiggled and pushed until the leg was free of the beam.

"I think we got it!" she said. "Do you think you can pull yourself onto the windowsill?"

"I don't know, oh God, it hurts so bad!" Carol sobbed.

If she hadn't thought the house might come down any second, she would have stopped to call for help, but between the driving rain and the smoke and flames still rising eerily from the tree, she knew there wasn't time. She had to get Carol, and anyone else she could find, out of there fast. Aren climbed back out through the window, then reached back in and wrapped her wet arms around Carol and pulled. Carol screamed as her leg turned. The sound gave Aren a queasy sensation in her stomach that she forced herself to suppress. She kept pulling until she could shift to the side and scoop Carol over the windowsill and into her arms. Aren walked her over to the soft grass and gently set her down. She smoothed back the hair in Carol's pain filled eyes just before they fluttered shut and she passed out. Rain quickly soaked the nightgown Carol was wearing and Aren wished she'd brought a blanket of some kind.

"You'll be okay now. I'll get you some help, okay?" Aren looked back at the house and had no idea where to begin searching for anyone else.

Headlights crested the hill coming up the road. Aren could hear the engine roaring toward them. She ran out to flag the person down.

"Hey, we saw the bolt of lightning and had to see if everyone's okay," a young guy said as he pulled up.

"Do you have a cell phone on you? I believe two more are trapped inside. We need to call nine-one-one." Aren swiped at the rain. "I got one person out, and she's hurt."

"Yeah, sure." He picked up his phone and reported the emergency. "Holy shit!" He shook his head at the sight of the house in his headlights. "I'll walk around the back and yell, see if anyone else shouts." He took off into the rain.

Aren ran back over to Carol's side. She found her awake and shivering. She was likely going into shock. The rain began to come down in relentless sheets. Lightning shot across the sky followed by another thunderous boom. Carol screamed and cowered and sobbed, her hands over her face. Aren ran over to the open window and crawled back inside. She dug around for a blanket or something to cover Carol up with. Aren found a quilt folded up on the floor. She grabbed it and then climbed back out of the window and ran back to Carol. She draped the quilt over her shivering body, not that it would do much good as it too would be soaked through in seconds.

"Carol, help is on the way. Stay with me, okay?" Aren looked into the wide eyes that stared up at her.

"Okay." She shivered so hard her teeth rattled. "What about Aunt Suzie and Uncle Frank?"

"Where was their bedroom? We'll go look for them," Aren said.

"Upstairs, the other end of the house." Carol looked over Aren's shoulder at the remains of the house.

Aren turned around and a flash of lightning lit up the landscape once again. From where she stood, it didn't appear that anything was left of the second story. It looked as though the level below had absorbed its mass. Branches full of leaves jetted out in every direction. The foliage was so dense that it was hard to imagine anything surviving beneath the weight. The flames had gone out, but the blackened tree continued to send steam into the storm.

Red and blue flashing lights caught her attention and the sirens sounded out a few seconds later. She could breathe again, now that she wasn't on her own. Aren ran out to greet the fire trucks and ambulances as they pulled up.

"Lightning struck the tree. I believe two more are trapped inside. They were on the second level at the far end of the house. Another guy stopped to help and he's back there looking for them," Aren informed the lead man of the crew. He bellowed out instructions and the group of firefighters went to work. Aren then ran over to the medics, leading them to Carol. "I believe she has a broken leg. I didn't see any other injuries."

"Did you extract her from the dwelling?" one of the medics asked.

"Yes, I did. The house was creaking, and I didn't dare risk it collapsing in on her." Aren pushed her hair out of her eyes and glared at him through the rain.

"Did you use anything as a back board or neck brace?" he asked.

"No, I just got her out. Look, the ceiling was ready to go! I got her out of there. Nothing seemed injured except her leg." Aren wasn't going to be blamed for hurting someone she'd tried to save. Not again.

"Next time let us do our job instead of trying to be a hero." He turned away to focus on Carol. "We'll need to transport her," he said to his colleague while shifting Carol onto a backboard.

Aren gathered up her rope and let the medics do what they needed to do. Hell, maybe she had been wrong to pull Carol out of the window. Shortly after she crossed the dirt road heading back toward her barn, she saw the ambulance take off and found herself praying she hadn't hurt Carol by moving her. If she hadn't been awake and watching the storm, she might not have gotten there in time to help her. It might come back to bite her on the ass, but she wouldn't regret saving someone.

She made it back inside, cold and fatigue mixing with an adrenaline crash, and she let a hot shower calm her. Once she was dry and warm again, she sat in the open loft door and watched the blue and red lights strobe through the rain as emergency vehicles came and went from the farm. By dawn, it was silent and empty, a husk of memories left broken under a clearing sky.

CHAPTER SIX

A couple of days after the storm, the sunshine returned along with sizzling July heat and humidity. Aren, clad in knee high rubber boots, jeans, and a tank top, trudged through the ankle-deep mud in the garden picking produce for the farmer's market later that day. Though it was only eight in the morning, she found herself soaked with sweat. Several times she'd twist with an armload of produce to set on the cart only to lose her balance due to the suction of the mud. Her arms would flail about, produce flying every which way, before she could regain her footing and set about the task of collecting everything she'd tossed. A few hours later and a few more close calls of a face-plant in the mud, she'd picked all that was ripe and climbed up into the driver's seat of the wagon. It was a lot of work, but hopefully she'd be able to sell most of it, and she definitely didn't want to let it rot in the field.

"Walk on, big fella," Aren said, releasing the brake on the wagon. Wyatt pulled the load easily through the muck. Once the wagon was up on the well-packed trail, they headed to the back of the barn where a hose and a worktable were all set up beneath a shady overhang.

"Whoa, whoa there, fella," Aren called to Wyatt, who stopped with the slightest touch on the reins. Aren locked the brake on the wagon before climbing down and pulling off Wyatt's headstall. She gathered up a couple of flakes of hay and a five-gallon bucket for water so Wyatt could eat while she prepped the wagon for a day at the market.

Whistling softly, Aren cleaned vegetables and arranged them by type into stackable wooden crates. Today's harvest was good, she thought to herself as she filled the back of the wagon to the limit.

"If everything sells today, Bailey girl, we should do pretty well this winter!"

Bailey simply cocked her head in reply and let out a single bark.

When she finished cleaning the vegetables, she threw the scraps to the pigs. Aren believed they looked forward to each market day because of their excited squeals at the sight of the bucket. She patted their heads and let them relish in the fresh treats. With that task completed, she ran upstairs and changed into clean clothes and her western boots before donning her Stetson hat and sunglasses once again. Aren grabbed the change box on her way back down the stairs and whistled for Bailey.

"Let's go, girl! We've only got three hours before the market opens and a long ride ahead of us." She slid the big barn doors closed, locking a padlock at each entrance. No one ever came out here, but old habits were hard to break.

Wyatt had long ago finished his hay and was scraping his hoof to go when Aren slid his bit into his mouth. She fastened the chinstrap and adjusted the blinders before climbing up into the wagon.

"Walk on, big fella." The wagon lurched forward and their journey was underway. Bailey ran across the pasture, jumping the four-foot fence to catch up to the wagon. One final leap had her sitting co-pilot, panting from the exertion. Aren reached over and ruffled her best friend's fur.

The route Aren took while riding was different from the one she had to take when Wyatt was pulling the wagon. The forest was too thick to cut that wide of a path for such a long distance. She'd miss the serenity that the forest ride always brought with it, although the route with the wagon took her close to the house damaged in the storm. Maybe she'd see movement and could find out how the family was doing. The night was still so fresh in Aren's mind. She could close her eyes and see the pain on Carol's face, hear the pain in her screams. Aren directed Wyatt out to the main gate at the road, and then guided him to the right heading toward town. The ride for the first several miles was pleasant enough along the well-maintained dirt roads. Aren caught herself whistling and looking forward to a day at the market. The people who shopped at the farmer's markets just seemed so much nicer than those shopping around town. The customers had long ago gotten used to the "cowgirl," as many called her, with the horse drawn wagon full of fresh veggies. The kids looked forward to seeing Wyatt and were never abusive toward him. The cash she brought in from sales enabled her to maintain her property taxes and buy items for the farm. It worked out well, and she even managed to stash away a bit for savings.

The farmer's market was in the parking lot of the feed store, two miles outside of town. Though the last few miles of her journey were on the shoulder of a paved road, the drivers seemed a bit more thoughtful than those in the heart of town. She still had the occasional idiot who honked as they passed, but it was rare. An hour and a half after they left the house, Aren directed Wyatt into the parking lot and found a spot to set up her booth.

She pulled three eight-foot folding tables from the back of the wagon and set them up with red checkered tablecloths to display her vegetables. Soon, all the tables were stocked full with wooden crates overflowing with fresh greens, tomatoes and other types of summer crops. She was proud of her haul and the work she'd put into making it happen, and at moments like this she was glad she'd stayed on the farm, even with all the baggage it brought with it.

All of the farmers who participated in the market, including the chicken lady who brought baby chickens and turkeys to sell, were friendly and sociable with her at the market. Aren had noticed, however, that she wasn't included in their social circuit outside of the market. She'd overheard invites being tossed around for weekend barbeques and holiday parties, and none were extended to her. She tried to brush it off and just enjoy the market for the little bit of social outlet that it offered her. She couldn't hope for more, and at least she had this.

"Hey, cowgirl, those veggies look terrific as usual." Tony, the compost and earthworm guy, smiled from across the aisle.

"Hey, Tony, it's all due to your magnificent worms!" Aren smiled when Tony puffed out his chest with pride.

"Twenty minutes until the market opens. Finish up your displays," the market manager announced to the group.

Aren took the time to browse the other tables. She stopped at Samantha Collins's table and smelled a few bars of her goat milk soap. Martie Andrews had fresh cheese and milk from her dairy cows, though Aren rarely purchased anything from her, since she had her own dairy cows. Ol' Joe Biddle had a beautiful display of heirloom organic corn and herbs. The chicken lady, Marie Hawthorne, had several pens full of day-old fowl. Aren spent a lot of time at her table. She loved to hear the baby turkey poults peep.

"Hey, Marie, I see you're adding waterfowl to your list." Aren picked up a solid black duckling. The fluffy baby nuzzled down into Aren's warm hands and closed its eyes.

"Yeah, I couldn't resist. I've had so many requests for ducks and geese that I had to add them. Now, if I can just get the pens finished so I can move the breeders out of the bronze turkey hutch." She laughed.

"I hear you there. Never a lack of projects. The chickens I purchased from you are starting to lay eggs. It's like a rainbow of colors, from dark brown eggs to bright green."

"I'm glad to hear that. I've had to buy another incubator to keep up with sales. What is it they say, expansion is a good problem to have?"

"Definitely a good problem to have. Well, I may not be able to resist these little guys much longer so I should probably mosey on down the line before market opens." Aren laughed, handing Marie the sleeping duckling.

As she walked down the row, Aren could hear the little duckling calling out for the warmth of her hands. She almost turned around and bought a few when the market manager announced open market.

She spent the next few hours making change and filling bags with fresh produce. She had pleasant chats with customers and even some laughs, and her heart lightened with the interaction. During lulls she'd refill the crates on the table and stack the empties into the back of the wagon. Since the market lasted for four hours, she always unhitched Wyatt and put him in a small corral that the feed store kept up as a display. They knew Wyatt would be there each week and always had a water trough set up, filled to the rim with refreshing, clear water. Kids, eager to pet the big horse, always begged their mom to buy carrots so they could swing by and say hello to him. Aren still kept her eye on him throughout the day, but he was good with the kids and probably liked the attention as much as she did.

All too soon, the market closed at seven o'clock sharp. Aren was thrilled to see she'd virtually sold out. There were a few small bunches of lettuce left and a couple of cucumbers, but the rest of the crates were surprisingly sparse. She broke down her booth, offering the leftover items to Marie for her poultry before heading over to the market director and paying her market fee of ten percent. She then slid the tables into place and stacked the remaining few crates into their space as well. Bailey yawned broadly and stretched with deliberate slowness when she was urged out of the back of the wagon for the final few items.

Aren collected Wyatt, waving good-bye to those who were finished breaking down as they passed by in their trucks. Once again, she heard them talking about meeting up at some restaurant or other, and she pushed aside the pang of loneliness. It had been a good day, and as she headed for home, she let that be the feeling she focused on.

CHAPTER SEVEN

The sun was still well above the horizon when Wyatt pulled up to the gate. Aren looked over to the house with the section of tree still tangled in the remains of the second story, but there was still no movement over there. She hoped everyone had been rescued and were recovering together. Aren shook her head to let the thoughts go as she climbed down from the wagon to get the gate. It wasn't any of her business. She'd done what she could. Running a farm on her own meant she didn't have time to sit around thinking. There were a lot of chores to do before the sun went down. She unhooked Wyatt from the wagon and got moving. As she rounded the front corner of the barn, she found Bailey lying on her back enjoying a tummy rub from Carol Matthews, who was propped up against the barn beside Bailey.

"Hey. I was just thinking about you. How's the leg?" Aren asked, shifting the load in her arms so that she could retrieve the key from her pocket.

"Broken, just like you'd said, but it should heal up in six to eight weeks. Luckily, it was a clean break. I'll get a walking cast at some point which will be nice. I'd offer to help you with that, but once I get the crutches under me, well, let's just say my balance isn't that good yet." Carol's smile was soft and sad.

Aren finally managed to pull the key from her front pocket and unlocked the barn door. She set the harness and change box in the tack room and quickly returned to her guest.

Carol looked at the ground. "I don't mean to interrupt your evening. I just wanted to thank you for pulling me out. I guess the ceiling in my room collapsed shortly after you walked away. They said that they likely wouldn't have gotten me out in time. I don't think they expected me to overhear their conversation."

"I'm glad you're okay. I took off because I was just in the way. That medic chewed me a good one for moving you. I must admit though, he was right. I could have really hurt you by not bracing your neck or back. Truth be told, I didn't even think of it. I could hear all the creaking and popping, and I just thought you needed to be out of that room." Aren looked at the thick plaster on Carol's leg and remembered the sound of her scream. It wasn't a night she was going to forget any time soon. "How are your aunt and uncle?"

After an awkward pause, Carol took a deep breath. "Aunt Suzie and Uncle Frank didn't make it. The main part of the tree collapsed the roof on them. They said that it was instantaneous, that they didn't feel anything. They said that they were still in bed together, that they died while snuggled up sleeping." Tears streamed down her cheeks.

"I'm so sorry." Aren couldn't think of a single thing to say that didn't sound trite. She was familiar with loss and her heart ached for Carol.

"Aunt Suzie always said, 'When the Lord comes a callin', there's no choice but to go home to Him.' I guess they're home with Him now. They're up in Heaven with my parents." Carol took a long, shaky breath and wiped at her tears.

Aren sat on the ground across from Carol. She wasn't sure what to do to comfort her. "Do you have any other family?"

"No, Aunt Suzie and Uncle Frank, they never had any children, and I was an only child. My parents were killed in a car accident a couple of years ago." Carol poked at the ground with a small stick.

One of the cows bellowed out a long, agonizing moo. Carol sat up, clearly startled.

"It's just the dairy cows. I'm behind on chores and they want to be milked." Aren smiled, still feeling awkward about not knowing what to say.

"Well, I should let you get to that. I just wanted to say thank you. Could I use your phone to call for a car? I lost my cell phone in the storm and haven't had a chance to replace it yet," Carol said, attempting to stand. Aren stood first and extended her hand.

"I don't have a phone," Aren said quietly, then continued as she helped pull Carol to her feet, "What are your plans now?"

"What do you mean you don't have a phone? Everyone has at least one phone," Carol said.

"Not me, so I guess not everyone."

"So, I'm stranded out here? Now what do I do?" Carol covered her face with her hands.

"Not stranded, well yeah, maybe stranded. It's too late for me to be on the roads tonight, but I can take you anywhere you need to go tomorrow. Do you have a place to stay in town?"

"Nothing lined up yet. I'm hoping they have a hotel in town that will take an IOU until I can get to my purse. Everything I have is buried in that room. A volunteer from the hospital dropped me off less than an hour ago. I was hoping I could reach in and get to stuff, but I can't reach anything, and believe me, I tried, cast and all. Luckily, I was able to add these clothes from the gift shop onto my hospital bill. I don't even know if my car survived the storm, or if it was smashed up too, I never made it over to that side of the house." Carol broke into tears again.

"Look, I don't know what made you take off the other night when you stopped by, but you're welcome to stay here as long as you need. I can open the house tomorrow and you can stay there if you like." Aren swallowed against the sense of panic that came with the offer. It was the right thing to do, but she hadn't had anyone around in a long time.

"Where do you live if not in the house?" Carol's face twisted in a look of confusion.

Aren pointed at the barn. "I live above the animals, up there, in the loft. It'll be interesting getting you up there for the night, but, like I said, tomorrow I can work on getting the power and water turned back on if staying over there would make you more comfortable. Hey, and look, no tall trees close by."

Carol forced a tiny smile before accepting the offer. Her eyes still brimmed with tears that threatened to spill over. Her chin quivered in an attempt to maintain control. Aren simply smiled with understanding, still unsure how to comfort her.

"I'm sorry I didn't stay for coffee that night. You were so kind to offer, so kind to share your evening and the campfire. I'm embarrassed for my behavior, taking off like that." Carol shrugged slightly. "My aunt had me a little off balance that night and when I saw your knife, I sort of freaked out."

The cows bellowed out again, this time in unison. Aren had an idea what Carol's aunt might have shared that had her nervous and she tried to stifle a sigh. She was glad that Carol came back by despite the rumors.

"Come on, let's find you a chair to sit in so I can get these cows to stop their belly aching. Then I'll take you up to the loft."

Carol sat with her leg propped up and watched with a curious expression as Aren milked the two cows.

"Doesn't that hurt them?" she asked.

"It'd hurt them if I didn't do it." Aren laughed. "The milk is produced regardless of how full they become. Eventually, their body would stop the production, but not before their udders would be filled to a painfully tight capacity."

"It just looks like that would hurt. Isn't there a machine that does that? I saw it on some 'Got Milk' ad somewhere. What on earth do you do with all that milk?"

Aren dropped into the usual rhythm.

"Yes, there is a machine, but I prefer to milk them by hand. It takes longer to clean the machine after each milking than it does just to do it this way. Some of the milk is used to feed other animals here, and some I get to use for cheese, butter, and to drink." Aren wondered if it made her sound like some kind of crazy backwoods person, but Carol looked interested rather than judgmental.

Carol continued to rattle off questions, often quicker than Aren could answer. After the cows were milked, Carol watched the rest of the feed chore ritual. More questions were shot off at a rapid-fire pace, and Aren tried her best to answer them all. She realized after a while that maybe this was Carol's way of not having to think about the heap of lumber across the street or the two lives it had claimed.

CHAPTER EIGHT

O kay, now you're going to have to hop. I'll stay on your good side. You grab a hold of the rail over there. You can use it as a crutch. We'll take this one step at a time."

Carol's leg was already throbbing. The large plaster cast was heavy and difficult to suspend in the air. It had been a long day and she was exhausted, both physically and mentally.

"I'm too much trouble. Honestly, if I could just call a cab and go to a hotel."

"You could call a cab, if I had a phone. You could go to a hotel, if you had your ID and money. But you don't and you're here. I'll take you anywhere you want to go tomorrow. I'll get you a hotel room tomorrow if that's what you want, but it's already too dark outside to do anything tonight. Now come on, one, two, three, hop," Aren said, helping Carol up the first step.

Carol's muscles were weak from supporting the heavy cast, affording her little control of her leg. The momentum of the hop swung the cast forward, smacking her toes into the back of the wood step. She cried out loudly, pain shooting up and down her leg.

"Okay, enough of this. Put your right arm around my shoulders."

"What are you going to—holy shit!" Carol felt her feet leave the ground. The next thing she knew, she was cradled in Aren's arms. Too tired to protest, Carol held on and rested her head against Aren's neck.

"I carried you once. I can certainly do it again."

Carol felt helpless, yet oddly safe in Aren's arms. Her back to the risers, Carol watched stair treads appear below as they ascended to the top. Aren gently set Carol back onto her good leg and handed her the crutches that she'd propped next to the railing. The loft was dark and somewhat eerie to Carol.

"Hang on, I'll switch on a light so you don't trip in the main aisle," Aren said before disappearing into the shadows.

Carol inhaled deeply, "It smells like grass, fresh cut grass." Lights clicked on, illuminating the vast space. "You sleep in the hay?"

"Nah, it's impossible to get out of my hair. Come on through here. My home is in the back." Aren guided her into the living area.

Carol looked around the loft. Neatly stacked hay lined each sidewall for about two thirds of the length of the loft. Bridles hung on hooks by the stairway, as did rope and other supplies that would be needed on a farm. The thought of Aren living up here confused her.

"You mean to tell me that you own this entire farm and you live up here, like a hired farmhand?" Carol continued to look around the space.

"Hey now, be nice to the hostess. Carol, welcome to my home. I like it up here. What do I need with a big ol' house like that to keep up? Besides, I like the hay and the loft doors and the openness."

"What are those, bear rugs?" Carol asked. She stood next to Aren, taking in the space.

"They're steer hides that I've tanned over the years. It helps to keep the draft out in the wintertime and the heat at bay in the summer," Aren answered. "Do you eat meat?"

"Yeah, I do as long as we don't have to kill it first."

Aren chuckled, pulling bowls off a shelf. But Carol noticed that Aren didn't say she *didn't* have to kill her own food.

"Can I help with anything?"

"You can sit down at the table and prop up that leg. I threw together a stew this morning so I wouldn't have to cook tonight, given that it's market day and all. I have some crackers and butter we can have with it."

Aren placed two bowls of stew on the table. Carol watched Aren rummage through the shelves in the kitchen area for the box of crackers.

"Well, I thought I had crackers around here somewhere." She sighed.

"The stew is perfect. Please, sit down and eat. I feel bad invading your space like this."

"How about something to drink? I have iced tea, water, and fresh milk," Aren said, pulling two glasses off a shelf.

"I've never had fresh milk. What's it taste like?" Carol asked, genuinely curious.

Aren stood there with a perplexed look on her face. "Well, I guess it tastes like store milk, only fresher. I'll pour you a glass and if you don't like it I can get you something else. How's that?"

"Okay," she answered sheepishly. "Aren, listen, I'm sorry to be such a pain, but—" Carol began.

"Carol, please stop apologizing. I don't do anything that I don't want to do, believe me. I wouldn't have made the offer if I hadn't meant to. I'm glad you came by. I was wondering what happened to all of you just this evening when I pulled in the driveway—"

Carol held her hand up in a stop gesture.

"What?"

"I just needed to know where the bathroom is. I have to, you know, pee," Carol said, her face heating with embarrassment.

The statement brought an eruption of laughter from Aren.

"Don't make me laugh. I do *really* have to go." Carol dropped her crutch on the floor while attempting to stand.

Aren ran from the back side of the kitchen counter to assist. She picked the fallen crutch off the floor, then held the crutches out for Carol. Aren guided her toward the bathroom. Carol was surprised by how attentive Aren was. Surely this wasn't the demeanor of a killer?

"I was tempted to tell you that the outhouse was downstairs and out the back of the barn," Aren said between giggling fits.

Carol began to giggle too, all the while hopping furiously to the bathroom. She darted behind the door, closing it quickly behind her. The crutch caught on a small rug in front of the sink, falling to the floor with a loud thud. Carol caught her balance using the sink for support.

"You almost had to loan me dry clothes, but lucky for you, I made it!"

Aren was still smiling when Carol opened the bathroom door. She had a nice smile, kind and open. Carol stumbled a bit with the crutch while making her way back to the table. She felt strong hands support her before she could completely lose her balance.

Once they were finished eating and the dishes were washed, Aren pulled a camp stove from somewhere beneath the counter. She lit the burner, then set a camping coffee pot on top of the flame. The moment it started percolating, Carol inhaled deeply. She loved the smell of coffee brewing.

"No coffee in the hospital?"

Carol opened her eyes and looked up. "Oh, they said they had coffee, but I tell you, it was the most deplorable tasting stuff I've ever had to endure, and only decaffeinated at that!" The simple surface conversation helped relax her shoulders a little. She didn't want to keep thinking about what a mess life had become seemingly overnight.

"Well, maybe you'll stick around for a cup this time. I'll try to keep my knife out of sight." Aren smiled, pulling out small containers for fresh cream and sugar.

Carol took a moment to look around the loft. "It stays surprisingly cool up here, considering the fact that heat rises, and it was hot today."

"They had this loft packed with bales of straw when I moved back. It had to be cleared out so I could store hay up here for the winter months. So, I separated the flakes and insulated the walls and ceiling both downstairs and up here. It took forever to finish the job. At the time it was for the animals, but it's worked out well for me too." Aren chatted freely, handing Carol a steaming mug of coffee.

After a sip of the steaming brew, Carol closed her eyes and smiled. "Ahh, now that's a cup of coffee. I do believe that you're the first person I've met who likes it as strong as I do."

Aren smiled. "I'm glad you're enjoying it."

A few moments of silence passed as they sipped their hot coffee. Carol looked through the open loft door out into the void of the night. The moon was high in the sky giving shadowy life to the landscape below. A tree caught her attention. Something didn't look quite right. Was it growing sideways? There was something hidden in the shadows beneath it. She set her coffee cup on the table the moment her brain registered what her eyes were seeing. The tree visible from where she was sitting wasn't growing sideways. It was the tree that had come crashing down on them in the middle of the night. That was the tree that had taken the last of her family away from her. That tree that had crushed her aunt and uncle, broken her leg. Carol felt the tears well up in her eyes, felt them spill over and run down her cheeks. She made no efforts to brush them away or control the emotion. She was too tired, too lost, too exhausted. What was the universe trying to tell her? Why was God stealing everyone away? The weight of it all was too much for her to carry. She didn't feel strong enough to deal with it. What should she do now? Where would she go? She had more questions than answers.

CHAPTER NINE

The sun was up and shining brightly when Carol's eyes fluttered open. She yawned, stretching her arms out wide before she attempted to climb from the comfortable bed she'd slept in. Specks of dust floated in the sunlight that streamed through the open loft door along with the gentle breeze. She was surprised when she sat at the edge of the bed to find that her leg wasn't throbbing too much this morning. The smell of fresh coffee teased her nose, drawing her into the kitchen. Aren was gone, and Carol was grateful for the opportunity to gather herself, since she wasn't exactly a morning person. She rummaged through the refrigerator for the cream container that Aren had used the night before. Excited when she found it, she poured a generous amount into her coffee and stirred in the two teaspoons of sugar. Turning around carefully, with a crutch under just one arm, Carol had a chance to take in the loft during the daylight. Aren had been right. It was a comfortable space.

Carol hobbled over to the table and found a note Aren had left for her. As she expected, Aren was off doing chores and would return shortly. Carol no sooner set down the note and settled into a chair at the table when she heard Aren's boots clomping up the wooden stairs.

"Well, good morning! Did you sleep all right?" Aren asked from behind.

"Good morning to you too. I slept better than expected. Your bed is quite comfortable. I'm afraid I don't remember much after I broke down at the kitchen table. Where did you sleep?"

"Bailey and I took your advice, and we slept in the hay like farm hands. It wasn't half bad." Aren's smile was genuine.

"Seriously? I would have taken the couch. I never meant to kick you out of your bed." Carol twisted around in the chair.

"Carol, look around, I don't have a couch. It's just me up here. I have my easy chair for those times when I can't be outside and a bed to sleep in. Besides, I don't sleep much anyway." Aren approached the table and set down an armload of items. "Listen, I was able to get into your house, and I found some stuff. I'm not sure if it's yours, though."

Carol lit up at the sight of her purse being pulled from beneath a large pile of clothes. "How on earth did you get in there? The ceiling caved in. I couldn't see a way to get to the other side of the room."

"There wasn't a way from the window I pulled you from, but I went around to the other side of the house and crawled in through a den or something like that. The bookcases supported most of the collapse, so I was able to weave through this and that until I got into what I hoped was your room. It was dark that night so I had no idea what the room really looked like. Anyway, here are some clothes I was able to pull from a suitcase in that room."

Carol dug through her purse and found her phone. The signal was good, but only one battery bar was left and she didn't have her charger. It was still plugged into the wall by her nightstand. She could always get another one. She squealed with the sight of her wallet and car keys and hugged them to her chest.

"Did you happen to see if my car was okay?" She had a feeling she wouldn't like the answer.

"Well, that depends upon which one was yours," Aren replied, her eyebrows rising above her sunglasses.

"Mine was the little blue car."

"Well, in that case, it's fine. Actually, they're both fine. The five-year-old jumps out in me every so often, sorry."

Carol smiled at the joke and then grew sad again with the reality of her situation. "Now, if I only knew where to begin. I never talked to Aunt Suzie or Uncle Frank about a will or their wishes or anything like that." Just when she felt like she could breathe again, reality became a heavy weight on her chest.

"Well, what did your parents have done? How did your aunt and uncle feel about their wishes?" Aren asked. She poured a cup of coffee for herself before sitting down at the table.

"My parents were cremated. They wanted to be cast into the ocean together," Carol explained, pulling up the painful memory.

"What were your aunt and uncle's thoughts about that type of service?" Aren asked over the top of her coffee mug.

"Uncle Frank didn't say either way, but Aunt Suzie wanted a proper funeral. She's pretty religious, adamant about her faith." Carol wiped a tear from her cheek.

"What faith was she?" Aren asked softly.

"Well, my mom and Aunt Suzie were raised in the south. They were raised Baptist and Aunt Suzie was as faithful as they come. She called it 'following the Lord.' At least, I think she was still Baptist. I remember her trying to get me to go to church with her a few times. Maybe I could call around to the churches in the area until I find which one she was a member of," Carol said, letting her thoughts rattle off her tongue as they came into her mind.

"That's probably a good place to start. I think there's a phone book in the main house. Who knows how accurate it is. It's probably been there since my teenage years. If you want to, we can walk over there in a bit and get you settled in. Or you're certainly welcome to just stay up here. I can go and get the phone book if you'd like. It's entirely up to you." Aren looked around like she wasn't sure what else to say.

"If you don't mind the company, I think I'd like to stay up here at least for a little while. That is, unless you'd stay at the other house too. Honestly, I don't want to be all alone right now." She knew full well she probably sounded needy, but Aren was her only tie to the world right now, and even that was tenuous given that they didn't know each other.

"Carol." Aren paused, lightly touching the scars on her face. "Carol, I...well, see, the thing is, this is my home. That's a house that happens to be on the same land, but I live here. You can keep the bed. I don't mind my little nest in the hay one bit. It's sort of like camping. That is, if you don't mind staying up here with me."

"Are you sure you don't mind the intrusion? I could go to a hotel too—"

"Nonsense, there's no reason for you to go through all that expense, and you just said you don't want to be alone. To tell ya the truth, I've enjoyed the company. It's been a long time since I had a visitor," Aren admitted.

"Yeah, well, it's only been one night. You could get weary of having me in the way," Carol replied nervously. She didn't want to be a hassle, and having to depend on someone wasn't her style. She also wanted to ask questions about Aren's life, about why she wouldn't live in the main house, about the rumors Aunt Suzie had mentioned…but there would be time for that, and she didn't want to get herself kicked out because she was nosy.

"Let's take it one day at a time then, okay? If you want to go to a hotel, then you go. You're no prisoner. If you want to move into the main house, where it would probably be more comfortable for you, well then, that's no problem either. If I get sick of you, well, I've been known to be pretty upfront and honest. We'll discuss it and go from there. How's that? Does that sound fair to you?" Aren asked, a half smile touching her lips.

"That sounds more than fair. I appreciate your kindness, Aren. I sincerely do." Carol returned the smile.

"So, do you want me to run down and get that phone book for you?"

"Phone book? No, thank you. It's really not necessary. I can just search for anything I need on my phone, although it's almost out of battery. Could you take me into town so I can buy a new charger for my phone?"

"Sure thing, I'll go and hitch up Wyatt to the wagon." Aren got up.

"Wouldn't it be quicker if we just took my car? It has a full tank of gas," Carol said.

"What does the timeframe have to do with anything? You got a hot date or something?" Aren said. "Besides, how are you going to drive with that leg?"

Carol looked down at her cast. There was no way she could push in the clutch with that bulky thing. "You could drive my car. Do you know how to drive a stick?"

"Noooo, not me." Aren laughed, holding up her hands. "I don't drive anything but the tractor. On these acres, life's a bit different than most anywhere else." Aren paused and seemed to consider her words. "I don't have a driver's license, just a state issued ID so I can vote."

"Do you not know how? I could teach you!" Carol liked the idea of giving something back to Aren after how kind she'd been.

A deep breath broke the momentary silence. "I'm blind in my left eye and don't see too well out of the right eye. I used to drive a car, use technology, but ever since this," Aren took off her sunglasses, pointing at the scars and the cloudy pupil, "well, I can't trust my depth perception or that I'll see something quickly enough that may run onto the road. I trust Wyatt though, who lends me his eyes when we're on the road."

"Shit, Aren, I'm sorry. It's a damned good thing I'm wearing a cast for all the times I've put my foot in my mouth the past twenty-four hours!" Carol stared down at the table, mortified. She recalled seeing the scars by the firelight that night and she'd chatted with Aren the night before but hadn't really paid attention to the scars on her face, nor the damage to her eyes. She'd just seen kindness and enjoyed the sound of Aren's laughter.

Aren smiled again. "Hey, like I said, life's a bit different on these acres. You'll get used to it. Do you still want to go into town? I can hitch up the wagon. Or I could just run over and see if I can find the charger."

"I'd really rather you not risk entering that house again. We'll just go on an adventure into town," Carol said, pushing herself up to her feet. Balancing on one crutch and her good leg, she hopped in front of Aren, pulling her into a tight hug. "Thank you, Aren, for all that you're doing to help."

Aren stiffened slightly and returned the hug lightly. "No problem." She shifted away and headed downstairs. "I'll be back to get you in a second!"

Carol sat down and rested her head in her hands. Only a few days ago, Aunt Suzie had asked what her plans were now that she'd graduated. Now Aunt Suzie was gone, and Carol was planning funerals. She let the fresh tears fall but pulled herself together when she heard Aren coming back in. She had to be strong so she could do what had to be done. There'd be time for grief later.

CHAPTER TEN

Aren looked over at Carol sitting beside her on the bench seat. Her eyes were closed and her head leaned back. She seemed to be enjoying the soft breeze and sunshine on her skin. The rhythm of Wyatt's hooves on the hard-packed road was musical, like the steady beat of a handcrafted drum.

"I'm surprised how comfortable the wagon rides. I guess I expected it to be rough like it appears in western movies."

"There's a big difference between rolling across an ungroomed field full of pits and rocks with steel rim wheels verses rolling down a well-maintained road on inflated car tires. I'll take this ride any day over what the settlers had to endure."

"I never thought about it that way. No wonder things bounced out of the wagons when the horses ran."

Carol's arm shot up, pointing at something off in the distance. Aren turned her head in time to see a deer emerge from the woods on its way to a small pond for a cool drink.

"This is so fun. It's like going on a hay ride to get pumpkins in the fall. How long does it take to get back and forth to town?" Carol asked.

"Round trip, it's about three hours." Aren stared ahead, her hands loose on the reins.

"Wow, that long. No wonder they invented cars. That would be some commute to work every day." Carol shifted in her seat and adjusted her leg. "Aunt Suzie said you came back from Tennessee or Kentucky or somewhere around there. What did you used to do there?"

"Seems like a lifetime ago." Aren frowned slightly. "I was a veterinarian. I'd decided long ago to work with animals. I started out as a vet tech and worked my way through veterinary school down at Michigan State University. After I earned my degree, I was recruited by an equine facility down in Kentucky to manage their breeding program. Looking back, I sold myself to the highest bidder. My work became about money and not about the animals, though I didn't realize that until years after I'd left." Aren squeezed her eyes shut. She hadn't meant to share that much.

"What brought you back here?" Carol asked. "Aunt Suzie said something about your sister taking ill."

"Your aunt Suzie said quite a bit, I guess," Aren replied a bit more curtly than she'd meant to. Her grip tightened up on the reins.

She watched Carol recoil, shift her focus to her fingernail, and look away. Aren felt bad for snapping at her. How could she have known what happened back then? But she wasn't used to people asking questions about her life, either. Still, it didn't mean she needed to be grumpy about it.

"She wasn't exactly my sister. We were each assigned to the same foster home when we were kids. Her name was Jennifer, and she died four years ago, cancer." Aren let the words out, words she hadn't said in years. A chill ran down her spine causing her to shudder.

"I understand if you don't want to talk about it. I shouldn't have pried." Carol lightly touched her leg.

Looking into Carol's innocent eyes made Aren smile a little. She was so sincere in everything she said. Aren hadn't experienced that since she'd lost Jennifer. The walls surrounding her heart softened a bit and the demons edged from her mind. "I'm sorry, I didn't mean to snap at you. I close my eyes and it seems like it was yesterday."

"What happened, if you don't mind me asking?" Carol asked, turning in her seat a bit to face her.

"How far back do you want to go?" Aren asked and then added, "Hey now, why aren't we talking about you? How did all of the questions get turned to me?"

Now it was Carol's turn to chuckle. "Because I already know about me. I would like to know more about you. Besides, you're keeping my mind occupied. If I remember right, it's how I dealt with my parents' death. Distraction is useful."

"You dealt with your parents' death by seeking out a complete stranger and asking incessant questions about her life? Who was the poor soul you interrogated last? Do you still talk to her?" Aren looked over to catch Carol's expression.

Carol rolled her eyes. "No, nothing like that. I kept my mind busy, that's how I dealt with my parents' death, by staying busy. At the time, I was just starting the master's program at school, so I dove headfirst into my studies." Carol ran her fingers through her hair, and the sight of it stirred something in Aren's heart.

"What..." Aren cleared her throat. "What was your major?"

"You'll laugh," Carol said, color showing on her cheeks.

"No, I won't laugh, come on, you're asking me all these personal questions and you won't even tell me what your major was at school?" Aren pretended to look hurt.

"I have earned a master's degree in library science," she said proudly, puffing out her chest and holding her hand over her heart. Then she started to giggle.

"What does one do with a master's degree in library science?" Aren asked, trying not to let Carol's giggles cause her to laugh.

"Someday, I aspire to be a librarian, perhaps even the director of a library, or maybe run a network of libraries!" She said it as though she'd be running for a political office.

Aren could no longer hold back the laughter. It wasn't Carol's area of study that caused her to laugh, but her over-the-top descriptions.

Carol looked up at Aren. "Seriously, I love books, love reading, love research. I want to know everything about everything. The work that goes into creating a book is mind-boggling."

"I never thought of it that way. I just pick up a book and read it, but I bet you're right about the work that has to go into creating one. So, why library science and not publishing?"

"It's the library that I love. It's a place for anyone and everyone to find something that intrigues them, regardless of their interests, situation, or income level. It was one of my favorite places to go as a child. I'd go home with an armload of books. I could go on great adventures in a castle, fight dragons dressed as a knight, or attempt to learn sign language, even study every breed of horse. Anything is possible with a library card."

Aren kept the conversation light the rest of the way into town, eager to avoid delving into Jennifer's death. She wasn't sure she was ready to talk about anything from that time in her life. She realized that Carol was as much of a distraction for her from her losses, her sadness, as she was for Carol. She was grateful for the temporary reprieve from her demons.

Chapter Eleven

Thank you for calling the Church of Our Lord, I'm sorry no one is available to take your call. Please leave a message and we'll return your call as quickly as possible."

Carol rolled her eyes and shook her head. It was the third church in a row with an answering machine. She waited for the beep.

"Yes, hello, my name is Carol Matthews. Susan and Frank Cordes were my aunt and uncle. I'm wondering if they were members of your church. My number is—"

"Hello, this is Reverend Todd. Are you still there?"

"Yes, I'm still here," Carol said.

"I apologize for the machine. Sometimes it takes me a minute or two to get back to the office."

"Hello, Reverend. My name is Carol Matthews. As I was saying, Susan and Frank Cordes were my aunt and uncle. I was wondering if they were members of your church. I'm trying to make arrangements."

"Hello, Ms. Matthews, yes, Suzie and Frank were members, both highly regarded. I'm sorry to hear of their untimely passing. It's a profound loss for all of us. I'm glad you called."

Carol squeezed her eyes shut and allowed herself to exhale. She'd finally found the church and was talking with an actual person and not a machine. But now she had to dive into the hard stuff.

"Thank you for your kind words, Reverend. I was wondering if you ever spoke with my aunt and uncle about their wishes should something happen to them? I'm embarrassed to admit that I'm ill-prepared for this and I'm trying to figure out where to begin so I can honor them." Carol caught herself staring across the road at the home splintered beneath the tree. She turned away and forced herself to focus on the phone call.

"It's a difficult time I'm sure, no one expects anything like this. Actually, yes, I have had conversations with Suzie and Frank about their final wishes. I understand that you were visiting when this tragedy struck and that you were injured. How are you doing?"

"Yes, I was in the house when the tree fell. My only injury was a broken leg, and it will heal with time. Now, as far as arrangements I—"

"Ms. Matthews, you needn't worry about any of that. They left me with detailed instructions on what to do should they both perish at the same time. I can take care of the funeral arrangements, unless you'd prefer to do so on your own. Actually, I've been trying to locate you, as I have some information for you and a sealed letter addressed to you. I tried to catch you at the hospital, but you'd already been discharged. I tried to call, but the number I had from the instructions was no longer in service. Are you still in town?"

"Yes, I'm still in town. They left me a letter? When did they arrange all of this?"

"Shortly after Suzie lost her sister. I believe Sara was your mother? Helping you throughout that process made them realize that they needed to be more prepared in the event of an accident. They didn't want to burden you with making difficult decisions should something like that happen to them. Suzie and Frank purchased a funeral insurance policy that should cover everything. The funeral home will need a copy of the death certificate once you receive it, and a claim will need to be filed. I took the liberty of talking with Kevin, the funeral director, to get things started. I hope you don't mind, but we ended up at a standstill until we could collect some contact information for you. Where should we have the death certificates mailed?"

Carol once again felt ill-prepared. She hadn't expected this much progress. She tried to remember the house number, but all she could recall was that she was on Thompson Road. She tapped her pencil on the tablet of paper in front of her trying to figure out a solution.

"Hello, Ms. Matthews, are you still there?" the reverend asked.

"Yes, I'm sorry, I'm still here. I don't have an address to give you. I'm staying with a friend who lived across the street from my aunt and uncle. Thompson Road is all I know. The house number isn't coming up on my phone. Would you mind mailing them to my aunt and uncle's house, by chance?"

"The farm across the street from Suzie and Frank is the Harris place. You're not staying at the ol' Harris farm, are you?" The reverend asked.

"I don't know the name of the farm. I'm staying with Aren. My leg was broken when the tree fell, and she pulled me out. She saved my life and offered to let me stay here while I make arrangements for the funeral, and until I figure out what to do next," Carol explained, somewhat confused by his response. Surely a preacher would be beyond believing rumors?

"How long have you known this friend? Perhaps you're not familiar with the history? I'm sure you could stay with a family from the church until after the services."

"Really, Reverend, I'm fine right here. Aren's been very hospitable." First the weird responses from Aren the day before, and now this. "What's the matter with me staying here?"

"I really wish you'd reconsider. You're not safe there. That place drives people insane."

"I'm sure there's a logical explanation. I'm fine right here."

"Very well, it's your life. I'll be sure to let you know when the service will be, and if you need anything at all, you just call. Bye now," he said before hanging up.

Carol got up from the table, confused by the change in the reverend's disposition once he'd realized where she was staying. Nothing she'd experienced from Aren so far caused her any concern. She was kind, courteous, and generous. She was also funny and calm. In fact, she was really pretty great. She grabbed her crutches and made her way over to the screen-covered loft door. Standing in front of it, she could see Aren working in the garden. She watched

Aren pick tomatoes from the last two rows, carefully setting them into wooden crates. Every few minutes, she'd take a full crate and slide it into the back of the wagon they'd taken into town. The wagon was now overflowing with produce. Carol could hear Aren whistling an upbeat little tune though she couldn't identify it. For someone treated so poorly by the townspeople, she was wonderfully relaxed, and Carol wondered what part of Aren's story she was missing.

After ten minutes or so, Aren had finished picking the vegetables and was climbing aboard the wagon. She heard Aren tell Wyatt to go to the back of the barn and she giggled, thinking of Mr. Ed responding. Carol carefully made her way through the main aisle of the loft. She hadn't tried the stairs alone yet. Carol used the railing for support as she lowered herself to the floor. She skootched her way to the top step, holding her cast up while using both hands and her good leg to work her way down the steps, seated, one step at a time. About midway down the stairs, she'd grown tired of trying to hold on to the crutches while working her way down. She tossed them to the bottom of the stairs. It was quite the effort, but she wanted to talk to Aren. She wanted to understand. She knew that Aren's past really wasn't any of her business, but she'd always been one to ask questions and look for answers, and Aren was turning out to be a puzzle she wanted to solve.

The whistling grew louder as Carol hobbled down the main aisle of the barn. The bay doors in the back were swung wide open and a soft breeze wisped through, lifting her hair from her face. Carol inhaled deeply. She loved the smell of a farm, the smell of the animals and fresh hay.

Carol could hear water running when she reached the back of the barn. Hobbling through the large open doorway, she watched for a moment as Aren scrubbed the dirt off the fresh vegetables before letting them dry in clean crates.

"Don't you ever stop working?" Carol asked from inside the doorway.

Aren shook her head. "There's too much to do to stop working. If I don't get all of this washed and canned up, then I won't have any veggies for the winter months. The animals have to be fed when they have to be fed, and the fields have to be tended almost constantly. When you do it yourself, you can't waste a minute of daylight."

"Can I help?" Carol offered, wishing there was something she could do aside from just sit with her leg elevated. She missed being active already and it had only been a few days. Six to eight weeks would surely make her crazy if she couldn't find something to do.

"I have a stool if you want to wash these up. Then, I could start blanching and peeling these for canning." Aren held a big tomato.

"Sure, I'd love to help!" Carol was glad Aren didn't send her away. It must be strange to have someone in her space all the time. "Why do you do all of this work when they have canned vegetables at the store? Wouldn't it save you time to just buy tomatoes?"

"When you preserve your own food, it tastes better, fresher, sort of like the milk. And I save seeds each year, so it costs nothing to grow the vegetables and reuse the jars. A little elbow grease and I have free food."

Aren grabbed the stool and tipped up a crate for Carol to rest her leg on. Soon, they were working together at a quick pace getting things ready to be put into quart jars. Once everything was washed, Aren set up a propane tank and a sturdy two-burner table. She grabbed two water bath pots from a shelf and filled each half full of water before lighting the flame to allow the water to heat to a boil. Throughout, she explained what she was doing and how it all worked. Carol enjoyed the lesson and opportunity to concentrate on something else.

"So, did you finish all of your phone calls?" Aren asked as she peeled tomatoes and stuffed them into quart jars.

"Yes, I did. That reminds me. I came down here to ask you a question. Is this the old Harris farm?" Carol looked up from her work in time to see Aren's head drop and her back stiffen.

Aren turned to face Carol before she answered. Her eyes had gone cold and dark. The scars on Aren's face suddenly seemed deep and rigid. Aren licked her lips before answering. "Yes, this is the old Harris farm. Why do you ask? What did they say about it?"

"That's just it. The reverend didn't say anything, but his mannerism sure changed, much like yours just did." She silently chastised herself for bringing it up. "I had to give him an address to send the paperwork."

Carol sat motionless, waiting to see if she'd pushed too far. Finally, she heard Aren draw in a breath.

"Phyllis and Ron Harris used to own this property." Aren turned back to her tomatoes and filled up another two quarts before continuing. "They had one son, Daniel. He dated a local girl and they were high school sweethearts. From what I could find in the newspaper archives, he caught her with another guy one night. The three argued and things got heated. There was a fight. After he pummeled the guy until he was unconscious, he turned his attention onto her. He beat her until she stopped fighting back. She died before she reached the hospital. Daniel was sentenced to prison for the crimes. He was murdered in prison fourteen years into his sentence by another inmate."

Aunt Suzie had been right about the farm being under a cloud. "So, did you buy this farm from them?" Carol asked hesitantly.

Aren sighed and rested the tomato on the jar top. "Kind of. They were my foster parents. Ron couldn't get work after Daniel's conviction. No one wanted to hire the father of a murderer. So, he and Phyllis decided to take in some foster kids to help them keep the farm. They wanted boys to do the farm work, but the state doesn't let you pick and choose. They took me in first, and then Jennifer four months later."

Aren trailed off after mentioning Jennifer's name. Carol sensed that Aren was done talking about the old Harris farm and went back to peeling her tomatoes. There was more to the story, but now wasn't the time to ask. Murder might explain the reverend's reaction, but it didn't explain Aren's scars, or the way the people in town treated her. All Carol knew was that the pain and wariness in Aren's eyes was real, and it made her sad. It sounded like she'd had a rough time of it, and a lot of loss in her life, much like Carol had. Oddly, there was comfort in finding someone who understood. She kept at the veggies, lost in thought.

Chapter Twelve

Aren released the cows out to pasture. She couldn't believe that it had been nine days since the storm. She thought for sure that she would have grown weary of having someone in her space for an entire week, but she found herself enjoying time spent with Carol. She realized how much she'd missed companionship and found herself looking forward to the evenings instead of dreading the loneliness in the loft when the chores were finished for the day. Aren made her way up the wooden stairs with her two stainless steel milking pails. About halfway up the stairs, she inhaled the most delightful aroma. Her pace picked up though she was careful not to spill the milk.

Carol was standing next to the dining room table, a crutch under each arm. She looked absolutely beautiful. Her short brown hair was tucked back behind her ears. Tiny earrings sparkled almost as much as her hazel eyes in the candlelight. A delicate sundress showed off a curvy figure, highlighting her breasts and hips. Aren's heart skipped a beat and butterflies stirred low in her belly. Carol's smile seemed to broaden when she saw Aren approaching, which made Aren's knees weak. The small dining table was set for two with a few more candles burning softly in the center.

"Wow, this is a wonderful surprise!"

"I thought that since I can't help out much in the garden or with many of the chores, the least I could do is cook you a wonderful meal. Well, I hope it's wonderful." Carol smiled.

"I'll get the milk strained quickly and then we'll see if it tastes as amazing as it smells." Aren hefted the pails into the back room and moved as quickly as she could. She didn't have time to change clothes and she winced at the way she probably looked and smelled. She never had to worry about it, but now there was a beautiful woman in a sundress waiting for her. She shrugged the thought away. It's not like Carol was trying to impress her.

Soon, the milk was in the refrigerator and they were seated at the table. Aren took a bite of the meal and allowed the flavors to dance on her tongue.

"This is wonderful! You found everything you needed to make this here?" Aren asked in astonishment.

"You have all sorts of great spices in that rack up there. I just pulled out a round steak and let it slowly cook all day in the Crock-Pot with a little of this and a touch of that. The summer squash cooked up nicely." Carol tilted her head. "I hope you don't mind me rummaging around for things."

"Oh, and mashed potatoes, my favorite!" Aren took a fork full of the potatoes. "If you cook like this, feel free to rummage all you want."

"I'm glad you like them. I've never mashed potatoes with a hand masher. I hope they aren't too lumpy. Now, all that's missing is a nice bottle of merlot." Carol smiled until she saw the look on Aren's face. Instantly, her smile faded. "What did I say?"

Aren scolded herself for letting her expression give her away. "Nothing, no, you didn't say anything wrong. I'm sorry. Please smile some more, I treasure your smiles. It's nothing you've done or said. I'm not a drinker."

"Would you consider telling me about it? I want to learn more about you, Aren," Carol said sincerely.

"Maybe later, okay? This is such a wonderful meal. I don't want any of my old stuff putting a damper on such a great evening. How about you tell me about your day instead?" Aren tried to keep her tone light. She wasn't ready to explain her hang-ups with alcohol or anything else.

Carol looked a little disappointed, but she smiled and continued to eat. Aren's heart sank a little knowing she'd dampened the mood of the meal.

"I made my way across the street again today, and the documents I'd been waiting for finally arrived in the mail."

"Oh yeah? Anything other than what you expected?"

Carol finished chewing her steak. She swallowed and reached for her glass of water. "There was a large envelope from my aunt Suzie." Her eyes welled up.

"I didn't mean to upset you." Aren reached over and touched Carol's arm.

"Aren, you didn't upset me. It's just a lot, like the past and present are colliding and I'm on this wild emotional roller coaster ride that I can't seem to get off of."

Aren pulled her hand back and picked up her fork. She had no right to push Carol or ask questions when she wasn't capable of sharing.

"If I'm honest, I haven't opened it yet. Her handwriting is so much like my mom's. I just held the envelope and cried like a baby."

"Past and present colliding. Now I understand. Your parents, you said they died in a car accident?" Aren asked, following another bite of round steak. She was getting better at this conversation stuff.

"Yes, just a couple of years ago. Aunt Suzie and Uncle Frank helped me with everything. I was a wreck. Aunt Suzie stayed with me for the summer. She helped settle their estate and sell the house. I couldn't afford to pay it off and keep it. I was still in school and didn't qualify for a loan to take it over. They had some life insurance, but it barely covered the cost of their funerals. They had some investments and a little in a savings account that paid for my master's program, but that was about all that was left beside the photos and other stuff like that. It was a draining summer, taking care of their estate after the accident. I miss them so much."

Carol shared with an openness that made Aren a bit envious. If only she could share her feelings so easily. She changed the subject and asked about Carol's university days and what books she liked, and it seemed to lift her mood.

Aren insisted on doing the dishes since Carol had cooked. She had to remind Carol of the need for her to stay off her foot before Carol finally gave in and allowed Aren to take the items to the sink. Soon enough, the dishes were done and coffee was percolating on the small Coleman stove.

Aren set up a couple of comfortable chairs in front of the loft door and left only the candles burning on the table allowing them to see the night sky through the screen. Once she successfully got Carol settled, using a hay bale as an ottoman, Aren fixed each of them a cup of steaming hot coffee.

"Here you are, m'lady," Aren said, handing Carol her mug.

"I do believe you are going to spoil me rotten," Carol said, smiling above the steamy mug.

"There's nothing wrong with a little spoiling." Aren smiled back, trying to ignore those butterflies swarming in her stomach again. "Thank you for cooking me such a lovely meal. It's been years since anyone has cooked for me. I appreciate it."

"It's the least I could do after all you've done for me." Carol reached over and tucked a loose strand of hair behind Aren's ear.

Aren took a deep breath and closed her eyes. A touch so tender knocked a few more stones free from the wall she'd built around her heart. She couldn't allow herself to get used to it, though. Carol would heal, she'd get back on her feet, and she'd move on. She wouldn't be interested in living on a farm with a woman who had more baggage than an airline. For now, she could enjoy having someone there who didn't know the whole story. She could pretend, for a while, that she could have a normal life. And when Carol left, she'd hold on to the memory of days filled with sweet smiles and laughter.

Chapter Thirteen

The chairs situated in front of the large loft door were left in place from the night before. Carol sat looking out over the pastures beyond the garden, where Aren was working with a big horse. She looked closer and realized it wasn't Wyatt. The large animal seemed a bit nervous, stepping off to the side and backing up often. Then, she'd watch Aren maneuver in front of the horse and say or do something, Carol wasn't sure what, but the horse would settle right down and allow Aren to lean in and embrace his mammoth head. After a moment or two, Aren would go back to saddling up the large horse.

The process unfolding before her eyes intrigued her. She'd taken a class in college on horsemanship and imagined that this was what they meant when they spoke of gentling a horse or starting a horse. Either way, watching Aren assure this animal that could surely squash her was exciting. Carol guessed that Aren was happy with the fit of the saddle. She watched as Aren went over to the fence and pulled off a long rope or leash. Aren affixed one end onto the horse's halter and led him out to an open area of the pasture. She waved a hand gently and the horse began walking circles around Aren to the length of the leash. Carol tapped the rim of her coffee cup trying to remember what the action was called.

"Lunging! You're lunging him!" She squealed out with excitement.

Aren looked up to the screened-in window and waved. Carol returned the wave from her observation post.

"Good morning!" She called down.

"Good morning to you!" Aren shouted back. "Want to come down and watch? I'll set you up a chair in the shade."

"Okay, I'll be right down."

By the time Carol hobbled down to the pasture Aren had already set up a nice Adirondack chair and matching footrest. The chair was weathered but sturdy and comfortable. Aren apparently used this chair often because she had a saddle pad cut to cushion the seat and back rest with another small padded fabric covering the foot rest. All three of the cushions were sun faded. Carol looked up from her new perch and took in the massive maple tree that seemed to shade an area three times the size of the space Aren was using to work the horse.

The image of her aunt's home came flooding into her mind. She'd never experienced fear like that before. She recalled that her first thought was that a tornado had struck the home. The sound of the thunderous boom that had woken her from a peaceful slumber had frightened her to the point of remaining frozen in bed. She remembered screaming when she heard the creaking, crashing, and popping as the second story was crushed above her. Carol was sure her time on this planet was over when the beam from the ceiling gave way and crashed onto her bed. Her next thought was of the relief she'd felt when she heard someone calling out. Seeing Aren's face had meant she wasn't going to die there, alone.

"Carol? Carol, are you all right?" Aren's voice pulled her from her thoughts.

Carol pulled her gaze from the tree canopy and blankly stared at Aren for a moment. She blinked a few times before she answered. "Yeah, I'm okay. I just got lost in my thoughts there for a minute I guess."

Aren knelt next to one of the armrests. She took Carol's hand in her own. Her touch was so gentle.

"Do you want to talk about it?" Aren asked, stroking the back of Carol's hand.

"Lightning striking a tree that collapses a house in on itself is what, a million to one? A billion to one odds? Why that night? Why when we were all sleeping? Why that section of tree and not the other half of the fork in the tree that would have fallen away from the house? Why did I get to live and not them?" Carol wondered aloud, returning her gaze to the canopy of the tree. She kept a tight grip on Aren's hand, not wanting to let it go.

"Do you believe it when people say, 'it was just their time to go'?" Aren asked. She shifted from the side of Carol's chair. Aren moved the empty footstool closer to Carol and sat down directly in front of her.

Carol looked at Aren and pondered the question she'd just been asked. "I don't know. I guess so. What do you think? Do you think the Lord calls us home or do you think that shit just happens and POOF, we're no more?"

Aren's free hand wrapped around Carol's. Her touch was so gentle. She continued to caress the back of Carol's hands when she spoke. "Are you asking me if I believe in Heaven? I don't honestly know if I believe or not. I read a few books after Jennifer died, trying to figure out an answer to that very question. Then, one day I was right in the middle of this self-help book when something dawned on me. Actually, it hit me as if I'd stepped on the wrong end of a garden rake."

"What was it? What did you figure out?" Carol asked earnestly.

"That all of these people who wrote these books had no more inside knowledge than I would have. These authors were no different than me. Some might have studied the bible, some might have studied spirituality, some were philosophers, but why on earth was I looking to them to give me answers that were really nothing more than their best guess? I mean, who really knows until we're dead, and then how would we come back to communicate that knowledge?"

"I see your point, but what about the people who died in the emergency room and then were brought back to life? Or the psychics that channel into the other world? Don't you think that they would have some firsthand knowledge? How could all the stories be the same if they didn't experience it?" Carol asked, offering a different perspective.

"I can't say what they did or didn't experience. I can't say why some of us are here and others aren't. Do the people here have some destiny to fulfill? I don't believe that's always the case. Not with the things I've witnessed in my lifetime. As far as the psychics and the near-death experience folks, I think a lot of that is offering people answers, telling them what they want, or maybe need to hear mixed in with a little power of persuasion. I think the light at the end of the tunnel is so beaten into our subconscious that when we wake up and we're told that we didn't have a heartbeat for a bit, we're certain we got to see that too. Who wants to be left out?" Aren asked. The sincerity in her expression warmed Carol's heart. She wanted to be wrapped up and held with the tenderness she saw in Aren's eyes.

"No one wants to be left out," Carol whispered.

"I can't answer any of the whys of it all. I will say that I'm sorry your aunt and uncle didn't make it, and I'm also so incredibly grateful that you did. I've grown quite attached to you." Aren smiled at her.

They looked deep into each other's eyes. Carol leaned in closer and her breath deepened. She swallowed hard and licked her lips. They were almost touching noses and Carol's heart was beating like a drum in her chest. Aren reached up to gently touch Carol's cheek.

"I should get back to working with Doc if we're going to take that ride together when you get your cast off," Aren said huskily.

The tension was broken, and Carol leaned back a bit. "You're doing all that work so that we can go riding together?"

"He's a young boy and while I've had him out a few times, he still needs a lot of work before I'd trust him off this property, but you'd ride Wyatt, not Doc. I'd trust you to be completely safe on Wyatt."

"Wait a minute. Doc, Wyatt…you're not a Tombstone fan, are you?"

"Oh, just you wait until you get to meet big nosed Kate!" Aren laughed and walked back toward the tethered gelding.

Carol watched Aren duck through the fencing. Her heart was still pounding in her chest. It was probably best that they hadn't kissed, but those lips were almost too much to resist. Carol had no business getting involved with anyone. She had no job, no home. She was grieving for her aunt and uncle, reeling from the way they died, and dealing with a broken leg. She was dependent on the kindness of a stranger so she could have a roof over her head.

She watched Aren work with the horse. Her shoulders were broad, her arms lean muscle from long days of physical labor, her waist was trim, and she had to admit that Aren had a nice ass. Aren stopped driving the horse in wide circles. She lowered her arms and turned her back on him. Doc slowed to a walk, approaching Aren from behind. He stood still, directly behind her nuzzling her shoulder ever so slightly. It was fascinating to watch. Aren turned to face him, embracing his large head, and at that moment, Carol wished she were that horse, cradled so tenderly in Aren's arms.

CHAPTER FOURTEEN

Dark shadows emerged from all sides. Aren could hear people calling for her, calling to her, telling her to run but begging her for help.

"Mom, Mom is that you? Is it really you?" Aren's voice sounded so far away. "Mom, look out! He's behind you! Run!"

Jennifer's face emerged from the shadows. She was so pale and sickly. Her once brilliant green eyes were now dark, sunken and haunted. She was pointing out into the fields. Ron was on the ground, face down, motionless. Phyllis was standing behind Jen screaming, her words unrecognizable. Aren reached for Jen, and she turned to run but her feet were so heavy. She couldn't move. She was trapped.

"Aren, Aren, wake up. Aren, are you okay?" Carol's voice pulled her from the shadows.

"Yeah, I'm okay. Are you okay? What are you doing up?" Aren rubbed her eyes.

"My leg was hurting. I had to take a pain pill." Carol looked at Aren, a concerned expression on her face. "You were screaming. Did you have a nightmare?"

"Yeah, a bad dream, nothing new." Aren stood and stretched her back. "Want a cup of coffee?"

Aren made her way into the bathroom. She washed her face, hoping to shake the dream. It had been four years and she still struggled with the reflection of herself in the mirror. Her cloudy eye, the scars, the person in the mirror wasn't what she saw when she closed her eyes and pictured herself in her mind. She wondered if she'd ever accept the face staring back at her. Coffee. She needed coffee.

Aren walked into the kitchen and turned on the light above the sink. She made coffee using the percolator, her mind far away.

"Are you staying up? You're not going to try to go back to sleep?" Carol asked.

"No point in trying to go back to sleep so I might as well get the day started."

"But it's only three o'clock in the morning. You can't make it on just a few hours' sleep."

Aren sighed. "Carol, it's like this most every night and somehow I always manage to make it through the day. I never sleep very long. You just haven't been awake any of the other mornings."

"What did you dream about? And please don't ask me if we can talk about it some other time, because some other time never seems to come." Carol sat down at the table.

Aren looked up from lighting the stove. "It was just a bad dream, no big deal."

"You have them often, don't you? Bad dreams, I mean," Carol said.

"Need distracting, do you?" Aren set the pot on top of the burner.

Aren walked over and sat across from Carol. She fidgeted with the spent matchstick still in her hands. For some reason, she couldn't meet Carol's gaze. It wasn't shame she felt, but perhaps fear. What would Carol think of her if she answered any of these questions with even a bit of the truth? She'd realized over the past week that she enjoyed having Carol in the loft. She was enjoying the conversations they shared and the amazing friendship that was building by the minute. She hadn't realized how lonely she'd become until she had someone sharing her life, and she didn't want to do anything to jeopardize that. The sad part was that Aren wanted to talk about all of it but figured there just wasn't any point in doing so. She wanted to let it out so she could let it go. She'd checked so many books out on the topic and knew she needed to release it before she could heal. Wyatt was a great listener, Bailey too, but neither offered much in the way of advice or feedback. The thought brought a grin to Aren's face.

"What are you smiling about?" Carol asked. "Did I miss a good joke?"

Aren leaned back in her chair. Maybe she needed to give it a try. "I've been alone on this land for over four years, Carol. You're the first visitor I've had. To be quite honest," she paused a bit before continuing. "Well, the truth is, I don't have any friends. The people in town don't think much of me, as I'm sure you've noticed. I'm the freak out on Thompson Road that lives on the cursed Harris farm. I don't drive a car and yet I have a small road atlas carved into my face. The thing people forget is that I'm partially blind, not deaf. I know what they say about me. I've heard the murmurs. I've seen the finger pointing. I've seen the look on people's faces when I walk into a store. They all think they know, but they don't know. They don't have a clue." Aren felt the matchstick snap in her fingers. She set the pieces on the table. "All I'm sayin' is that it's weird having someone sitting at my table asking me sincere questions about my dreams. It's been a really long time since I've talked to anyone like you want me to talk to you." Aren pushed at the broken matchstick pieces with her finger.

"That's what friends do. They talk about things. They talk about funny things and serious things and difficult things. Don't you want a friend?" Carol reached for Aren's hand.

Aren got up from the table and walked around the room. She stopped at the open loft door and looked out into the darkness. The room was comfortably warm, yet she suddenly felt chilled. She wrapped her arms around herself and drew in a deep breath. Her heart was pounding in her chest.

"I miss it, ya know, friendship. As much as I've told myself over the years that I hate people, that I'm better off alone, I do miss it." She finally managed to push some words out.

"Then let me be there for you. Let me in. Let me be your friend."

"Why? What's the point? The funeral's coming up. Then, in a few weeks, you'll get your walking cast. I imagine you have a life you want to get back to. So, I ask you, Carol, what's the point? What's the point of sharing all this stuff? What's the point of opening all these old wounds? You talk about friendship, but you won't be here to be my friend. You'll be off somewhere living your life and I'll be here, alone, trying to stuff everything back inside."

"I'm sorry, Aren. I never saw it from that perspective." Carol sat silent for a minute. "Maybe we can use this time to help each other heal. How about I start with some unedited honesty?" Carol rubbed her face with her hands, "I'm lost, at a crossroads. You see, I don't have a life to get back to and I don't even know where to go from here."

Her voice was barely a whisper, but Aren heard every single word loud and clear. She stood still, looking out the loft door into the darkness.

"I have a few friends from high school, from college, and I have no doubt that they'd help if I asked, but they've all moved on with their own lives. They've all scattered to different corners of the country, starting their next chapter, starting new jobs, some have started families." Carol's voice was stronger again.

"So, you don't have anyone special waiting for you? No one to return to? No home?" Aren turned to face Carol. Maybe Carol wouldn't leave so soon after all.

"I hadn't planned anything beyond visiting my aunt and uncle. As soon as I graduated I gave up the apartment I was renting. For years I've known exactly what I want to do with my life, but the problem is that I don't know where I want to do it. My parents are gone, now my aunt and uncle are gone. I'm in this lost limbo. Where do I go? Where do I settle down and create my life?"

"What about Pennsylvania? Don't you have a life there? I overheard you talking on the phone yesterday afternoon. I was working in the garden. I took Bailey for a walk in the woods to give you some privacy. I wasn't eavesdropping, I promise." Aren returned to the table. She sat down in the chair next to Carol.

"Ah, Pennsylvania. Yes, I called for a status on a job application. I had applied for a position in a small community library outside of Philly right before I'd left campus. A friend from college thought it would be so great if we could work together, but I don't live there, I don't have roots there. Besides, the role has already been filled. I just thought if I could find a direction to head toward, something to shoot for, that I'd have a goal, an end game. I guess you could say I was looking for a sign. Aren, I feel like such a burden. I've completely invaded your space. I know that I need a job, but I can't even drive my car right now to get back and forth to work. I've looked for an apartment in town, but without a job... It's just that you've been so kind and I don't want to take advantage." Carol buried her face in her hands, "You missed an epic meltdown after that call. Everything that's been bottled up inside exploded. Emotions erupted everywhere. I cried, I got angry, I screamed, I threw my crutches down the main aisle and then had to crawl across the floor to go get them. It was quite the pathetic scene."

Aren felt bad that she hadn't been there for Carol after the call. Taking off for the serenity of the woods wasn't to offer Carol privacy. Aren had walked away because she was hurt. She thought Carol was leaving the state. She was reminded that the friendship that was building, the companionship, was just temporary, that she'd lose it. Now, she felt guilty for being so selfish.

"Maybe that was the sign, the job being filled. Maybe you should stay and start your life here." Aren looked up from the small piece of matchstick she'd been rolling between her fingers.

"Could I live here, in this town, with all of the bad memories?" Carol's eyes asked the question as much as her words, her eyebrows raising expectantly.

"Are there good memories? Are there enough good memories to outweigh the bad? Wouldn't it be nice to stay somewhere where you're surrounded with good memories?"

"Is that why you bought this farm? Are you surrounded with good memories here?"

"My situation is different." Aren's jaw muscles tightened up.

"How so? Talk to me. Please tell me something."

"I will. I'm doing my best." Aren couldn't look up. She focused on the matchstick.

"How about something simple? Why do you live in the barn and not the house?" Carol's voice was soft and tender, like a delicate touch.

"There's nothing simple about that question. I'm not ready to talk about the house." Aren sat back and tried to keep her voice steady.

"The barn then, do you have good memories in the barn?" The look on Carol's face, the expression in her eyes, seemed to be pleading for an answer.

Yes, the barn was a source of many good memories, but that wasn't why she didn't live in the house. The house, that night, it was all still so vivid in her mind even after four years. The barn had always been her safe place. Maybe that would be a good place to start.

"This barn, especially the loft, became my sanctuary from the world shortly after I was assigned here." Aren allowed her thoughts to escape, unedited. "When things became too much or I just needed to feel centered, feel safe, I'd come up here to the loft. Sometimes I'd climb up high in the hay, almost to the peak, and arrange the bales like a fort, so I was protected from all sides. The hay was my own little castle, like the ones you talk about in books, the creaky floorboards, my moat. I'd lay on my back and watch the dust particles reflect the sunlight, like floating flakes of gold dancing in the breeze. Sometimes, I'd sneak away for a few minutes so I could regroup, other times, I'd spend hours up here, become lost in my thoughts or think about nothing at all and just be still." Aren looked over to the stacked hay.

"Do you still do that? Climb up to the top of the hay?" Carol asked.

"I haven't done that in years. I haven't even thought about it in years. The last time was probably right before I left for college."

Aren felt Carol's hand cover hers on the table. The touch was tender and her hand was warm. It felt good. All of it felt so good, the conversation, the interest, the gentle touch. Maybe, Carol pulling her out of her shell, even an inch at a time, was just what she needed. Maybe, just maybe, she could lower the drawbridge and let someone in, perhaps a little bit. Aren covered the top of Carol's hand with her free hand. She looked up into Carol's kind, understanding eyes.

"Carol, just so you know, you're not a burden. I like having you here. Stay for as long as you want, okay?"

"Thank you, I appreciate it. Thank you for sharing too, it means a lot to me."

Aren squeezed Carol's hand before releasing it. She stood from the table and walked over to the open loft door. "The sun's coming up, I'd better get to it."

Aren wasn't sure what else to say. It was all so new, and sharing feelings, hell, acknowledging feelings, wasn't her strong suit. It was Carol's though and maybe Carol was right, maybe they could help each other heal.

CHAPTER FIFTEEN

A few hours later, Carol was mulling over the conversation with Aren while sorting laundry. She had so many questions to ask, but knew she needed to give Aren time. She picked up the last of her dirty clothes and the large manila envelope fell from the edge of the pile. It was the packet from her aunt. She hadn't been ready to open it when it had arrived the other day, but today she felt stronger. She felt like she could handle what might be inside. Laundry forgotten for the moment, Carol picked up the envelope. She touched the ink that spelled out her name, reminded once again of her mom's handwriting. Carol looked out beyond the garden and took in the house, still buried beneath the tree. She gathered up her crutches and the envelope, making her way to the small dining table. Carol took a deep breath before opening the envelope and letting the contents spill out onto the table. There was a letter on top.

My Dearest Carol,

Honey, if you're reading this, then something has happened to both me and Uncle Frank. If that's the case, I hope it was quick for us. I can't imagine a better way to cross over to the other side than with Frank at my side. He's always been my rock.

Sweet Carol, we're so proud of you. You remind me of your mama more and more. I miss her every single day. We put all of this together after your mama's passing. Our hope is that we made it all a bit easier on you than it was when your folks passed on. The papers included with this letter outline our wishes. There's a sheet in here with the name and number of our attorney and accountant, and they can handle everything for you.

Sweetie, watching you grow up over the years has been such a pleasure. Being your God parents has been our honor. You're more than just our niece, you're like a daughter to us and we can't think of anyone else we'd like to share our little legacy with.

I love you, Carol. We love you. Hopefully, you've found your rock and your happiness by the time this letter finds you. You deserve nothing less.

Love you to the moon,
Aunt Suzie

Carol set the letter down on the table, tears running down her cheeks. She slid it off to the side before reviewing the other documents. Maybe Aren was right, maybe this town could be where she belonged. She turned her attention to the rest of the contents of the envelope.

"Holy shit," Carol said over and over while reviewing the papers.

After some time to settle her emotions, she picked up her phone and dialed the first number on the list.

"Thank you for calling Smith, Harper, and Dahl Law Firm. How may I direct your call?" A smooth male voice chimed in her ear.

"Yes, hello, I was wondering if Savannah Dahl was available."

"May I tell her who's calling?"

"Oh, yes, sorry, my name is Carol Matthews. Susan and Frank Cordes left me her number."

"Thank you, one moment please."

The transferred call was answered on the second ring. "This is Savannah Dahl."

"Hello, my name is Carol Matthews. Susan and Frank Cordes were my aunt and uncle. They passed away recently and left me with information that included your name and number." Carol tried not to ramble, but it was a lot to get out.

"Hi, Carol. I am so sorry for your loss. I read about the lightning strike in the paper. I understand that you were injured as well. How are you doing?"

"I have a broken leg, but should make a full recovery, thank you for asking. The reason for my call, well, what do I do? Where do I start?"

"First, let me say that I'm glad to hear that your leg will heal. Second, I understand you'll have questions. I took the liberty of pulling up the file after I read the article in the paper. Your aunt was quite adamant about having her affairs in order, ensuring that you didn't have to figure it all out on your own. We'll need a few copies of the death certificate. Have those been ordered yet?"

"Yes, I've ordered them, but they hadn't arrived last time I checked the mail. I can check again today."

"Yes, please do that. We'll need original copies in order to file claims with the homeowner's insurance and a few other entities on the list. We have some forms for you to sign as well if you'd like us to represent you and handle the claims, transfer of assets, etc. It won't be long after we get the ball rolling that you can start repairs to the home."

"This is such a relief! I'll be in town the day after tomorrow for the funeral. Would that be soon enough? Could I stop in before the service to review and sign the forms?"

"Absolutely, that will be fine. If you can email me your contact information, I'll have the papers ready when you arrive. I'll explain the process in more detail when I see you. Thank you for calling."

Carol returned all of the papers to the envelope and slid it into the dresser drawer that Aren had cleared out for her. She turned around to find the half-sorted laundry on the bed. She finished sorting and started a load, ruminating the whole time on what lay ahead. She spent the rest of the afternoon looking up phone numbers for tree removal services and contractors. The project gave her a renewed sense of purpose. She would let things unfold and see if this could be where she belonged. One thing for certain, she couldn't wait for Aren to get back so she could share the news.

CHAPTER SIXTEEN

Aren was busy bagging up produce at the farmer's market when she glanced up and saw the cab pull in. The funeral had been at one o'clock today and she'd offered to go. She had even ironed black slacks and a shirt, but Carol insisted on going alone. She'd needed to meet with the attorney and had a few other appointments before the services, so Aren had taken her to the attorney's office and left her. It was torture, wondering all day how Carol was doing. She hadn't felt that helpless in quite some time. She quickly finished with her customer and excused herself for a moment before running to the taxi.

"Carol, slow down, let me help you. Are you okay?" Aren asked as she saw Carol trying frantically to climb from the back of the cab with her crutches. Aren heard the driver repeating the total and leaned into the passenger window to pay him.

"I can pay for my own cab. Driver, don't leave. Keep the meter running."

"What? Why? What happened?" Aren was thoroughly confused. This wasn't what she expected at all.

"The things they say about you. I wasn't prepared to deal with it, certainly not today of all days and at my aunt and uncle's funeral of all places. I felt blindsided and I didn't know what to say to them. I don't know how to defend you. Please tell me that none of it's true, Aren. I need to hear it from you! I need to know, is any of what they say about you true?" Tears streamed down Carol's cheeks.

Aren's head dropped forward, her jaw tightened. She'd known this day was coming. It had all been too good to be true. The friendship, the companionship, she knew it would come to an end eventually, but she definitely hadn't expected it today. She felt horrible that her stuff had ruined an already somber time. Maybe if she explained, maybe if she opened up and talked about it, maybe Carol would understand.

"I don't know exactly what they said, or which version you were told. I don't know how to answer a question that has more answers than you probably want. Can we talk about this later? Please? I'll answer the questions, I'll do better." Aren was almost begging. She had never been more grateful for the dark sunglasses. She knew tears were welling up in her eyes, though she could do nothing to stop them.

"I need the truth, I need honesty. I can't stay with you and not know what happened." Carol's eyes were pleading again, like they had the other night, after the nightmare. She'd asked for honesty that night too.

"Right here? Really? Right now? Okay, fine, let's do this. Ask. Ask your questions. Or do I have to guess? What am I being accused of now? Who have I murdered this time? Or maybe it's about the bodies buried somewhere on the farm? What have I stolen this week and from who? Ask your questions, Carol!" Aren's chest was tightening up and old, hardened anger was bubbling over. She was sick of it. Sick of the stories. Sick of being assumed guilty. She couldn't stand the thought of losing Carol to a bunch of twisted tales, but if she wanted to believe that crap instead of Aren, then so be it.

"People are staring at us. I didn't mean to cause a scene, certainly not here. This is one of your favorite places. I should go. You have customers waiting." Carol sounded defeated and she looked completely drained. "I was wrong to stop here. It's just, well, I missed you all day and it's all so confusing."

"It's not confusing, it's bullshit. Everyone has ghosts, and a lot of people never talk about it. Why can't the past be in the past?" Aren stuffed her hands into her front pockets.

Carol reached up and pulled Aren's sunglasses off her face. Carol's eyes seemed to bore into hers, like she was trying to read her mind. Aren stood statue-still and held Carol's gaze. A tear escaped. She was having a hard time holding it together.

"You pulled me out of a crumbling house. You opened your home to me. It's like the you that I'm getting to know and the person that they talk about are two completely different people. How can that be? I need to know what happened, okay? I stand here and look into your eyes and all I see is kindness, tenderness. I don't understand how they see someone so completely different."

"I'm the only one left to pay for all the sins, and *someone* had to pay."

"What does that cryptic shit even mean? What sins?" Carol flailed her arms sending one of her crutches thudding onto the gravel drive.

Aren bent down and picked up the crutch. She stood and offered the crutch to Carol, all the while searching Carol's eyes for a hint of understanding. When Carol was balanced again, she lifted her arms and slid the sunglasses back in place on Aren's face.

"Will you stay?" Aren asked, her words quivering with the overwhelming emotion she felt.

Carol nodded, adjusting her crutches. "Everyone is staring at us." She pulled a few bills out of her purse and handed them into the cab. "Thank you for waiting, you can go. This should cover your time."

"Let them stare. My only concern is you."

"Nothing to see here, folks, just a post funeral meltdown." Carol called out to the crowd of onlookers. Those who had been staring averted their eyes and returned to their shopping. "I didn't mean to come at you like that. I should have waited until later, and asked questions like a normal human being, I'm so sorry. You seem to bear the brunt of my meltdowns lately. Thank you for not shoving me into the back of the cab and sending me on my way."

"Would you like to come and sit on the back of the wagon while I finish up here? I have about an hour to go. Or I could just pack up the booth and take you home now. You tell me what you'd like to do and we'll do it," Aren said. Seeing Carol cry and not being able to do anything about it was awful, but it was worse knowing that part of it had to do with her.

"I'd like to stay. I can sit with Bailey until you're done. I feel better just being here with you." Carol gave her a small smile. "Distraction, right?"

Aren nodded, led Carol to the booth, and helped her get seated in the back of the wagon among the empty crates. Bailey wagged her tail and nuzzled Carol, eager for a good tummy rub.

"Thank you, Marie, that was very thoughtful," Aren said, resting her hand on Marie's shoulder.

"That woman looks good on you, cowgirl. I'll catch up with you later, looks like my booth is getting busy again. It'll all work out. Have a little faith." Marie smiled and winked at Aren before jogging back to her poultry.

Aren's face grew so hot she could rival the sun. She was thankful to see customers needing assistance and jumped back to work.

CHAPTER SEVENTEEN

Wyatt pawed the dirt, showing his impatience to get going. Aren finished packing the rake and shovel she'd carried to clean the corral before climbing up into the driver's seat. She looked over to Carol and smiled.

"Walk on, big fella." They were on their way home and there was still plenty of tension between them. Aren hoped it was something they could figure out. She didn't want this to be the beginning of the end.

"How are you feeling? How was the service? Did your appointments go well?" Aren asked once they were on the shoulder of the paved road heading home.

"I'm doing okay, all things considered. It was quite a lot for one day. The service was nice. My aunt would have loved it had she been anyone but one of the guests of honor. The reverend did honor every one of their wishes, as promised. It was different, going to this funeral than it was going to my parents' funeral." Carol adjusted her leg before continuing. "I'd spent time with my aunt and uncle over the years, but I didn't know them like I did my parents. I don't know how to explain it better than that, but this was easier to accept and I don't feel the profound emptiness or the loss that I felt when I lost my parents." Carol was quiet for a few minutes and then looked over at Aren, "I almost feel guilty for not feeling sad *enough,* if that makes sense. I mean, God, they left me everything and here I sit talking about not feeling that sad."

"I think it's much different when you lose a relative outside of your immediate family. There's certainly no reason for you to feel guilt. You feel how you feel, and I wouldn't judge you for it either way." Aren flicked the reins.

"Did you lose an aunt or grandparent, someone besides your folks?" Carol asked. "I'm sorry, did you even know your parents? How did you end up in foster care, if you don't mind me asking?"

Aren smiled wryly. "You do like your questions, don't you?" She took in a deep breath and knew it was time for her to share her truths. Carol had probably heard the worst of it already, and there was a good chance only a smidge of it was true. At least she could set the record straight.

"Yes, I did know my parents. I don't know if either of them had any brothers or sisters and I never thought to ask. My gut tells me that my mom was disowned for marrying my father. And, knowing my father, I doubt his own family wanted much to do with him either." Aren let the sound of Wyatt's hoofs keep her calm. "My parents left their hometown and moved to Detroit when they were married. My father got a job with General Motors working on the assembly line. My mom was a housewife, and she took care of him, me, and our tiny house. I never met my grandparents on either side. I never knew anyone in my family beyond my parents." Aren looked up to the dark clouds in the sky. "Looks like it's gonna rain tonight."

Aren sat in the quiet for a moment. Her jaw tightened with the prospect of revisiting a world she simply wanted to leave behind. She looked over at Carol and watched her chew on her lip. She seemed to do that when she wanted to ask something but wasn't sure if she should.

"Ask." Aren looked over at Carol.

"Aren, you've been nothing but kind to me. I shouldn't have let them get into my head like that. I was wrong to go off on you like I did."

Aren sighed. "It's not going to go away. You'll always wonder if you don't ask. Better to get it out in the open." Aren's heart was pounding in her chest. Her tense muscles ached. "Want to tell me what happened to set you off?"

"It was after the service. I'd already called for the cab. The reverend and a few others gathered around, asking me questions about you, telling me things about you. It was like they couldn't wait to gossip, to share every ugly tidbit someone had heard or made up. I was already emotionally raw, drained from a long day and I felt blindsided. I didn't know what to believe. I didn't know how to defend you. What version is the truth. Then, when my cab finally pulled in, the reverend said he'd personally caught you stealing money from the church." Carol twisted in her seat to look at Aren. "That was a new one that I hadn't heard before. I'd heard other things, from my aunt, but the stories just don't line up with the person I believe you to be. Is any of it true?"

Aren was well aware of the stories told about her, about the family. She was grateful that Carol started with the money and not murder. "Ah, the good reverend. I wasn't stealing the money, I was returning it. Money that someone else had taken."

"Excuse me? Who stole it? How did you come across it?"

"After I came back from Kentucky, when Jennifer was sick, Phyllis was already drinking pretty heavily. She was broke. I thought that if I stopped giving her money that she'd be forced to sober up. She rationed for a while, then one day she comes home with several bottles of booze. Big bottles. It didn't make any sense. She drank herself into a stupor that night. I waited until she passed out, and then dug through her purse. There was all this cash in there and a few checks. The checks were made out to the Church of our Lord. I gathered the cash and the checks, added what I thought was spent on booze, plus some extra—I mean, Jesus, she stole money from a church. Anyway, I got into the rental car late that night and drove to the church. When I walked inside, I saw the contribution box on the floor, and a tiny lock beside it that looked to have been busted with the rock that lay next to it. I picked up the box and was putting the money back when the good reverend walked in with a police officer at his side. I tried to explain, but he'd already called the police and he wouldn't listen to a word I said. Thankfully, the police officer did. The officer talked to him, explained that the church had the money back, so there wasn't much they were going to do. The police officer was a guy I'd gone to high school with. He was always nice enough, good ol' Joe. To this day I'm relieved that it was Joe and not some rookie who had listened to the tall tales about the farm."

"You never told them it was Phyllis?"

"Oh, Joe suspected as much, but the money was returned so he didn't pursue anything," Aren said. The memory of it was still so embarrassing. "I will forever be grateful to sober Phyllis for taking me in, but drunk Phyllis was not my favorite person. She caused me so much grief."

A carload of teenage boys zoomed by, laying heavy on the car horn. One of the boys threw a glass bottle at Wyatt's hooves. The bottle exploded around the horse's legs. Wyatt jumped to the side and bolted with all his strength into a full gallop.

"HANG ON!" Aren yelled.

Wyatt had shifted into the ditch when he'd leapt into the air. The wagon was on a steep angle with the two right wheels bouncing their way down the rocky wash. Aren could hear crates bouncing around in the back of the wagon. She was sure she'd lost several in the hundred yards or so that they had already traveled. The cross street ahead was approaching fast, and there was a culvert jetting out that would surely flatten the wagon tires if it didn't destroy the wagon completely. Aren pulled gently back on the reins, trying to calm the terrified horse.

"Come on, Wyatt, whoa, fella, easy now." The pounding of Aren's heart nearly drowned out her words as the horse thundered forward. "WYATT, whoa, easy down!" she yelled.

Finally, Wyatt began to respond. He slowed to a canter and then slowed further to a trot before easing down to a brisk walk.

"Whoa, whoa there, fella," Aren said again in a calm voice, though she was anything but. He finally stopped completely, his sides heaving. Aren locked the brake and wrapped the reins to keep them from falling to the ground. Aren turned to Carol. "Are you okay?"

"Yeah, I think so, just bruised and scared." Carol shifted in her seat to arrange her leg, and she winced as she did it.

Aren jumped from the wagon and ran up to Wyatt. She stood in front of him rubbing his face, and he nuzzled his head into Aren's chest. She held him for a moment before she checked his legs for cuts from the glass. Once she was satisfied that there weren't any cuts, she lifted each hoof and checked for rocks.

"The exploding glass must have scared him more than anything. I'm not finding any cuts," she said to Carol from the front of the wagon.

"I can understand it scaring him, shit, it scared me. Is he going to be okay now? You know, to get us home without running again?" Carol asked while trying to get the cat tail fuzz out of her hair.

"Yeah, he'll do great, you'll see. Let me just run back and get the crates that fell out." She scanned the wagon. "And your crutches. I'll be right back," Aren said, heading for the lost items.

"But what if he runs again while you're back there? What do I do?" Carol called out. Aren turned around and looked up at Carol who sat there looking frazzled. Her hair and her black dress were covered in cat tail fuzz. She'd had a tough day and this hadn't helped. The least Aren could do was help her feel safe. Aren walked back up to the wagon and climbed back into the driver's seat.

"I'll get us out of the ditch and get him over onto that side street. That way he'll be out of the traffic, okay?"

Carol nodded earnestly in agreement.

Aren released the brake and urged Wyatt forward, her heart still hammering in her chest. He easily pulled the wagon free from the ditch. Once on the side street, Aren circled Wyatt around so he could see the main road. She halted him on the shoulder in case cars needed to get by.

"How's this? He'll be able to see me and I'll run fast to get the loose stuff," Aren said. "Here, you hold the reins. If he moves forward, then you just very softly pull back and say 'whoa, fella.' Don't pull too hard. You could hurt his mouth."

"This is great. Thank you, Aren, for putting up with me." Carol smiled.

"Think nothing of it. I'm happy to help you feel safe," Aren replied as she jumped down from the wagon.

It didn't take Aren long to collect the loose items and repack the back of the wagon. Within ten minutes, they were safely back on their way home.

"How often does that happen?" Carol asked once they were traveling again.

"Not too often, maybe once every few months. Usually, it's only a horn, which doesn't bother Wyatt too much anymore. The glass bottle, now that's a new one. I can honestly say I've never had anyone throw anything at us before. Although, you've increased my odds now, since I only went into town maybe six times a month and four of those were for market. We've been in town at least six times since you came to stay with me. And please, don't apologize. I'm enjoying it, just some levity in a veiled attempt to calm my heart rate." Aren smiled.

"Well, I appreciate all the extra trips you've taken for me. Thank you again for taking me in to get this dress. It felt nice to dress appropriately for the funeral," Carol said, still pulling bits of cat tail off her clothes.

"My pleasure and it really has been wonderful to have you stay with me. I didn't realize how much I missed having someone to share things with." Aren flicked the reins and headed for home.

She exhaled slowly, willing her heart to settle down. She was angry. Angry with the relentless rumors that plagued her for so many years. Angry at the kid who threw the bottle, angry for the loss of her vision and the need to travel like this in the first place. She wanted nothing more than a normal life. A normal life that could maybe include Carol, but tonight she realized how her way of life could affect Carol. She could have been injured, thrown from the wagon. Aren could never have forgiven herself if Carol had been hurt. Maybe a normal life wasn't in the cards for her.

Chapter Eighteen

Later that evening, after chores were finished and their bellies were full of another Crock-Pot delight, they made their way back to the chairs still situated in front of the screened-in loft door. The low-hanging clouds had opened up and were releasing a soft, steady rain. The air felt damp and smelled so clean and refreshing after a hot, humid day. The breeze was a bit chilly given the dampness. Aren got up and grabbed a light blanket to drape over Carol's lap.

"You are so thoughtful. You do so many things out of observation more than request. It's sweet," Carol said, nuzzling under the blanket.

Aren was glad they only had candles burning. "I saw you shivering and thought you'd enjoy a warm fuzzy."

Carol reached over and took Aren's hand in her own, resting both in her lap beneath the blanket.

"Can I ask you something?"

Aren sighed. She was tired and it had been a rough afternoon. She looked over to Carol knowing it had been a rough day for her too. Finally, she nodded.

"You mentioned that you were grateful to sober Phyllis. Would you tell me more about that? Something that was good in your life? Something that made you happy on this farm?"

Aren considered that. A happy story? Seriously? "Yes, of course."

"I'd like to know that you've had some happiness in your life." Carol held Aren's eyes. Her expression was so sincere, so tender.

"I've had happiness in my life, right here, on this farm." Aren squeezed Carol's hand.

"Tell me about it. Please?" Carol leaned her head on Aren's shoulder.

"When I was assigned here as a foster kid, I was terrified. I'd only ever lived in the city. Detroit of all places, downtown, serious big city. I knew nothing of life on a farm. They dropped me off here, with my Hefty bag of belongings, and introduced me to Ron and Phyllis Harris. They were so nice, so soft-spoken and kind. Phyllis loved to sew, loved to cook. She let me help and I treasured every minute of it. I'd measure fabric, cut it exactly as she asked, and then iron it exactly as asked once it was sewn. She made quilts, clothes, everything and anything needed for the family. She wouldn't make me wear ruffles or super girly stuff either. She made clothes that I liked, clothes that Jen liked. She respected our differences. She was a great cook, too. She had a spice rack that was unbelievable and much of it was homegrown. Sage, basil, chives, oregano, you name it, Phyllis grew it in her herb garden and then dried it, and bottled it. Many of those herbs are the spices you've used to make your amazing Crock-Pot dinners." Aren turned to Carol and smiled. "Phyllis would let me help cook meals, too. Breakfast, lunch, and dinner, anything I'd ask to help with. Dinner was always meat, veggie, and potatoes or rice, each seasoned perfectly with spices that made your taste buds dance. I was in awe. I hadn't experienced anything like that in my life before living on this farm." Aren pulled her hand free from Carol's. She walked into the kitchen and poured two cups of coffee. She added cream and sugar to Carol's cup before returning to the chairs. Aren handed Carol her cup of coffee, then sat down beside her.

When Aren sat back down, Carol reached over and pulled her free hand back into her lap. Carol gave Aren's hand a gentle squeeze. Aren squeezed back. She felt so completely accepted and at home at that moment.

"Keep talking," Carol said, her eyes softly smiling.

Remembering the good things was painful too, but in a good way. "Ron was just as amazing, if not more so. I respected him, admired him. He was the first man in my life to ever earn that. He asked for honor, honesty, and a good day's work. Not once did he ask us to do something he wasn't willing to do himself. He was slow and methodical in his lessons. He showed us how to run a tractor and hook up the accessories. What to watch out for and where to push a little harder. How to work the fields, respect the soil, feed the soil, rotate crops, and appreciate the harvest. He taught me how to care for animals, tend the livestock, and gentle the horses. He never used a whip or a strong hand. We harvested timber that was overcrowded in order to create a healthy forest, milled that timber into useable boards and worked together side by side, something that was completely foreign to me, yet he was patient and gave me time to become accustomed to his ways. He taught me how to be one with the land. He was always kind and so knowledgeable. I sincerely admired him and enjoyed working at his side."

"Was Jennifer included like you were?"

"Yes, yes, she was. She bonded more with Phyllis when we were younger, whereas I was perfectly happy working by Ron's side, but we helped wherever we were needed. They treated us like part of a family, never like hired hands or foster kids."

"Did you ever meet Daniel? What was he like?" Carol asked, her head still resting on Aren's shoulder.

"No, we never met him. I've only ever seen pictures of him, heard stories, looked up the newspaper articles at the library. He was sentenced well before we were ever assigned here as foster kids. Phyllis traveled every week for his assigned visitors' day. It was the only thing I ever heard them fight about. Ron had no interest in Daniel after the conviction, but Phyllis, she said he'd always be her son."

"Were you happy that you were assigned here?" Carol asked, sounding sleepy.

Aren pulled her hand free and wrapped her arm around Carol's shoulders. Carol snuggled as close as she could get given the separate chairs.

"Yes, I was happy to have been assigned here. Throughout high school, I was happy to call this land, this town, this farm, my home even with the stigma of living on the Harris farm and what Daniel did. During those years, Ron and Phyllis were a source of kindness, structure, and stability that had been missing all my life. The impact they had on my life was huge, and I miss those years to this day."

Carol's breathing evened out and deepened. Aren sat there in the chair holding her, grateful for the chance to explain some of her truths. She felt understood, at least for now. There was plenty more darkness lurking, but being able to remember the good had lightened the tunnel she'd been in for so long. She waited for hours before she helped Carol to bed, not wanting the moment to end. They hadn't talked about Carol's plans for the future, nor how long she planned on staying. But she could be grateful for this time that felt wonderfully normal, and she'd cherish the memory of it when Carol was long gone.

CHAPTER NINETEEN

The sun was high in the cloudless sky, the breeze elusive. Heat and humidity returned with a vengeance. Carol was seated in the shade of the barn, thinking of everything and nothing all at the same time. It had been several days since the funeral and it had affected her more than she cared to admit. Saying good-bye to Aunt Suzie had been especially difficult. They'd become close since her mom's passing. Seeing the two caskets in the front of the church brought back a flood of memories, and they kept threatening to drown her.

"Come on, it's too hot to work. It's been an intense few weeks. Let's take a play day." Aren's voice pulled Carol from her thoughts.

Carol spun around in her seat. Aren stood behind her holding the handle of a large pull wagon in one hand and a small bucket in the other.

"Where are we going?"

"It's a surprise. You'll like it, I promise. Come on, hop in."

"You want me to ride in the vegetable wagon like a veggie? I can follow along just fine with my crutches."

"Humans are ninety percent water. We're basically just walking cucumbers anyway. I know you can use your crutches, but you'll be staring at the ground and not the scenery. Please, trust me, ride in the wagon. You can hobble all the way back if you want."

Carol pushed herself up out of the chair and hopped to the side of the wagon. Aren had arranged pillows, transforming the wagon into a rolling lounge chair. She accepted Aren's hand as she lowered herself onto her chariot. She leaned back against the tall wooden slats and situated her legs around a small picnic basket resting in front of her. Aren slid the wooden side panel back onto the old wagon before sliding Carol's crutches in along the side. The smile on Aren's face had Carol intrigued. She'd been quiet and thoughtful since the day they'd shared so much, and nothing more had been said about their pasts. And yet, something had shifted between them, too. There was a closeness now that made it so her breath caught whenever Aren was close. It was both scary and exciting, but she wouldn't get ahead of herself.

Aren pulled the wagon onto a trail Carol had never noticed before. The trail led into a stand of dense forest where the trees towered over them. Large boulders jutted out on either side. It was breathtakingly beautiful. Carol looked up into the canopy and watched a squirrel leap from branch to branch. "They're like little acrobatic stars, aren't they?"

"See what you would have missed if you were staring at the ground looking for a place to land the crutches? You haven't seen anything yet." Aren twisted around, a big grin on her face.

The trail started to drop, twisting and turning into a valley. The side walls grew taller and were lined with trees growing out of jagged rock. How trees managed to flourish with a tiny bit of soil in the crack of a rock was beyond Carol. The temperature suddenly seemed to drop too, at least ten degrees as they made their way deeper into the valley. Carol closed her eyes and leaned her head back, treasuring the cooler air. Her eyes popped back open when she heard the sound of running water. A babbling brook, perhaps? Carol looked around for water but found none. Aren pulled the wagon around the large root base of an enormous old tree. The trail dropped down again and the sound of running water grew louder, closer. Around another tight bend and suddenly the trail ended at the edge of a large pool of water surrounded by tall trees. Sunlight streamed in through tiny openings in the canopy. A tall waterfall fed the pond on the far side. It was magical.

"Oh, Aren, this is incredible. Is this part of your farm?" Carol sat up, trying to take everything in.

"Indeed, it is. It's my little hidden secret, and now there's two of us in this world that know this paradise exists. We had a really wet year my second year here. The rains were so heavy that the river overflowed the banks. The deluge cut a groove and forked the river upstream about a mile away, and this is the result of that fork. The water never stopped flowing down here, like this little valley was a perfect home for it. The pool is deep out in the center, and as much as I try, I can't swim to the bottom. I don't know if it opened up a spring or if it was just that deep of a valley, but the waterfall keeps feeding the pool and the water flows on, out the other side over there. I've never been able to find where it ends, the terrain gets too dense, and there are too many ferns and wild raspberry bushes. All I know is that this water is clean and cool, and the pool is full of happy fish."

Aren pulled the side off the wagon and leaned it against a tree. She lifted Carol's crutches out and then held out her hand. Carol accepted the help up. Once she had the crutches situated, she made her way closer to the water's edge. It was crystal clear. She could see tiny minnows swimming in the sandy-bottomed shallows.

Carol turned around in time to see Aren spreading out a blanket on the trail head. She must have been sitting on that blanket all the way here. Aren set a few pillows down on the blanket and then rested the picnic basket in the center.

"What I wouldn't give to be done with this cast. The water looks so inviting, I'd love nothing more than to dive in."

"How about a no splashing float? I dug through my stuff and found supplies that could work as a waterproof cast cover. I feel silly not having thought of it sooner. I know how much you've been craving a hot shower. If it works, you get both."

"Seriously? Do you think it will work?" Carol felt giddy with the prospect of floating in the clear, cool water.

"I think it will work great. Here, let me help you down on the blanket and we'll get it taped up."

Carol held onto Aren's hands while lowering herself onto the blanket. Aren was so thoughtful, so gentle, and this was such a private, romantic spot, it made Carol feel special, like Aren was sharing a part of her that no one else got to see. Aren lifted her casted leg and slid a thick plastic sock over it. She created a few pleats in the plastic and then pulled out a roll of tape about two inches wide. She taped up the pleats, sealing any gaps and then taped around the top of the plastic where it met Carol's skin just below the knee. Aren's touch was so gentle, and Carol couldn't remember enjoying such an innocent touch so much. It almost tingled.

Aren popped up off the blanket, returning the tape to the bucket. She reached down in the bucket and pulled out a folded piece of plastic.

"I bought a couple of these as a test to keep ice out of the water troughs, but it was a completely failed experiment. The horses thought they were play toys and I was worried they'd choke on the plastic."

Aren unfolded the plastic float ring, and with just a few breaths of air, she had it inflated.

"Are you okay getting your shorts and shirt wet?" Aren flopped down next to Carol and started pulling off her boots.

"What's the alternative?" Carol could feel the heat rising in her cheeks. "Seriously, this is fine. My swimsuit is still buried beneath a tree." The thought of standing before Aren in a bra, panties, or even naked, with a plastic and tape-covered cast wasn't the romantic image she wanted for a first experience like that. If, of course, that was in the cards. Which it wasn't.

"No one would see you except me." Aren must have read her mind.

"I'm good going in just like this. Thanks, though." Carol fanned her face, pretending to be hot and not completely embarrassed.

Carol watched Aren pull off her socks. She stood and unbuckled her belt, then unbuttoned and unzipped her jeans. The jeans fell into a puddle on the blanket and then Aren tossed her hat down and removed her sunglasses. There she stood in fitted boxer shorts and a white tank top. It was probably the sexiest sight Carol had ever seen, in spite of the ghostly white legs.

"I have never seen such tan arms and such pale white legs in my life." Carol tried to suppress her pounding heartbeat and tried for teasing instead. "Is this the first time they've ever seen the sun?"

"Keep it up, Ms. Matthews. Shorts and livestock don't much go hand in hand." Aren picked up the float ring before squatting down and scooping Carol up in her arms.

Aren waded out into the pool of water cradling Carol in her arms. Carol felt like she was being whisked away by her knight in shining armor on a hot summer day. She kept her arms wrapped around Aren's neck as the cool water enveloped her and crept up her back. It felt amazing, refreshing, and she hoped it would help cool the desire she felt to pull Aren in and kiss her.

Aren stopped walking as if she'd read Carol's mind. Carol felt Aren's arm that was supporting her back slide down lower, closer to her butt, and then Aren's hand was wrapping around Carol's thigh. Carol's heart pounded; her breath hitched. And then Aren pulled the arm away that was supporting Carol's legs. She slid the floating ring over the plastic wrapped cast up to Carol's knee and then she took two more steps until they were both neck-deep in the crystal-clear water. The cool water did nothing to calm her beating heart or soothe her disappointment. These new feelings would have to be nipped in the bud. Her life was far too messy to get involved with anyone, even someone as hot and sweet as Aren. Wasn't it?

CHAPTER TWENTY

I'm going to let you go for just a minute. Are you okay to float here or would you like me to take you closer to shore?" Aren asked.

"I can keep myself from drowning if that's what you're asking. Where are you off to?" Carol's expression was suspicious.

"It's a surprise. Wait here. I'll be right back." Aren pulled her arms away.

Aren watched Carol lean back and use her arms to gently float in the water, and the inflated tube supported the plastered leg perfectly. She looked more relaxed than Aren had ever seen her. Aren swam underwater toward her favorite spot, back behind the waterfall. When she came up for air, she was hidden behind the cascading falls. She checked the rock ledge for any unwelcome visitors. Over the years, she'd encountered a few snakes, a racoon eating a fish, and once, a very aggressive badger, though today the rock ledge was free for the taking. She stood there for a moment, behind the cascading water, watching Carol float out beyond her reach. She was the first person allowed to peek over the fortress walls that surrounded her heart. Except Jennifer, of course. Though, back then, Jen just leapt over the top and was inside before Aren had known what happened. She was more guarded now, more cautious, though she had to admit that she liked the way it felt to care about someone and to be cared for. She dropped under water again and made her way back to Carol.

She resurfaced next to Carol, scooping her up into her arms. "Close your eyes."

"Now what are you going to do?" Carol asked, her arms tightening around Aren's neck.

"You'll see. Close your eyes, come on, trust me. I am a doctor." Aren was excited to share her special spot with Carol. She hoped that Carol enjoyed it as much as she did.

"Oh, good one, I'll remember that."

Aren watched Carol squeeze her eyes shut. She found solid footing and walked them toward the waterfall. She kept Carol, specifically her leg, as far away from the spraying water as possible as she ducked behind the cascading falls. She stood up in a smooth, swift motion and lifted Carol up onto the rock outcropping behind the falls.

"Okay, open your eyes," Aren said, hopping up on the ledge next to Carol.

"Where are we? Holy shit, are we *behind* the waterfall?" Carol seemed to twist her head in every direction taking in her new surroundings.

"Yes, we are."

"Another one of your safe spots, protected from behind with a clear observation post," Carol said, looking around the dark space.

"Hadn't thought of that, but I suppose you aren't wrong. Anyway, welcome to the coolest, most air-conditioned spot on the farm. When it's a hundred degrees out there, it's crisp and cool in here." Aren leaned across Carol and adjusted the float ring to better keep her leg out of the water. "See, you have goose bumps." Aren trailed a finger down Carol's arm before leaning back. "Though, I have learned to check first and make sure the spot isn't already occupied."

"If you're the only one who knows this place exists, who'd be back here?"

"Oh, I've met a couple of racoons and a badger. None of whom wanted to share the space, and who were very obvious about it, so I've learned to check first." Aren smiled.

"It's definitely nice and cool back here, but it's not the reason for the goose bumps." Carol turned her head to Aren, her eyes sparkling. "It's also quite romantic, back here, behind the falls."

Aren sat there silently, her heart pounding in her chest. She felt Carol's hand wrap around hers. Aren turned to face Carol. Yes, it was romantic. Carol was absolutely beautiful, smart, intelligent, understanding, and undoubtedly sexy as hell. But what if this town wasn't her home? What if she left? Was it already too late? Were the feelings already too strong?

"Can I ask you a weird question?"

"What the hell." Aren smiled. "Go for it."

"Are you attracted to me? Sometimes I think you are, but then you pull away. I know my life is a little messy right now...okay, a lot messy. God, the meltdowns, and you're certainly getting to know me at my worst, one of my lowest points, but the good side is, it can only get better, I swear. And you're so sweet and thoughtful. You brought me out here to this spot, then back here, behind the falls. Well, what I'm wondering is, Aren, why haven't you kissed me? I'm making a big leap here in assuming you're attracted to women, and hopefully attracted to me. Shit, I'm rambling, I'm stopping, see, silent." Carol pulled an imaginary zipper across her lips. She looked absolutely adorable as color touched her cheeks.

Aren squeezed Carol's hand. "I brought you back here to the pool and behind the falls to share a part of me, so you can see what makes me happy, what fills my tanks. I'm trying to be more open. I guess I need more practice."

"Oh shit, I'm sorry, Aren, I totally misread this. God, I feel stupid."

"No, you didn't totally misread anything. I am attracted to women, more specifically, to you. I assumed you were too, attracted to women, that is. That first day when I retrieved your clothes, when I checked on the cars, I saw all the rainbow stickers. Why haven't I kissed you? You're all but stranded here. I haven't wanted to do anything that could or would make you feel uncomfortable or make you feel taken advantage of. You can't drive with this thing on your leg," Aren said, tapping the plaster cast. "I don't want you to feel trapped with a predator. I like having you around way too much to do that to you. I like the friendship we're developing and it's nice having you here in my life. I don't want to lose all of it over an unwanted advance."

"What if it's not unwanted? What if it's welcomed?" Carol looked into the waterfall.

Aren squeezed her hand. "Can I ask you something?"

"Anything."

"Are you staying, Carol? Is this home? Or are you still searching?" Aren looked out through the waterfall too, at a world blurred by water in motion.

"I don't know. I hope it's home, but I'm not entirely sure—"

"And that's what scares me. Yes, I want to kiss you, I want to touch you, but then what happens if you decide it's not home?"

"Can you give me more? Help me understand what you're feeling?"

"I don't know how to put it into words." Aren was thankful for the dark shadows behind the falls, thankful for the noise that hid how nervous her voice sounded.

"Would you try? Anything will help."

"Talking about emotions, hell, *feeling* emotions, is something I haven't done for a long time. Somewhere, over the last few years, it all just sort of shut off and I focused on what needed to get done. Then you show up on my doorstep and turn my world upside down. You poke and prod, you ask questions and I find myself thinking about the answers. But if I open up, if I let my guard down and really start to feel again, only to have you say good-bye... God, the thought of that already hurts too much." Aren exhaled. Where on earth had that come from? Relief and anxiety jumbled together.

Carol lifted her hand and kissed Aren's knuckles. "I won't make promises I can't keep, and I don't know what's going on in my life. I can see how unfair it is to ask you to take a chance, I really can. Can we keep moving forward? Just keep being us, helping each other heal. No pressure." Taking anything romantic off the table felt wrong, but what else could she do?

"I'd like that. And I hope you understand, it's not like I'm asking for marriage or anything, I've just never been one to do casual sex or whatever. But if I let my emotions get involved and you leave, it would be damn hard to recover."

Carol nodded, and her expression was so warm and understanding. Aren wasn't used to feeling this raw, this open. It was unsettling and settling all at the same time.

"I've got a picnic basket up on shore with your name on it and you never told me about how your appointments went the other day. Are you ready for a snack?"

"I could be hungry." Carol smiled.

Aren slid off the ledge and back into the water. She found her footing and stood up, reaching for Carol, who wrapped her arms around Aren's neck. They made their way through the falls and back to shore and holding her close felt so right. She wanted to do this over and over again, but maybe it just wasn't their time.

CHAPTER TWENTY-ONE

A few days later, Carol woke to the sound of heavy rain and the teasing smell of coffee. She thought she heard a car pulling in as she mixed sugar and cream into her morning coffee. Before she had a chance to gather up her other crutch and investigate, she heard Aren bounding up the stairs two at a time. Her arms were again overflowing with items from Carol's room at her aunt's house.

"Good morning," Aren said around an armload of items.

"Good morning. What is all this?" Carol asked. "I thought I heard a car pull in."

"You did. I brought your car over from across the street. They must have finished clearing the tree away yesterday and stabilized what was left of the ceiling on the main level. The crew was rained out this morning, but said it was safe enough for you to look around before everything was ruined by the rain. I told them I'd let you know, and then I snagged your keys since I'd feel comfortable driving you across the street and back. I don't really need a license for that." Aren set the pile on the table. "These are some more of your clothes out of that room you stayed in. I imagine you're sick of wearing the same few things over and over. Do you feel up to going through the house now?" Aren shook the rain from her hat.

Carol moved to the door and looked across the field at the house. "Everything will be soaked if we wait. Wow, they have the second story all removed. It's all open to the elements."

"You could tell me what you'd like and I could go and get it for you." Aren stood behind her and rested her hands on Carol's shoulders. The touch was comforting.

"No, I should go. You'll come with me, won't you? Forget I asked, you're driving," Carol said, laughing at herself. The thought of going through the debris of her aunt and uncle's lives was daunting, but it had to be done.

"I have a long rain slicker hanging on a hook at the bottom of the stairs. That should keep your cast dry. I don't think we need to tape it up."

Aren helped Carol into the car before climbing into the driver's seat. Carol smiled when she saw Aren looking for the brake release in the location it would be had they been on the wagon. She smiled again when Aren blushed before reaching between the seats to release the brake. After a slight slipping of the clutch, they were off on their first motorized adventure.

Carol's heart dropped as she walked into the house. Pictures of her parents still hung on the wall in the living room. She walked over and traced the frame with her fingertip.

"These are my parents," Carol said absently, removing the picture from the wall. She held the photograph close to her heart while scanning the other photos for her parents or relatives. She came across one of herself as a small girl on the back of a Shetland pony.

"I was nine years old here. The pony I'm riding was part of the purchase agreement when my aunt and uncle bought this place. They had to take the pony if they wanted the land. They soon realized why he was named Cujo. He'd wait until you were leading him around, and if you didn't pay close attention, he'd bite you square on the butt cheek. Got my uncle a few times, then my uncle got him." She swallowed against old emotions. "Cujo went to the great horse heaven in the sky." Carol pulled that picture off the wall as well. Aren held out her hand to hold the pictures. "Thanks, but I'll hold these two." She didn't want to let them go.

Aren nodded and left with the box of items she was carrying. Carol made her way to the bookcase, looking at a few other pictures.

She thought she heard a car pulling up. She turned around in time to see a car pull in directly behind Aren. The reverend stepped out of his car and walked up behind Aren.

"Just like one of the Harris folks. Couldn't be bothered to show up for the funeral, and sure couldn't wait to raid their belongings either. I have the jewelry they were wearing. Do you want to steal that too?"

Carol stepped to the side, trying to see better. Aren spun around to face him, her face red and her fists clenched.

"How dare you assume I'm here for my own benefit!" Aren said. "You're some piece of work. Putting on this front of holiness and righteousness, all the while stirring up shit, spreading rumors that you know to be untrue. Stealing from the church? Seriously? I put back way more than was stolen. How dare you? How dare you hit Carol with all that nonsense on the day of her family's funeral. To what end? Do you think you'll run me out of town? Piss me off enough so I'll come after you?"

Carol saw the veins in Aren's neck popping out. She stepped into the reverend's space. He backed up a step or two. Aren wasn't wearing her sunglasses and the scars around her eye looked dark and jagged. It was the first time she ever looked scary. She was grateful it wasn't her on the other side of that emotion.

"Good luck with that. I wouldn't waste my energy on someone like you. The least you could do is to give Carol some time to grieve. Let her have some time to mourn at her family's funeral before you start in with your Harris farm bullshit!"

Carol watched the reverend back up a few more steps until he backed himself up against his own car. "I had some items for Carol from the funeral home. I got a call from one of the workers who attends the church. He said that you asked them to stop working this morning, said that *you* were here picking through stuff, not Miss Matthews."

"You know damned well that she's been staying with me and rather than ask me if she's here, rather than ask if she's inside, you assume the worst. Why couldn't you just call her on her cell phone and make arrangements to drop the stuff off? No, you have to rush out here so you can say you caught me in the act. Caught me red-handed all over again. Look, I know that the Harris boy killed your niece, but I wasn't any part of that. I came along years later. I know you had your differences with Ron and Phyllis, before and after. I've heard it all and I'm willing to bet I got about half the truth." Aren pointed at her face and stepped closer to the reverend. "And I've paid my price too for knowing that family. Believe me, I've paid and paid, time and again. You weren't the only one that was hurt by Daniel's actions. But you were so angry that you couldn't see anyone else's pain. You couldn't see that Ron and Phyllis needed you. Needed your compassion, your guidance as their spiritual leader. They needed the community's help, but no, you denied them. You ruined their name as much as Daniel did. You wouldn't let it go and now you're ruining my name and punishing Carol just for being around me. Enough. It needs to end. Please, just set the envelope down, get in your car and get the hell out of here. Leave Carol in peace to sort through what she wants. I won't ask you again."

Reverend Todd didn't argue. He dropped the envelope, scooted around his car, climbed in behind the wheel and took off toward town without saying another word to Aren.

Carol was sitting in the living room next to the glassless window, tears streaming down her cheeks. She tried to wipe them off when she heard Aren coming up the porch, but she knew that Aren would know she'd been crying.

"I'm sorry you had to hear all of that. I didn't mean to upset you," Aren said, squatting over the glass shards in front of Carol's chair.

"You didn't upset me. These aren't sad tears, well, maybe some of them are, but not because of you. They're *for* you. I feel so bad for you," Carol said, wiping away another stray tear that trailed down her cheek, "He was so cruel to you, so hateful because of something that you had no control over. That girl that was killed, she was his niece?"

Aren nodded silently. Carol touched Aren's cheek as she shook her head in disbelief. "You offered to go to the funeral, to be there for me, even though you knew you'd have to face that hatred? You put up with everything I said to you at the market that day, yet you stopped the work here today just so I could have time to dig through this heap for a few pictures and some clothes?"

Aren remained silent, looking at the floor. Carol squeezed her hand, and with her free hand, lifted Aren's chin so she could see her eyes.

"Aren, you are the most selfless person I've ever met," Carol said softly. She wrapped her arms tightly around Aren's neck. "I'm done here. I don't want anything else. Please, just take me home."

Chapter Twenty-two

The rain continued to fall through that afternoon and into the evening. Carol followed Aren down for the evening chores and sat on a stool watching Aren as she began to milk the first of the two cows.

"Were you and Jennifer lovers?" Carol asked once Aren had the milking under way.

Aren's arm dropped too far while working the milk out of one of the teats, and she nearly knocked over the milk pail, catching it just in time to save the milk. She shook her head and looked over to Carol. "You've got to warn me when you're going to ask questions like that out of the clear blue."

Carol tried to keep a straight face. "I'm sorry, it just popped into my head."

"Why do you ask about Jennifer?" Aren asked, her brow furrowed slightly.

"I think you had a nightmare about her last night. I woke up to you screaming out for her," Carol answered quietly. "I still want to learn more about you."

Aren leaned her head against Cinnamon's side, closing her eyes for just a moment. The mere mention of her name tugged at Aren's heart. The thought of reliving all of that through words seemed much like slicing open a healed scar. Only her scars weren't really healed, they were more like severely infected, festering scabs.

"We don't have to talk about this if you don't want to. I'm sorry. I didn't mean to pry," Carol said in a hesitant tone.

"No, no, you're not prying. I want you to ask any question you have. I'm not known for letting my demons come out to play, that's all. Sometimes it just takes me a bit to figure out the words." What more information could she offer that wouldn't slice open old terrors? "Jen. How do I describe Jen? She was the closest thing to family, real family, like you read about in books, that I've ever known. I knew all of her secrets and she knew every one of mine, and despite that, we still loved each other, unconditionally."

Aren milked for a few more minutes before continuing. "We did sleep together once, my junior year of high school, well, we slept together often, but we made love just that one time. It helped both of us learn a lot about ourselves. She learned that she still liked men, sexually anyway. I learned that I couldn't have the one person I loved most in this world."

"So, you were in love with her?" Carol asked softly.

"Oh yeah, head over heels in love. Have you ever been in love with someone who loved you but wasn't in love with you?" Carol shook her head. Aren nodded slightly. "It rips your guts out. Watching her kiss some guy she just met or seeing her hop into a car and take off with some guy, knowing that he was going to touch her in a way that you had once, but likely never would again." Aren paused again for a few moments before continuing. "Loving her was like being in one of those deep caverns you explore. One wrong turn and you're forever trying to find your way out, all the while walking deeper and deeper into the heart of the cavern. Some years later they find your bones just two turns from the exit. I can't necessarily say I regret making love to her, but I can't help but laugh when I think of Bugs Bunny saying 'I knew I should have turned left at Albuquerque!'" Aren used her Bugs Bunny voice for the last sentence.

Carol chuckled. "Were other women able to help heal your heart?"

Aren shook her head. "Other women, I tried. I went out on a few dates, took some of them to bed, enjoyed the moment, the sex, but none of them could win my heart. I was still in love with Jen, totally committed to her. It took me some time to realize that back then. I guess I was just waiting for her to see the light of day, to realize that the men she picked were abusive, drunks, or perpetually unemployed. Waiting for her to see that I could give her a stable, secure life. I went to school, landed a good job, saved a ton of money and kept waiting for her to call and say, 'come and get me, I love you!'"

"But you never did get that call, did you?" Carol asked.

"We talked almost every day on the phone. We were the best of friends and I loved her with every ounce of my heart, body and soul. She'd tell me about the men she was dating at any given moment. I'd listen and tell her how I hoped this one worked out for her. I'd tell her about the horses and my work. She'd ask if I was doing anything besides working, like going out and meeting people. By people she'd mean women. I'd tell her I'd met some, gone out on a few dates, but it wasn't right and she'd just tell me I was a hermit and needed to get out more. Sometimes we'd talk several times a day if there was a lot of news." Aren continued to milk the cow out of habit, while movie reels played vividly in her mind. "It was young love, and usually that just fizzles out, right? You move on. But for me, that intensity never went away."

"Had you ever told her how you felt?" Carol asked.

Aren grew quiet for a few minutes before answering, "No, Carol, I never told her how I felt. What was the point? She didn't want to be with me, be with a woman. She didn't want a life with me. She wanted to go out and socialize, she wanted men. I wanted a home and quiet time, romance. I wanted a life with her. No, I got other calls instead. When Ron's health took a turn, I started to get calls to send money home because Phyllis couldn't pay the bills. Then Ron died, so I got a call to send money home because Phyllis couldn't afford Ron's funeral, send money home, so she could go to the doctor…" Aren trailed off.

"That's when you found out she had cancer? Where did it originate?" Carol asked.

Aren led Cinnamon out and brought in Ginger for her turn at the milking stand.

"She had cervical cancer from an ignored case of HPV. She refused all treatment. I tried to take her on a small vacation, fill the one bucket list trip, but she became too sick. She passed away a couple of months after I came back."

Carol became quiet, just sat there watching Aren milk the cow. After a few minutes went by, she asked, "Why didn't you return to Kentucky after Jennifer passed away? Why did you stay here with all the memories? Stay with all the judgment?"

Aren sat on her milking stool quietly. It was time to share, time for her to be honest. Jen would want her to open up to someone. She inhaled deeply, exhaled slowly. She finished milking Ginger and sent her back out to the pasture before she spoke again. "I'm going to ask you a sincere question. I'm not trying to be a smart-ass here. Would you like the short or the long version?"

Without skipping a beat, Carol gave her answer. "I want the long version. And just so I'm clear, I'll always want the long version. I want to know about your life."

Aren shook her head. "Well then, let's finish the chores really quick. I'll call Bailey in for supper and then tell you the long version over dinner and coffee."

Chapter Twenty-three

They decided to heat up the leftover stew from the night before. Aren got a pot of coffee percolating while their meal heated in a saucepan on the other burner. She fixed Bailey a bowl of dog food with some stew stirred in and set it next to her water bowl. Instead of sitting at the dining table, they sat in their favorite chairs facing the screened-in loft door. The rain continued to fall steadily.

"I'm glad there's been no lightning with this storm," Carol said, sitting down with her stew and milk.

"I understand why, but I must admit, I love a good thunderstorm. Your thunderstorm was a scary exception, but I love to hear the thunder and watch the landscape light up. I was up watching the storm that night. That's how I knew the tree had been struck, that it had fallen." Aren motioned toward the house with her spoon.

"And I'm very thankful that you love to sit up in the middle of the night and watch the storms or I might not be sitting here in such great company." Carol smiled sweetly. "Now, before you can weasel out of it, you promised me a long version."

"Ah yes, so I did. You asked me why I stayed here and didn't return to Kentucky. I need to go back in time a bit for the long version. I told you that Ron and Phyllis took in foster kids because Ron could no longer get work. They had taken a second mortgage on the farm to hire an attorney for their son's trial. I don't know how much they received each month for Jennifer and me, but they had that income for four years for me and five and a half for Jennifer. We were both fourteen when we were sent here for fostering, but

Jennifer was two years behind me in school, so they received money for her until she was nineteen and a half. She was held back one year and I'd skipped a year. I graduated high school at seventeen and went on to community college and worked for that last year until I turned eighteen and I could leave."

"So, you were fourteen when you went into foster care?" Carol asked.

"No, I was twelve, almost thirteen when I went into the system. I was fourteen when I was sent *here* from a different foster home. That's a different long version." Aren took their bowls into the kitchen and set them on the counter to wash up later. After pouring two cups of coffee, adding cream and sugar to one, she returned to continue answering the original question.

"So, I guess they could pay the bills with the income from the farm and what they received from having both me and Jennifer here. I think things started going downhill after I left for college. Ron finally landed a job down in Lansing, though I don't believe the pay was all that great. He commuted back and forth five days a week all the while trying to keep animals fed and cared for here on the farm. Jennifer helped where she could. She'd feed and milk cows, but she had school too, so he'd take morning chores before his commute and have her do evening chores. They also had acreage planted with crops that needed care and cultivating." Aren took a long sip of her coffee. "Phyllis wasn't worth much on the farm. She'd say she signed on to be a farmer's wife, not a farmer. So, she would only do stuff in the house. She kept a clean house, kept laundry up and always had a meal on the table at supper time, but she wanted nothing to do with learning how to run a tractor or milk a cow. This left a lot on Ron's shoulders, and I think that over the years the stress just got to be too much for him. The state wouldn't send any more foster kids to the house because Phyllis had taken to drinking a fair bit by this time and when they made a few surprise visits, let's just say she wasn't the least bit sober. They almost pulled Jennifer out, but by then she only had another month of school, so they let her finish high school and choose her path. Ron and Phyllis pulled a guilt trip on her and talked her into staying on at the farm and helping them for all the 'help' they'd given her over the years. I tried to tell her to come to Kentucky with me, but she felt obligated to stay and help." Aren paused and took a deep breath.

Carol reached over and took hold of Aren's hand. Carol pulled her hand onto her lap and squeezed it gently.

"Are you chilly at all? I can get that blanket for you," Aren asked.

"Actually, I'm sitting here wishing for a reclining love seat. You always hold me when I share something emotional. Tonight, I'd love to be holding you while you share this chapter in your life with me," Carol said. Her voice was tender and soft.

Aren gently pulled her hand free and urged Carol up out of her seat. After some coaxing she also got Bailey to move over to the dining room with Carol. She pulled the two chairs back to their previous location in front of the potbelly stove before she bolted down the stairs. Aren ran for the back of the house. There was an Adirondack love seat that would be perfect for Carol's request. She hoisted up the wooden loveseat over her shoulder and made her way back to the barn. It was more difficult to get up the stairs than Aren had expected. She was quite winded when she got to the top step with her load.

"Have you gone completely insane? You could seriously hurt your back doing goofy shit like that! Just because I mention something doesn't mean you have to jump right up and do it!" Carol said.

"Let me catch my breath before you chew me out," Aren said, breathing heavily, "I'll finish moving that in a minute, I have to run down and get the foot stool that goes with it." And with that, she was back down the stairs before Carol could stop her.

Aren set up the new couch with fluffy pillows for the back rest and cushions from the dining room chairs on the seats. She decided not to use the slanting foot stool, choosing instead to keep the bale of hay in place so Carol wouldn't have pressure on her leg. Only then did she invite Carol to sit on the new loveseat and snuggle deep into her arms beneath the light blanket. If she was going to have to delve into the darkness of her past, at least she could enjoy some comfort in the present.

CHAPTER TWENTY-FOUR

The rain continued to fall. Carol nudged Aren to continue her story. When Aren didn't take the hint, she prodded her with words.

"Jennifer stayed out of obligation after she graduated high school. So, you were what, a sophomore in college at the time?" Carol asked.

"No, I was a senior. Much like you with your master's degree, I had to have something to keep my mind busy, and I dove into schoolwork. I had taken most of my associate's degree in the next town over, and I tested out of a couple of classes, and I was working on my senior year at Michigan State for my undergraduate degree. I was accepted that year into the veterinary medicine program. I had applied for a bunch of scholarships and grants, and I got enough to get me through. I remember calling Jennifer to tell her the good news. I pushed myself hard back then, and all I did was study and attend classes. I pretty much lived in the library on campus. I had my DVM by the age of twenty-three or twenty-four and was off to Kentucky," Aren said, not a hint of boasting evident in her voice.

Carol was thoroughly impressed. She'd worked hard to get just her master's degree in the same amount of time.

Carol pulled away just a bit and squinted at her. "You're not trying to get out of telling me the rest of the story, are you?"

"No, I'm sorry. I got sidetracked is all..." Aren said. "So, Jennifer stayed on after high school and got a job. She gave the

Harrises most of her check each week. Ron kept working in Lansing and commuting back and forth, and Phyllis stayed the 'farmer's wife' leaving all the outside chores to Ron and Jennifer. A year or so later, Daniel was murdered in prison. Now keep in mind that Phyllis had traveled all that way to see him on every visitor's day since he'd been sentenced. Anyway, she took Daniel's death really hard. I was already in the DVM program and couldn't get back for his funeral, and honestly, I had no interest in going to the funeral, but it was a good excuse. Anyway, it stirred up quite a hornet's nest. Reverend Todd refused to host the funeral at his church. Ron and Phyllis were members, but obviously they hadn't attended since the murder. They couldn't face the reverend or the town, but they couldn't afford to move, either. Anyhow, after the funeral, Phyllis went deep into the bottle. Jen told me that she'd drink breakfast, lunch, and dinner. It got to the point that she didn't recognize the Phyllis who had taken us in. Once she got to drinking, she'd become belligerent and cruel. Ron pushed himself so hard to keep things afloat that he passed away from a massive heart attack a little over two years later. Jen found him out in the field, face down. I was already in Kentucky by that time and I came back for his funeral. I admired him. I wanted to be there for him, for Jen. He was always good to me. He had his company life insurance of ten thousand dollars, but that just caught them up on their debt from the previous few years. Phyllis couldn't even stay sober long enough to make any arrangements for the funeral, so Jen and I took care of that. The house was falling apart. There were rotten sill boards and peeling paint. Jen did all she could to keep things up, but she was working so many hours that it was quite overwhelming for her." Aren pulled her arm out from behind Carol and got up to refill their coffee.

Carol sat there taking in all she'd heard, adding the new information to previous conversations. She felt so bad for Aren, especially for her heartbreak over Jennifer. The new understanding of how much she loved Jennifer explained a lot, especially why Aren corrected her when she'd called Jennifer her sister. Each conversation seemed to build on the previous one, adding new pieces to an extremely intricate puzzle, a puzzle that seemed far from complete. As intricate as the puzzle was, it seemed that the more she learned, the closer she felt to Aren. For Carol, the town—the place—didn't matter, it didn't make a home. It was the people, the special person, who mattered and who made it home. More and more every day, Aren was revealing the person who could be her home. It was a startling thought, but not an unwelcome one. Aren returned, handing Carol a cup of coffee. Aren pulled her attention back to the story by continuing right where she left off.

"So, we attended Ron's service, and I could see that Phyllis was falling apart. I stayed an extra few days and cleaned the place up as best I could, but there was just way too much work to be done everywhere. I begged Jennifer to come back with me. I begged Phyllis to check into rehab. I even told her that I would pay for it. She refused to go, and like any addict, denied she had an issue, all the while sloshing vodka all over the floor. Jen said she couldn't abandon Phyllis and refused to join me in Kentucky. I felt so bad, but I just couldn't stay. I can't stand liquor, can't stand the smell, can't stand what it does to people. I know I should have stayed to help, but I also knew I had to go, even if Jen refused to leave," Aren said, shaking a bit.

Carol wrapped her arm around Aren just a little bit tighter. She knew it was good for Aren to let this out. "I can't imagine how difficult it is for you, to share this. If you can, please keep talking, I want to hear *all* of this story," Carol said softly, gently touching Aren's cheek with her fingertips.

Aren nodded, looking tired. "It wasn't long after Ron died that Jen called saying that she thought she needed to go to the doctor. Well, maybe it had been a year or so. It's all a blur now. Once the results came back, I used vacation time and took leave from work. I took over everything on the farm because she was too sick to do much of anything. She was so tough, so strong, she never complained, but her eyes told me it was getting difficult to fight. She just went to sleep one night and never woke up."

"Who found her when she passed on?" Carol asked.

Aren shifted around a bit in her seat. "I did. I checked on her every morning. She looked so peaceful. The pain was gone from her face and I stayed with her until the coroner came to take her away. Phyllis never even climbed the stairs to say good-bye."

Carol turned to face Aren. She could just make out her facial features in the candlelight. The sadness in her eyes was heart wrenching. Her jaw muscles were rigid, her chin quivering. Carol guessed that she was trying to keep the emotion at bay. There was still something missing. "So, why did you stay after Jennifer passed on, especially with Phyllis drinking like she had been?"

Aren took in a deep breath. Carol could feel her beginning to shake again. Once again, she wrapped her arms around Aren and held her.

"Later that night, after Jen's death, Phyllis was beyond drunk. I can't tell you how much liquor she'd consumed that day. The power had been shut off earlier that afternoon because the bill hadn't been paid. I lit a few candles and Phyllis kept screaming and hollering about how it was all my fault. If I'd just stayed and worked locally, Ron would probably still be alive, and Jen wouldn't have worked herself to death. It was my fault because I had to go off and get a fancy job. After all they'd done for me, how could I desert them like that? She screamed that I'd leave to go back to Kentucky, and she'd have nothing. The bank was threatening to foreclose on the farm and Phyllis was in no shape to get a job." Aren shook her head and sighed. "She screamed and carried on for some time and then, just like that, she totally changed. She became really calm and started talking nonsense about going to be with Daniel. That they could have the whole damned farm because her son would take care of her." Aren took a few deep breaths. "Next thing I know she smacks an empty vodka bottle on the counter. Glass shattered all over the kitchen. She had the jagged neck of the bottle in her hand. Before I could stop her, she jabbed the jagged end of it into her neck." Aren turned to look at Carol. "I know what you've heard. I know people say that I stabbed her in the neck, but they weren't there. There's no way I could ever do something like that. They didn't hear it, what it sounded like. The sound when glass cuts skin and tendons is indescribable, but I hear it, over and over in my sleep. No one in their right mind could ever do that to another human being." Aren wrapped her arms around herself, haunted by the memory.

"Tell me about it, Aren. It's time to let go. Tell me what happened that night," she whispered.

"I tried to get the bottle out of her hand, but every time I'd come near her, she'd jab it at me before sticking herself with it again. It was dark and I couldn't see very well. The candles were in the dining room and living room, and we were in the kitchen. I kept trying to get it away from her, and then I felt the impact in my arm, but I kept wrestling her for the bottle. The entire time she's screaming at me to just go, get out, blaming me. There was this stench of blood, and she sounded funny, like she was under water." Aren rolled her neck and touched her face. "I remember this intense burning on my face, and I realized she'd struck my face with the bottle. I couldn't move because my face burned like it was on fire. My eye felt like someone was stabbing it with a red-hot poker. She swung out again, and there was more burning, more fire. I reached out, tried to stop it, but my hands wouldn't work and I couldn't see and everything burned. Then there was this sickening sound and at the same instant I felt a warm liquid spraying me and I heard Phyllis gurgling and choking. I ran to the dining room and got a candle so I could find her. There was blood everywhere, blood just pumping and pumping out of her neck. She gurgled some words, though I couldn't tell you what she was trying to say. I found my cell phone, called nine-one-one. I tried to stop the bleeding but there was so much pumping out. Then, just like that, she stopped gurgling and it was over." Aren barely finished the sentence before jumping up from her seat. "Carol, I need a break. I need light. The candles are too much. Do you mind if I blow them out? Just for a bit? I need real light."

"Shit, absolutely. I had no idea about the candles." She pulled her leg free from the bale and started to stand up.

"I'll get it. You can stay, I'll be right back. I just need a second." Aren disappeared down the main aisle. Suddenly, lights clicked on, row after row. It was brighter than Carol had ever seen it. She watched Aren come back up the aisle and walk around the table, blowing out the candles.

"What can I do to help?"

"Let me get the other loft door, that will help air it out some." Aren took off down the main aisle again. "I just need to be in the light and to not smell that smell. The candles went out, that night, when I ran from room to room. That smell, when the candle smoke rises... It usually doesn't bother me, but tonight, it's all too much."

Carol got up from the chair and made her way toward Aren, stopping about midway. *The hay, the hay is safe.* "Aren, would you build us a hay castle? Let's sit in the hay."

"What? Now?"

Carol worked her way to Aren at the far loft door. She hoped this wouldn't sound childish. "Please, can we go sit in the hay? Let's smell the hay instead of the candles. Let's make a safe place in the hay."

Aren turned around to face Carol, her eyes wet with tears. They looked haunted, terrorized and rightly so. There was no doubt in Carol's mind that Aren was reliving every single second of that awful day.

"I don't want you climbing up the hay. What if you slip or fall?"

"What about a hay spot down here, beneath one of the lights? We can stack bales around us. What do you say?"

Aren nodded and led her to a single stack of hay beneath one of the large lights. She stepped up onto the stack and pulled a few bales off a taller stack close by to create a U shape out of the bales. The breeze from the loft door was just enough to keep it from being stifling. Carol propped up her crutches outside the stack and crawled into the space, not much bigger than a double bed. She worked her way to the back corner of the U and patted the space next to her. Silently, Aren joined her. Carol pulled her into her arms and held her until her breathing settled. She couldn't believe that it had been Phyllis, someone Aren had once trusted and admired, who was responsible for that injury, responsible for all those scars, inside and out. She couldn't imagine how much alcohol, how much rage and desperation, it would take to make someone do something like that.

Carol was surprised when Aren started talking again.

"They took me to the hospital and told me the next day that I had been in surgery most of the night while they stitched my face back together, along with my hands and arm. They did their best to repair my hands, and some of those cuts were quite severe, but they couldn't save the sight in my left eye. There was too much damage. The police were there too, questioning me over and over. They wanted a detailed order of events, then they'd review things in the right order, then tell me I said the wrong order and then change the order again. It was hard to keep track. I guess they got what they wanted since they eventually left. There were complications, infections. They missed a few fragments of glass." She rubbed at her face, wiping away tears and sweat. "I had to get arrangements made for Phyllis and Jen. I had to keep the animals here cared for. I just shut down, blocked everything out, and did what I had to do in order to keep going." Aren stopped, unable to continue.

Carol pulled her in close and let Aren cry. She found herself crying too, sobbing right along with Aren. She held her until her breathing changed and she fell asleep. Carol sat up for a while, in the brightly lit loft, absorbing everything she'd learned tonight. For the first time, she understood the seclusion, the walls, the barriers, and was thankful that she knew about the safe place in the hay. How could someone go through so much, experience so much tragedy, and still have such a good heart? Aren was funny and sweet, too, things that life should have wiped away but hadn't. The more she learned, the more she was in awe of the beautiful person Aren was.

CHAPTER TWENTY-FIVE

Aren squinted, adjusting to the bright overhead lights. She carefully lifted Carol's arms off to the side before sitting up. Carol was hunched over and sound asleep. She looked adorable with hay stuck in the side of her hair, though she'd be sore tomorrow if left to sleep here. Aren got up on her knees and scooped Carol into her arms.

"What are you doing? Where are we going?" Carol's voice was garbled by a yawn. She draped her arms around Aren's neck.

"I'm going to take you to bed," Aren said.

"Hmm, I'd like that." Carol's head rested on Aren's shoulder. She sounded as if she were mumbling in her sleep.

Aren worked her way to the edge of the bales. She lowered one leg, shifting her weight so she could get her other knee off the bales and beneath her, without dropping Carol. Carefully, she walked up the main aisle and into the living area. She bent over to lay Carol closer to the center of the bed and Carol's arms released. She rolled over onto her side, her casted leg still dangling off the bed. Aren lifted her leg up and then covered Carol with a light blanket. Part of her would have liked to curl up against her and pull her tight, but she was too raw from the night's emotions to do anything like that.

She walked quietly over to the loveseat, picked up the two coffee cups from earlier, and made her way to the sink while replaying the conversation from a few hours ago. She felt ridiculous, embarrassed for freaking out like that. Running around turning on all the lights, then hiding in the hay like a terrified child. What Carol must think.

She turned on the countertop light before walking to the other end of the barn and shutting off the large overhead lights. She stood there, next to the light panel, looking out the far loft door into the darkness. Now Carol knew how her face had become scarred, knew all the gory details about what had happened that night. What she wouldn't give to know how Carol felt about it. She hadn't cried in years. She'd learned not to. It was a sign of weakness. It was safer not to cry. She walked back up the aisle, grabbing Carol's crutches along the way.

Aren plopped down on the Adirondack sofa with a tall glass of milk. Bailey moved closer, leaning up against her leg.

"What do you think, Bailey girl? Did I share too much? She must think I'm crazy." Aren patted her dog's neck.

"No, you definitely did not share too much, and no, I don't think you're crazy."

Aren jumped to her feet and spun around. Carol sat at the edge of the bed, softly illuminated by the countertop light. She reached for her crutches.

"I'm sorry, I didn't mean to wake you."

"You didn't wake me. My bladder did. Are you okay? I can stay up and sit with you."

"It's just after three in the morning. You should at least try to get a few more hours of sleep."

"Do you need some time alone? If you do, I'll go to the bathroom and go right back to bed, but if you'd like company, I can take a nap later." Carol made her way across the space, through the dining area.

Aren shook her head. "I don't need time alone. I've had my fill of that, four years was enough. Coffee or milk?"

"Let's start with milk and see what the morning brings." With that, Carol closed the bathroom door.

Aren walked into the kitchen and poured a second glass of milk. She was grateful that Carol woke up and glad to have her there. Carol nudged her when she needed nudging, pushed her when she needed a good shove. It felt good to have someone care again. She put on a pot of coffee just in case they decided to stay up talking.

Carol sat next to Aren on the Adirondack sofa and smiled when Aren covered her legs with the light blanket from the bed.

"How are you feeling this morning?" Carol asked.

"Spent. A little embarrassed. Worried about what you must think of it all." Aren looked out into the darkness. The new moon turned the landscape into a deep void, leaving her with nothing out there to focus on.

"Oh, Aren, you have nothing to feel embarrassed about. How you survived that, came out the other side, is beyond me. I think you're the strongest person I know." Carol twisted in her seat.

"I know I didn't quite finish explaining why I didn't return to Kentucky."

"I figured it was because of your injuries."

"That was certainly a big part of it." Aren set down her empty milk glass. She kept her focus on the black void beyond the screen. "You see, by the time everything healed properly, I didn't think I'd have a job to go back to. They'd canceled my insurance even before I was completely done healing. I didn't know if my hands could be steady enough to do my work. I was embarrassed, too. I couldn't face my colleagues with the scars and the cloudy eye, all of which looked much worse back then. My vision was no good anymore, and I didn't know if I could see well enough to work with a microscope or to operate. Besides, this was where Jen was. I'd already abandoned her once. Phyllis was right, you know. It was my fault. I was responsible for all that happened to them. I was selfish and walked away. If I'd been here, none of that would have happened." Aren had never said the words out loud, and it was a relief to do it, even though it hurt.

Carol tugged at Aren's chin until she turned her head. She had a way of expressing so many emotions with a simple look in her eyes. At this moment, with her forehead furrowed, she looked stern. Aren held her gaze and waited for the words that would confirm everything she felt about herself.

"None of that was your fault! You're not responsible. They could have sold this place and moved to a small house in town. Nothing said they had to stay here on this land. They could have moved to Lansing where Ron worked. They could have moved closer to the prison when Daniel was still alive. Hell, they could have sold the farm and moved to an island in the middle of the ocean. Aren, you are not responsible for their choices, not one of them. Not for Jen's choices, not for Ron's or Phyllis's. They each made their own way, just like you did when you went to school."

Aren nodded slightly. Carol released her chin and held her hand. She was grateful for the touch. A therapist had told her the same thing years ago, but the guilt continued to eat at her. The voices continued to scream at her, torment her dreams in the darkness of night. No one else could understand what she'd been through, especially that night. "I know what you're saying makes sense. I know we all choose our own paths. I know different choices could have been made by each and every one of us, but the logical side of my brain and the guilt that I still feel in my heart simply agree to disagree. I imagine that a different person, a saner person, would have bolted at the first opportunity after that night. Maybe I should have found some place to start over, found a different way to use my education, or even just walked away and never looked back. But as twisted as it sounds, to me, this farm is home. I know it sounds crazy, but once upon a time it was the best home I'd ever known. And there's something else, not quite a promise, but a mutual dream, that I felt compelled to honor."

Aren needed to stand up. She went into the kitchen and rinsed out the two coffee cups from earlier. She held one up to Carol, who half-smiled and nodded in return. Aren fixed the two cups of coffee and made her way back to her seat.

"I have a thousand questions about what your life must have been like if this was the best home you've ever had, especially after that night, but I know that's not for today," Carol said.

"No, that's definitely not for today, I don't have it in me."

"Will you tell me about the mutual dream? Can we keep talking, even if just for a little bit?" She snuggled into Aren's shoulder.

"How do I explain this one? Well, when you're a kid in the system, you completely lose any hint of control over your life. The system, the social workers, everyone but you, decides where you'll sleep, what possessions you're allowed to keep, everything about your existence. There's simply no control, so you start to crave it. You dream about the day that you can determine your own destiny, the day that you answer to no one but yourself. That's utopia, I get that, but as kids, you can dream of utopia. When Jen and I were sent here, we were both from big cities. Tight spaces, rough neighborhoods, intense situations, and zero control. Out here, in the country, it was different. This way of life was completely foreign to us, but Ron and Phyllis somehow knew how to get through to us, knew how to teach us the what, why, and how, of what needed to be done. We fought it at first, dug in our heels, each in our own way, but after a while we started to see the benefits too. We started to pay attention, accept the lessons, ask questions. We found out that if we worked hard and got the chores done, we could have some freedom, some control of our time. We could take the horses out and ride, we could hang out in the tall grass and talk for hours, we could make friends and spend time with them. We also figured out that the more we did on the farm, the less we had to buy off the farm. Milk, eggs, meat, vegetables, and then there's wood for heat, wood for buildings, hay for feed, so many things were right there, provided by nature and a lot of hard work. Learning how to be self-sufficient meant we had more control, and we both loved that. We saw a way to our utopia, a way to achieve control over our own lives. All we had to do was to buy a farm. So, we looked at what jobs made enough money to buy land or a farm. I had a knack for working with the animals, and veterinary medicine seemed a perfect fit. Jen looked at the medical field too and was taking classes in nursing. We were going to work hard and bank the money, and our goal was to eventually buy ourselves a farm, but then life happened. Things started going downhill, spiraling out of control. Jen refused to leave, Ron died, Phyllis fell apart and then that night happened, and the world crashed down around me. So, while I was healing and tending to this farm, it occurred to me that *this* was a working farm. This was the dream, and this was where Jen was. I could honor the dream, honor our goal. I could buy this farm and maybe gain just a little bit of control in a very uncontrollable time of my life. So, that's what I did. I paid off the debts Phyllis had run up all over town and worked with the bank to buy the farm."

"Why on earth would you pay off Phyllis's debts? She did nothing to deserve that kindness."

"I didn't do it for Phyllis, I did it to help clear the name of the farm, maybe bring some honor back, though I don't think it had the effect I'd hoped for." Aren sighed. "Anyway, that's why I didn't go back to Kentucky, and why I stayed in a town that barely tolerates me. It's home, and it's mine."

She leaned her head against Carol's and drew in a few deep breaths. She was done talking for the time being. She just wanted to sit here, hold Carol in her arms, and watch the horizon welcome the morning sun.

Chapter Twenty-six

C arol lifted the spoon to her lips and tasted the soup. Something was missing. It was her first attempt at a cream-based soup in a Crock-Pot. She'd used leftover chicken from the day before and added a variety of vegetables to the potatoes in the recipe, but something was missing, it was bland and lifeless. Carol was digging through the spice rack hoping to be inspired when her phone rang.

"Hello." She caught it on the third ring.

"Hello, is this Ms. Matthews?" a male voice asked.

"Yes, this is Carol Matthews."

"Well, ma'am, my name's Trevor Lee. I've been working with Cliff on your house. I'm wondering if you have some time to meet me over here. I have a few things that belong to you."

"Certainly, what time?" Carol looked out the loft window. A shiny new skeleton of pine was taking shape where the crushed home once stood.

"I'm here now, working, so anytime is fine," Trevor said.

"Okay, I'll be over shortly." Carol wondered what on earth he could have that belonged to her.

She made her way down the loft stairs, an expert now at hopping down the stairs on one foot while holding the rail with one hand and her crutches in the other. She could smell the sweet scent of fresh cut hay as soon as she opened the lower barn door. The chugging sound of the tractor grew closer. Shielding her eyes from the sun,

Carol searched the fields for the tractor. She felt like a teenager with a super crush, hoping to sneak a peek. Her breath hitched at the sight of Aren perched confidently atop the tractor. Carol watched her twist in her seat, maybe checking the haying equipment behind the tractor. It didn't matter, she saw what she wanted to see, a sexy lean cowgirl. The black hat, the sunglasses and that white tank top that hugged her perfectly made her the sexiest thing she'd ever seen. The desire to rip that tank top off was becoming more and more difficult to resist. They were growing so close with the conversations and the gentle touches, and she loved cuddling up to her at night. It was hard to be patient yet she knew it was best to wait, for both of them. But there was no longer any doubt in her mind that she wanted more.

Aren must have spotted her. She stood tall, climbed up onto the tractor seat, and waved with both arms. Carol could see her beautiful smile from here. *What a goof. What an adorable, loveable goof.* Carol waved back. She needed to be on solid ground before jumping in, they both did, but soon just wasn't soon enough. She watched Aren lower herself back into the seat before turning and making her way up the path to the road.

Carol worked her way across the street. It wasn't much farther than the mailbox and she was becoming an expert on the crutches. As Carol made her way closer, she could hear men calling out numbers, saws running, and loud rock music. She couldn't imagine being able to focus on the details with all that commotion. Carol looked around the job site, wondering which guy was Trevor.

"Ms. Matthews, over here." Trevor waved. He was jogging toward her. "I owe you an apology."

"I'm not following you. What's going on?" Carol looked at the young man. A bandana kept long scraggly hair out of his face, and he was missing a few teeth. She imagined he had quite a life story.

"Well, see, the thing is it started raining and I had a box of stuff on the tailgate of my truck, but I tossed it in the truck with my tools and my gear so it wouldn't get soaked. I guess I forgot all about it, but then I went to grab my impact driver this morning and saw the box. When I looked inside, I knew I'd screwed up royally. The boss gave me your number."

"Trevor, what's in the box?"

Carol followed Trevor to the back of a rusted old pickup truck. There was a tattered box sitting on the tailgate. He motioned Carol to the box.

"You see, when we were pulling off the second story, I was sent up in the boom after they removed the tree. I saw this stuff in the rubble and thought you might like to have it."

Carol looked in the box. She instantly recognized her aunt's purse. Beneath it was her jewelry box and a photograph of Aunt Suzie and Uncle Frank that had always been on their dresser. She lifted the photo and there was Uncle Frank's wallet and his key ring in the same wooden dish he'd pull them out of when she was a kid and it was time to go to town for coffee with the guys, which always meant ice cream for her. Tears welled in her eyes as she ran her fingers over the fragile mementos of another life.

"Again, I'm really sorry it's been in my truck all this time." Trevor reached up and ruffled his scraggly hair.

"No harm done. I'm not the least bit upset. I'm quite grateful to have these things. Thank you for rescuing them from the rubble. I appreciate it more than you could know." Carol smiled, hoping to reassure him.

"Do you need me to carry this stuff across the way for you? I don't mind, seeing how you have crutches and all," Trevor said.

Carol reached into the box and picked up her uncle's key ring. She looked over to the driveway. There sat the Impala, in the same spot her uncle had parked it in after his last trip up to the coffee shop. Carol thought about it for a second. The Impala was an automatic, no clutch. She had wheels!

"Actually, would you mind carrying it over to that car?" Carol jingled the keys.

"No, ma'am, not at all." Trevor smiled, his tongue briefly poking through the space where a tooth had once been. Carol tried not to stare. She turned and led them to the Impala.

"Well, I'd best get back to work. It was nice to meet you, Ms. Matthews. I'm real sorry for your loss." Trevor set the box in the back seat.

"Thank you again, Trevor. I appreciate it."

Carol climbed awkwardly behind the wheel of the car, her crutches riding shotgun, the door closed. She held the keys in her hand for a moment. She drew in a deep breath. She could smell Aunt Suzie's perfume and Uncle Frank's soap. She touched the worn spot in the leather of the steering wheel, where Uncle Frank always rested his hand. The package of spearmint gum that he always had in the cup holder was sitting there, one piece missing. It was comforting and sad at the same time. Carol slid the key into the ignition and started the car. She looked into the review mirror and saw Aren's barn and the open loft door. More and more, that was feeling like home. Time to get back to that soup and figure out what was missing.

CHAPTER TWENTY-SEVEN

C arol Matthews?" the nurse called into the waiting room.
    Carol stood up, positioning her crutches beneath her arms.
"Please follow me. We'll take a few X-rays and then the doctor
will meet with you in exam room four."

"Thank you," Carol said, following the nurse to the X-ray area.

After the four X-rays were taken at various awkward angles,
she waited on the exam table in room four. It seemed to take forever.
Finally, the doctor entered the room.

"Hello, Ms. Matthews, I am Dr. Kumar. Well, there's good
news, very good news. Your leg is healing up much better than
expected. Looks like you'll get to go home with a walking cast
today."

"Holy crap! That is great news! Are you serious?"

"I do not joke around about broken bones," Dr. Kumar said,
very matter-of-fact.

"How exciting, let's get to it! Oh, it's been so hot, I'll be so
excited to get this thing off! What are my restrictions?"

"Well, it's been just over five weeks since the fracture, and
while the fibula was fractured, it was aligned almost perfectly and
has knitted quite well. The notes from the hospital state that the
tibia was also fractured, but it must have been an anomaly on the
single X-ray that was taken. I can find no break of the tibia bone in
any of the X-rays taken today. I checked each of the four different
positions and nothing shows up. You were very fortunate, Ms.
Matthews. While the cast wasn't completely necessary, it certainly

helped speed up recovery since you avoided any weight bearing on that leg. I'd recommend the walking boot for at least a few days to a week. The fibula isn't a weight bearing bone, but maintains ankle stability, so beyond that, I'd let discomfort be your guide. Certainly, come back in if you experience any sharp pain or feel you are unable to bear weight."

"Oh my God, that's the best news ever! Thank you so much!"

"You are most welcome. Please, give me one moment to gather the proper tools and we'll have you test out the boot. If all is well, you'll be on your way."

The cast came off in no time at all. The nurse, who insisted Carol call her Kelly and not just nurse, was so kind. She gently washed the lower leg and applied some soothing lotion to the chafed area. Carol savored how the air felt on her skin. It was short-lived. Kelly slid on a thin sock up to her knee before fitting her in the walking boot.

"You'll want to keep a sock on your leg to protect the skin from sweat. Here are a few extra-long socks. If it feels sweaty, change it. You can take it off to shower or when you won't be walking on it," Kelly said.

"Thank you. I appreciate that." Carol tucked the spare socks into her purse.

Kelly handed Carol her crutches. "Let's take a few steps up and down the hall, just to see how it fits."

Carol used the crutches to support her weight at first. It felt a little weak, but it also felt amazing to step down on that leg. She supported much less of her weight with the crutches by the end of the long hall, where Kelly swapped the crutches for a cane. Carol tried the hallway again with great delight, and she felt more stable with the cane. Another step toward freedom. She couldn't wait to share the news with Aren.

Carol left the doctor's office and headed back to the farm. Aren was just coming up from the back of the property on Doc when she pulled up to the barn. Carol watched Aren, so relaxed in the saddle, while the horse trotted up to the hitching post. God, she couldn't get any sexier.

"Hey, you, what did the doctor say?" Aren asked, sliding down off the horse.

Carol opened the car door and stepped out. She put the cane on her good side, as advised by Kelly and started walking toward Aren in the new boot. "It went this good!"

"Look at you. That's fantastic news!" Aren walked up to Carol. "What's the first thing you'd like to do?"

"Doc's saddled up, so could we maybe go for a ride? Dr. Kumar said I had no restrictions. The cane is just for balance while I get used to the boot, and the boot is just for a couple of days. Apparently, the shin bone wasn't broken, just the little one on the side and it's pretty much healed." Carol felt like she was begging, but she didn't care. "Can we?"

"I might have a stirrup that will hold that boot, if you're sure you want to."

"Oh, I'm sure!"

Carol walked with Aren to retrieve Wyatt and then followed her again to gather the tack. She felt giddy to be back in the saddle again. Aren fitted the larger stirrup onto the saddle and then helped Carol mount up on Wyatt. The stirrup worked perfectly.

"How's Doc doing on the trails? I'm excited to ride him," Carol said, stroking Wyatt's neck.

"He's doing pretty good. Maybe someday you can ride Doc, but he's still pretty green. I know Wyatt will keep you safe. Doc may spook if something scares him, and if he threw you, I'd never forgive myself. That's why I'll be riding him until I know he's safe enough for you." Aren moved easily into the saddle and Doc's ears twitched like he was listening.

"Ah, so because I don't know how to milk a cow, or drive horses with a wagon, you assume I don't know how to ride?" Carol laughed, adjusting to the saddle. She raised herself up out of the saddle, and found that her foot and leg felt good and sturdy. They headed off the farm and onto a trail at the back.

Once the horses were warmed up, Carol looked over to Aren. "I admit I've never trained a horse or lived on a farm, but I never said I couldn't ride!" With that, Carol nudged her heels into Wyatt's sides.

"Let's go, boy!" Wyatt opened up, extending into a strong gallop. Carol turned in her saddle, and Aren and Doc were right at her side.

They allowed the horses to have their head and enjoy the run while in the open field, but Carol gently pulled back on the reins as they approached the woods. She'd never been on these trails and knew Aren should lead.

"That was amazing! I loved it!" Carol's heart was pounding. "I've never ridden a draft horse before. I learned to ride on a variety of skinny gaited horses. I love feeling the muscles working beneath me, and the gallop wasn't nearly as rough as they told us it would be."

"Where'd you learn to ride?" Aren asked.

"My parents insisted I was active in something. I wasn't really into sports, didn't care much about the piano or any other musical instrument, but I loved horses. I had every Breyer horse I could get my hands on, neatly displayed on shelves in my bedroom. After a lot of convincing, they finally agreed to send me to horse camp. I attended each and every summer. We'd spend all summer riding, grooming, and caring for our assigned horse. I can't recall a happier childhood memory than those spent out on the trails." Carol smiled and tilted her face toward the sun.

"What was your childhood like? Did you enjoy life as young Carol Matthews?" Aren asked as they plodded along down the trail through the dense woods.

"I had a great childhood. My parents were strict but fair. Schoolwork always came first. I had certain chores that I had to do every day before I could change into my play clothes and go outside with my friends. I grew up in the suburbs and all the kids in the neighborhood hung out together. We'd take turns when deciding whose pool we'd swim in during the summer and whose mom had to tolerate our wet boots and clothes in the winter. I had a complete storybook childhood." Carol smiled. "Now my teen years, I think those were years that my parents would have liked to exchange me." She flinched at her choice of words but kept going. "But my childhood was great."

"Were you a rebellious youngster with no respect for your elders?" Aren asked.

"I was a snotty, self-centered bitch," Carol admitted. "I took off, snuck out, drank, smoked. I was every parent's worst nightmare. I was struggling with my identity, with my sexuality. I was angry at the world and thought that the world owed me. I was absolute hell on wheels."

"What snapped you out of that? I can't even imagine that side of you," Aren said.

"My parents gave me a choice. Counseling or reform school. I started counseling at seventeen. After the first session, I knew if I kept up my attitude that I was going to crash and burn or end up in jail. I had an amazing counselor who listened without judgment. She was the first person I told about my sexuality. Believe me, it was much easier telling her than it was my parents. I quit drinking for the most part, I quit smoking completely. I found respect for myself. I found that I liked myself a whole lot better as a respectful and considerate person than I did as a partying asshole." Carol shook her head.

"What did your parents say when you told them that you were a lesbian?"

Carol grew quiet for a moment. "I never did tell them. They died in that car accident and I hadn't mustered up the courage to tell them yet. I never told Aunt Suzie and Uncle Frank either. My mom and Aunt Suzie were raised in the South and both were faithful Southern Baptists. Aunt Suzie probably more than Mom, but some things are just not okay with the Baptist church or in the South in general, and being gay was a big one. I'd already been enough of a disappointment with my behavior. Now there's no one else in my family left to tell. Do you think I'm a coward?"

"You're asking me, the person who couldn't tell the woman she was in love with, that she was in love with her, if I think you're a coward?" Aren twisted in her saddle and smiled. "You'll get no judgment from me, young lady!"

"Pretty boring, aren't I?" Carol asked.

"Not at all, it's great that you had a joyful childhood. I admire you for knowing your limits and accepting the help when you questioned your identity. You're smart, you're beautiful, you're amazing to talk to, and you ride like no one I've ever met. I could hardly call anything about you boring," Aren said.

Aren turned Doc off the forest road. Carol followed suit, patting Wyatt's neck. Aren whistled for Bailey who was still on the forest road up ahead of them. Carol looked up in time to see Aren looking over her shoulder, a mischievous grin on her face. She watched Aren bend her knees and knew what she was about to do. Carol beat her to it as she nudged Wyatt's sides, urging him into a full run. "Race you home!"

Chapter Twenty-eight

As they were unsaddling the horses, Aren thought about Carol's childhood. She'd never known anyone with a normal childhood, which made it abnormal. She wondered how a woman like Carol could even be interested in someone like her. Someone with so much hurt, anger, and disaster in her past. She didn't feel worthy of someone with Carol's light, sweet personality. She shook the thought and focused on checking the last of Doc's hooves for rocks.

"How long has it been since you've been in the house over there?" Carol asked.

"I haven't gone back inside except to clean up, drain the water lines, and steal the pot belly stove. So, I guess it's been about four years." Aren momentarily paused the good brushing she was giving Doc's coat to look at the house.

"Did you ever think of just knocking it down and building a small cabin?" Carol picked up another brush from the tack box and started brushing Wyatt.

"Still not liking life in the loft, eh?" Aren asked, laughing.

"No, no, I like the loft just fine, but wouldn't it be a nice luxury to have a full-size kitchen sink, not just a single bowl, and a stove with an oven, or a refrigerator that held more than a couple of gallons of milk and a bit of butter, or a freezer that wasn't four hundred yards away? When is the last time you made bread or baked anything? Do you know how hard it is to plan something for dinner to surprise you when all I have to work with is a Coleman stove, outdoor fire pit, and a Crock-Pot?" Carol asked.

Watching the progress on Carol's aunt and uncle's house did have Aren thinking more and more about fixing up the old farmhouse. There were some good memories within those four walls. Laughter and teasing over who washed and who dried the dinner dishes. Then, once they had decided, the silly silent water fights that would begin as they flicked water at each other when the other wasn't looking, and then giggling about it until Phyllis would put a stop to the fun. Aren thinking about helping Phyllis unload groceries and noticing that she'd picked up the double stuffed Oreos that Aren had begged for all week. She thought about Thanksgiving and how after dinner she'd go out with Ron to cut down a young pine for a Christmas tree. They'd tie it onto the sled to drag up to the house. Later that night, they'd make hot chocolate and decorate the tree. She hadn't had a Christmas tree since her senior year in high school. The thought of putting one up always made her feel empty and alone. Maybe it was time to change that. Maybe, if Carol stuck around, she'd have company this year.

"I'm sorry. I shouldn't push." Carol's voice pulled her from her thoughts.

"You're not pushing. I've been thinking about it lately too. The rebuild going on across the street has somewhat inspired me. That and you." Aren smiled. "Getting all that stuff out the other day helped me remember the good things too."

Aren led Doc and Wyatt to the pasture gate. Carol opened the gate so that the horses could go run and play. Aren walked back toward the front of the barn carrying halters and lead ropes. "I'll be right back."

Maybe it was time to see if the good memories could silence the bad. She took the loft stairs two at a time. There was a key hook at the top of the stairs where cobwebs and dust covered the old keys. Aren grabbed the set for the front door and made her way back downstairs.

"Come on, let's see if I can stand being in there with all the ghosts."

Bailey ran past them as if she knew she was going to her old home.

They walked silently side by side around the front of the house that faced the road. A driveway leading to a two-car garage was off to their left. The porch was covered in soft beige vinyl siding, the windows were trimmed with a deep barn red. Aren loved how the colors complemented each other and was glad she'd had the house re-sided after she'd purchased the farm. Aren helped Carol up the steps, taking each step one at a time since the new boot didn't flex at all. Aren was shaking so much that she had to use both hands to get the key into the lock. She unlocked the door and shoved the keys into her front pocket. Before she could ask, Carol had tucked her hand into Aren's. The gentle squeeze gave her the confidence to turn the knob and start to push the front door open.

"Come on, Bailey, let me open the door would ya?" Aren said, prodding the dog away from the door. Bailey burst by them into the house, pushing the doorknob out of Aren's hand.

Stepping into the foyer, Aren could smell the musty odor of a long ago closed up house. She stood still for a moment and took another breath. Was it her imagination or could she still smell the sweet fragrance of fresh picked herbs hanging to dry? Dill, cilantro, sage, and basil were some of her favorites to help strip from the stem once dried. The fragrance of each seemed determined to hang on and always made her feel like summer would never end. Aren closed the screen door behind them, but left the solid door open to allow some fresh air in.

"Let me open up the curtains and windows. Maybe it will help push out some of this musty smell."

Aren opened windows in several rooms around the house. She found Carol still standing in the entryway, her head swiveling around as she tried to take it all in. Aren stood next to her and sought out the comfort of Carol's hand. The interior of the house didn't look nearly as nice as the exterior. The walls were still painted in a seventies' gold color from about three feet up to the ceiling. From the three-foot mark to the floor was wallpaper with the gold color as a background to orange flowers and drab olive-green stems and leaves. The furniture in the living room was vinyl and showed evidence of heavy use. The arms of the couch and chairs were ripped, with fuzzy stuff poking up through the tears. The side tables were solid wood and were all covered with stains from sweating cups and glasses. The carpet, probably the greatest cause of the odors, was stained from spills over the years.

"I see why you didn't take the couch."

Aren looked down at Carol and smiled. "Yeah, that couch is nasty. This main level is in rough shape. The entire thing would need to be gutted. Are you up for a look around?"

"Yes, if you are," Carol said.

"Okay, you asked for it," Aren said. She kept hold of Carol's hand.

Aren led them into the living room off to the right of the foyer through a large archway opening just a few feet from the front door. Carol pulled a little to the left and stopped. Aren turned to see what had caught her attention. The family photo wall. She'd forgotten that was up there. Carol walked up to the photograph of a young Aren sporting short, light brown hair and sparkling blue eyes. She touched it as if she were touching the person sitting still for the picture.

Aren rolled her eyes. "Yes, that's what I looked like before Phyllis messed up my face. I didn't used to look half bad."

"You're still beautiful. It's just, your eyes were so bright, so full of life." Carol stepped to the next photo over. Jen with her trademark half grin. Her hair was dark brown with a few highlights from the summer sun, her eyes a brilliant green. "This is Jennifer, isn't it? For some reason I expected her to be blond."

"Yep, that's Jen." Aren's chest tightened, and her heart ached. She hadn't looked at a photo of Jen since the day she died.

"She looks like a wild child there, but I can see how you'd be attracted to her. They let her get tattoos?"

Aren shook her head. "Henna. She used henna ink to do those designs. It washed off in six weeks or so."

Carol moved farther down the row. The next photo was one of a young man posing with his football gear on, his helmet held in the crook of his arm.

"Is this Daniel?" she asked, backing away from the photo a step or two.

"Yes, that's Daniel. Ron wanted the picture taken down, but Phyllis fought to keep it up there." Aren followed Carol down to the final photograph on the wall.

"Wow, so this must be Ron and Phyllis. Am I right?" She looked at the photo of the two standing on the same porch they had climbed just moments ago.

"Yeah, that's them. They were good people, well, Phyllis was good until she started drinking. They gave us some stability at a time in our lives when we needed it most. They were good parents for Jen and me. I miss that version of them. The house didn't look like this when Phyllis was sober. It was always so clean and tidy. This," Aren said, motioning to the living room, "is the result of the Phyllis she became after her world turned upside down."

Aren stood next to Carol looking at the wall of photographs. It seemed like a lifetime ago. It was weird, seeing her face on the wall just as she saw it in her mind when she closed her eyes and pictured herself. Her memories of the house were much the same because what she pictured in her mind when she thought about it was what it had looked like when she was in high school and not the neglected mess she saw today. She looked at each of the photographs again and it dawned on her that she was the only one on that wall still alive. She looked at the faces of the family she remembered and silently said good-bye. It was time to move on. It was time to stop punishing herself for everyone's decisions, everyone's actions. Even if Carol left tomorrow and her life became empty again, it was time for something different.

Chapter Twenty-nine

They continued their tour of the home downstairs. The dining room was decorated in the same fashion as the living room. The kitchen was Carol's favorite room in the home. It was a large country-style kitchen with tons of counter space, a big breakfast nook that opened out to the back deck, and an island in the center with power and room for stools on one side. The floor was covered with low pile carpeting that was light beige.

"There's a laundry room and large pantry over there," Aren said, pointing through a door to the right. "And that door in the nook goes out to the back deck that has a view of the barn. I used to spend a lot of time on that back deck studying." Aren's shoulders were tight, her hands stuffed in her pockets.

"This is a weird color of carpeting for a kitchen. Look at how the stains show up," Carol said, pointing to spots all over the floor in front of the large stove. She followed as the spots grew larger, and then she noticed the large area of dark stained carpet. She felt the blood drain from her face.

"Holy shit, that's where Phyllis died isn't it?" she whispered.

"I cleaned it up the best I could, but it had already set in by the time my hands healed up enough to scrub it. I couldn't drive anywhere to get a shampoo machine, and to be honest, I didn't want to come back in here," Aren replied, staring at the spot.

"Then the spots beyond the big spot were from you, from your face and hands?" Carol asked. "That's where you were standing that night in the dark. I can see the archway leading into the living room and the front door from here. I can see where the light was glowing behind you down the hallway," Carol said, re-creating the scene Aren had described.

Aren nodded. She took Carol's hand and pulled her out of the kitchen, away from the visions of that dark night. They entered the hall that led back to the front door. Carol tugged at Aren's hand, forcing her to stop and turn around.

"Aren, stop. I'm sorry I brought that up. Please, look at me. I need to see your eyes."

Aren's eyes finally lowered enough to meet Carol's gaze, but her jaw was clenched tight. Carol tugged again, pulling her closer. She wrapped her arms around Aren's waist and held her for a moment. After a few seconds, Aren hugged her back and exhaled.

"Do you want to go? Is it too much?" Carol asked.

"No, I'll be okay, but that's enough time in the kitchen for today. Let's keep going."

They turned back toward the front door. About midway up the hall, there were doors, two on the left and one to the right. Farther down the hall, to the right, was the stairway leading upstairs. Aren led them down the hall explaining that to the left was a small half bath and then the stairway to the basement. She stopped in front of the door on the right, placing her hand on the doorknob.

"This was Phyllis and Ron's room. I warn you that I haven't done anything to the room. I didn't clean up at all in here or even open the door while Jen was sick. It was completely Phyllis's space after Ron died, and I was too angry to care after that night." Aren pushed the door open. The stench of a closed-up bar mixed with dirty clothes and mold was almost overwhelming. The room was dark with very little light filtering in from behind blackout curtains. Carol stayed back while Aren made her way into the darkness. She heard Aren trip over something, mumble and curse under her breath, and then suddenly the room filled with light and the reality of the mess became apparent. Aren seemed to wrestle with the lock on the window before she managed to free it and lift it open. Once that window was open, she worked her way to the other two windows, stepping over a dead mouse and more empty bottles before she made her way back to Carol's side. Aren explained that there was a full bathroom off to the left and a walk-in closet, but she wasn't interested in exploring the rooms. They looked at one another and silently agreed to simply pull the door closed and let the room air out some.

"Jen and I each had rooms upstairs. All that's in my old room is a dresser and a bed. I think some of my clothes are still in the closet, just old work clothes. I didn't have any use for them after that night, so I just left them hanging up there."

Carol followed Aren up the steps, taking them one at a time and carefully, in case any had come loose over the last four years.

The upstairs was expansive. It matched the size of the lower level but with far fewer rooms. There were four bedrooms in all and two bathrooms, one between the bedrooms on each side. The center of the upstairs was open with a much nicer couch, two recliners and various end tables facing an old television. Above the couch was a wall hanging bookcase filled with VHS tapes. To the right and left of the recreation room were three doors, one with a Do Not Enter sign.

"I'm taking a guess that that's Daniel's old room," Carol said, pointing to the door on the right with the sign.

"Good guess. Jen and I tried to sneak in there once but both that door and the one from the bathroom were always kept locked. Phyllis probably has the key in her room somewhere. We heard her in there often singing songs she probably sang to Daniel to get him to sleep. We even tried picking the locks, but we just couldn't get in. I have no idea what the room looks like. I hope it doesn't look like Phyllis's room downstairs." Aren grimaced. "The other room on that same wall was Phyllis's sewing room and there is a full bath between the two rooms. Jen and I had bedrooms over here on the left. We shared the bathroom between the two rooms."

Aren walked to the farthest room on the left and opened the door. Carol stepped in behind her and looked around. It was a plain room with beige walls and dark green carpeting. There was a double bed between two windows on the far wall and a long six-drawer dresser centered on the wall on the far side of the bed. To the left was a door leading into the bathroom. A closet with bifold doors lined the fourth wall.

They walked through the bathroom, which was surprisingly clean, and into what used to be Jennifer's room. The bed was neatly made with fluffy pillows across the headboard. Bailey was curled up in the center of the bed. There was a lamp on a nightstand off to the right of the bed with a few prescription bottles lining the top. The floor was covered in a dark purple carpet. The closet doors were neatly closed and what looked like a night shirt hung on a peg on the back of the door that led to the recreation room. Posters of various bands mixed with taped up photographs covered the beige walls from the ceiling nearly to the floor. The dresser held perfume bottles and various knickknacks that Carol thought must have had special meaning. It looked eerily like a room someone had just left for a moment, frozen in time.

"What's that smell? It's an earthy fragrance, but it doesn't smell musty like downstairs." Carol continued to take deep breaths trying to identify the scent.

"That's patchouli oil, I'd recognize that scent anywhere. Jen wore it as a perfume for as long as I'd known her. She loved the way it smelled." Aren walked over to the dresser and held up a bottle of the essential oil.

Carol stepped into the room and looked at the multitude of photographs. She recognized Aren in many of the pictures. Some were taken on the front porch, others on horseback or driving a big old tractor. Both girls seemed happy in the pictures. Some were of Jennifer with groups of people. All the pictures gave Carol a bit of insight into what happier times looked like on this land and in this house. She started to understand why Aren could call this the best home she'd ever had, even after all that had happened. The smiles in the photographs reminded her of the smiles from her own childhood. Seeing this room, these pictures, added several missing pieces to the puzzle. Carol could have studied the photos for hours, but she pulled herself away and looked back at Aren. She looked lost and sad. Carol's heart sank. Her eagerness to see inside this house seemed to cause Aren so much pain. She walked back over to Aren and tugged at her hand.

"Is it hard, seeing all of this?"

"I think it was needed. It was time to see it again. Maybe time to finally say good-bye."

"You cleaned up this room after she passed away. That had to have been a difficult thing to do."

"Yeah, before the power was cut off that day. They took her body away and it just felt wrong leaving everything messy. I washed all the linens, remade the bed and cleaned things up a bit. A few hours later, they shut off the power. It's never been back on since."

Carol walked over to the bed and scratched Bailey's neck. "Bailey was Jennifer's dog?"

"Yep, they were inseparable. Where you'd see one, you'd surely see the other. She'd only had her for a little over a year when she passed away, but Bailey remembers her. When Jen was having a tough time those last few weeks, I could barely get Bailey out to pee, she wouldn't leave Jen's side. Hell, it's been four years, and this is where she wanted to get to from the moment I opened the front door." Aren shrugged and rolled her neck. "Well, that's the house, except the basement which is just a storage facility really. Do you mind if we get headed back? I can hear the cows bellowing from here."

Carol followed Aren down the stairs. Seeing Jennifer's room, seeing the kitchen, the photographs, drove home the point that everything she'd heard from Aren weren't just stories, they were her life, her memories, her experiences. She finally felt like she understood the need for the safety of the loft so much better. She had no idea how Aren could ever walk into this house and not feel pain, not feel loss, not feel anger. She couldn't imagine that there were enough good memories to overcome the pain. Carol decided at that moment to never push about the house again. It wasn't her place, and as Aren's friend, it wasn't right. Whatever might develop between them, she understood Aren's pain now, and she'd do all she could to keep bringing light into her life to chase away that old darkness.

CHAPTER THIRTY

Early the next morning after all the chores were finished, Aren borrowed Carol's cell phone from the table in the loft and walked back over to the house while Carol slept. Bailey girl was right on her heels, not wanting to be left behind. She knew from all the books she'd read that she had been avoiding the memories in the house by moving into the loft. But the walk-through with Carol the day before helped her realize that not only had it been long enough, but maybe it had gone on for far too long. She'd lain there thinking about it all night, trying to put words to what she was feeling. Thinking about the events, thinking about her life and the town, thinking about her perceptions. Somewhere in there, she'd given up on everything. She'd stopped living, stopped dreaming, and had become satisfied with merely existing. She'd grown accustomed to the same routine day in and day out, maybe even depended on it. Nothing new, nothing exciting, nothing to chance. The more she thought about it the more she realized that life was passing her by, and she was the only one to blame.

No more. Whether Carol stayed or not, it was time for her to start living life again, time to start dreaming again. Definitely time to stop hiding from the world. She still had money stashed away and now seemed like the perfect time to use a bit of it. Aren unlocked the door, the key much steadier in her hand today. She walked into the house and headed directly for the kitchen. In the drawer between the stove and the refrigerator, she found what she knew would be there, a dusty old phone book. She chuckled out loud, realizing that so much had changed around town in those years that half the phone numbers may be no good. Aren flipped through the pages and found an advertisement for a waste management company and dialed the number.

Aren breathed a sigh of relief when the person answering rattled off the company greeting. She shared her need with the lady and gave her address.

"Now, I just need a credit card number," the nice gal said.

"I don't have one. Couldn't I put a cash deposit down or something?" Aren asked. She felt so out of touch with society since Carol had come into her life.

"Well, I'll have to talk to a supervisor. We typically only take credit cards as deposit. Please hold."

Aren tapped her fingers on the counter listening to a bad classical remake of Billy Joel's 'Piano Man.' While she waited, she also looked up the number to the electric company. She had a feeling they'd want a credit card too. A wave of anxiety hit at such a scary first step. Time to rip the Band-Aid off.

"Are you still on the line?" a new voice said, interrupting her thoughts.

"Yes, I'm still here," Aren quickly answered.

"Are you the same lady out at the ol' Harris place that paid off all of Phyllis's debt back when she passed on?" he asked.

"Yes, I am. This is Aren Jacobs. I was one of the Harrises' foster kids," Aren said, swallowing hard. Would he hold it against her?

"I remember you. I'm the one who helped you that day. I'm the office manager now. You don't need to worry about a deposit. Just call us when you need it picked up. We'll weigh it and send you the bill. I trust you'll take care of it. Do you get mail at the physical address?" he asked.

Breathing a huge sigh of relief, Aren answered, "Yes, I do get mail out here. It's been a long time since it was anything but fire starter, but I still have a mailbox."

"Have you been living out there all this time or did you just get back in town?" he asked.

"I've been out here all this time. I'm finally tackling the inside of the house and realize I don't want to keep most of it. I'll have to gut it and start over." Aren had never been this open with a stranger before. She shook her head. Being around Carol was changing all kinds of things.

"Well, good. I hope everything works out for you. I'll have a truck deliver the container sometime today. Take care and let us know if you need anything else."

Aren thanked the man and shook her head, smiling. Well, maybe ol' Maggie had been right. Some from the old days did remember. She called the power company next, and that proved much more difficult. After some kind words and lots of convincing, she arranged to have the electricity turned on later that day as well. She'd have to give the driver a deposit to prove she was better than the account history, but she figured she'd get it back in a year when they reevaluated the account.

Satisfied that the two calls she needed to make were complete, Aren closed the phone book and put it away. She thought about the house, if she was going to do this, she needed to make it her own, all of it. New paint, new carpet, fix what was broken and make it the start of a new beginning. She wanted it gutted, especially the floors.

Before she'd left for college, Aren recalled helping Ron cut down an old stand of oak trees that were at the end of their life. They'd cut the trees down and pulled them out of the woods with the old tractor. Then, he'd had a company come out and mill all that wood into one-inch-thick planks. It had filled an entire bay of the garage. Ron had loved to woodwork, but she didn't see anything new in the house that he might have made. Maybe he'd sold it all when times were tough.

Deciding to find out, Aren walked into the living room and went through the door that connected the house to the garage. Ron's old pickup truck was still parked in his spot closest to the door. The other bay was empty, less a small set of shelves that held oil and antifreeze. Aren climbed up the old wooden steps that led to the large loft above the garage, where Ron's workshop had been. Dust and spider webs covered everything. She smiled when she saw the huge stack of raw oak slabs just beyond Ron's old, rusted tools. Now, she had new flooring for the entire lower level.

Aren called out for Bailey on her way back to the front door. There was a lot of work to do, but she was excited to get started. Excited to start living again. The more time she spent with Carol the more she wanted her to stay. She was beautiful and open and exactly the kind of woman Aren could fall in love with. Now that she had a walking boot and more freedom, she could start pulling her own life together, and Aren hadn't had the courage to ask what she'd been thinking about her future. She'd been content to let things flow and see what happened, but the more time they spent together, the more she wanted something...more. Was it worth taking a chance on opening her heart? She wasn't sure yet, but she wasn't about to put it aside, either. She and Bailey headed back to the loft to return Carol's phone.

CHAPTER THIRTY-ONE

Aren was cleaning the last of the box stalls when a sweet floral scent caught her attention. She dropped the scoop of the littered straw into the wheelbarrow and set down the stall fork. Carol walked up the aisle and she looked amazing. The dress hugged her figure perfectly, yet she looked professional, like she was headed off to work. Her hair lifted a bit with the crosswinds in the barn, making her look almost ethereal. Aren couldn't take her eyes off her.

"Wow, you look great. What are you all dressed up for?" Aren came around the wheelbarrow to stand in the aisle. She didn't want to get too close since Carol definitely smelled much better than she did.

"I'm applying for a job today. There's an opening at the library in town. Can you believe it? Honestly, does the boot look completely silly with this dress?" Carol twirled around.

"I think you look absolutely beautiful, boot and all." Aren couldn't help but stare. She looked stunning.

"You're sweet. Well, I'm off. Wish me luck." Carol pulled the car keys from her purse.

"Good luck." Aren watched Carol walk to the car. She caught herself praying that Carol would get the job. Then, she'd have a reason to settle here and call this home.

Aren finished up in the barn before she ran over to the main house to open the gate. The truck delivering the dumpster should arrive anytime. She was kind of glad that Carol had errands to do today. She wanted to have some time to sort through a few things on her own.

When the truck arrived with the dumpster, Aren was glad she'd chosen the biggest one because even it looked small for all the stuff she wanted to toss. While the truck was sliding the dumpster off the slanted rails, the power company truck pulled in. Aren signed all the forms and gave the guy the deposit money before he would reconnect power. She was really doing this. A little anxiety crept in with the excitement, but excitement won. It was time to move forward. It was time to start living again.

Aren wanted to get to work and fill the dumpster immediately. Action had become her habit, so she stopped and stood still for a second, forcing herself to slow down. She walked into the living room and removed three of the four photographs from the wall. She wasn't sure she'd ever hang them, but she wanted to save these memories. She set the framed photos on the counter.

She made her way up the stairs, to Jennifer's room. There were a few photographs taped up on the wall that she wanted to save. Aren took her time looking at the pictures. She could hear the laughter they often shared. She thought about how good it had felt to have someone finally know her, really know her. Jen had opened that world up for her and she would always be grateful for that. She started pulling the photographs off the wall, saving a few off to the side, memories that made her smile, memories that deserved to be saved. It was time for the rest of them to go. Time to let it all go and say good-bye.

An hour later, Aren stood in the doorway looking around Jen's old room, the walls bare. She thought about Carol. Carol would have grabbed her hand or wrapped her arm around Aren. She would have asked if she was doing okay. Aren realized how much she'd grown to like that. Carol would poke and prod, ask her how she was feeling. Did she have words to explain that right now? Such a mix of emotions. Excited and scared, then grateful came to mind, and sad too, but there was something else. Acceptance. Maybe there was finally some acceptance. She picked up the few photos she wanted to save and made her way back downstairs.

It was time. Aren looked at the chair in the living room that Phyllis always sat in. Stains surrounded it where drinks had spilled over the years. Aren picked up the chair and carried it out to the porch. She heaved the chair into the dumpster, and it crashed down on the other side with a great deep metallic thud. It felt good, therapeutic. She went back in for the couch. It was much heavier than she expected. She plucked off the cushions and launched them off the porch, into the trash container. She tugged and dragged the couch out the door and onto the porch, tipped it up on end, and heaved it up onto the side of the dumpster. Finally, the weight of it shifted, and it teetered on the edge before falling in with another loud thunderous boom. She ran back in, grabbed the photo of Daniel off the wall, and threw it in. She heard the glass shatter upon impact. *Wow, that felt great!* She worked her way around the living room, saving some pieces that could be refinished and launching the rest. Before long, she wrapped a bandana around her face and began the daunting task of pulling up the living room carpeting. She'd brought down the portable radio from Jennifer's room and had a country station playing while she worked. She used her chore knife, cutting the carpet into long runs and then rolling it up and throwing each section out into the dumpster.

While taking a short break and enjoying a cool glass of water from the now running tap, she took in the wallpaper. It had been on the walls for at least forty years. She picked at a corner and found it barely stuck. She began pulling off sections of thick fabric-backed paper and found it much easier to remove than she expected. Before her break was over, she had most all the wallpaper peeled off, less a few stubborn areas. There was still some glue on the walls that would have to be sanded or scrubbed off, but that was easy enough to tackle.

Aren was in the kitchen staring at the carpeting when Carol walked through the front door, a confused expression on her face. Aren turned down the radio on the island.

"Well, this is a surprise. This is the last place I expected to find you. You ordered a dumpster. Holy shit, look at this place!"

"It's time, Carol. I'm doing it. I've decided to clean it up, fix it up, make it mine. A little elbow grease, some paint." Aren looked around the room, seeing the possibilities.

"It's so unexpected, after yesterday," Carol said, walking from room to room. "Look at all you've already done. This is great!"

"I thought about it all night. I'm actually excited about it." She dusted herself off. "Thank you, Carol, you helped more than you'll ever know. I'd hug you, but you look amazing and I'm a filthy mess."

"You look great, Aren, even when you're a filthy mess. So, would you like help? I can get changed and be right back. Or is this something you'd like to tackle on your own?"

"I already tackled the part that I needed to do on my own. There may be others, but I'd welcome your help. Thank you though, you're very kind to consider that. By the way, how did it go at the library?" Aren took a sip of her water.

"There was indeed an opening and I was able to talk with the director. She's very nice. I submitted my application and résumé. Fingers crossed I hear something soon." Carol's eyes lit up.

"Did someone move or retire or something?" Aren asked.

"Moved, because her husband lost his job. I never dreamed there would actually be an opening. They were just about to start a nationwide search. Some people applied and were even hired, but then turned it down because their spouse couldn't find work with it being such a small town. Talk about things falling into place when something is meant to be!" Carol looked so happy she could burst.

"Things falling into place when something is meant to be, I like the sound of that," Aren said.

"So, when did you set this up? You're sneaky. We only talked about it yesterday," Carol said. She walked over and opened the refrigerator. The light inside popped on and she could hear the humming of the electric motor. "The power is on!" She squealed.

"I borrowed your cell phone and called for the dumpster and the power early this morning. I hope that's okay. I've realized a few things about myself, since you've been here. The loft helped me get through a dark time, but I feel like I'm maybe coming out the other side finally. Being in here, looking around, it's funny but I'm starting to see a blank canvas. I no longer see total darkness. I don't feel that torment nagging at me constantly. I'm actually excited!"

Aren smiled, "I've even decided to put in hard wood floors. I'm pulling up this carpeting and with the stuff I'm finding beneath it, well, let's just say I'd like a clean surface to walk on. Here, you've got to see this."

She took Carol up to the loft above the garage and showed her the wood and the router table. She explained her idea for creating beautiful flooring.

"Then all there is to do is sand, stain, and seal the floors. It's all right here waiting to be put to good use. We'll pick out colors for the walls and see if you can paint as well as you can ride." Aren smiled.

"I'm so excited to work on this with you. I finally feel like I can help you with something." Carol's eyes darted every which way, taking it all in.

Aren looked around the kitchen too and then looked into Carol's sparkling eyes. She'd already helped her so much more than Aren could ever express. She took a sip of water to control the emotions that suddenly welled up.

"Let's go to the loft so I can get changed. I bought deli subs as a treat. I put them up on the loft table. I figured you hadn't eaten yet, but I assumed you'd be in the garden." Carol spun around in a circle again. "Wow, I'm still in shock! Please tell me that I can have kitchen rights! I'm giddy at the thought of cooking something for us, just you wait!"

"You have unlimited kitchen rights." Aren smiled.

She looked around the house and while it was in an early stage of transition, she felt like it was possibly the final stage too. Ever since she'd purchased the farm from the bank four years ago, she worked hard to claim it as her own. She fixed up the barn so it would last another hundred years. She mended fences and created pasture rotation to keep the land healthy. So many changes made this her land, her farm, and now it was time for this one final change. It was time that she created a home, a permanent place where new memories could be made and shared. This land didn't always have to be remembered as the ol' Harris farm, now it would be one hundred percent her farm.

CHAPTER THIRTY-TWO

The August heat had been setting in with temperatures in the nineties for the past few days. Even with the straw insulation, the loft had been sweltering in the evenings. Carol had just returned from an interview with the library staff. After changing into shorts and a tank top, she walked out to the garden looking for Aren in the early afternoon sun. She believed her interview had gone well and was eager to share her good news, but Aren wasn't there. She felt the sweat dripping down the sides of her face while she continued her trek around the barn, calling out for Aren. She noticed the cows lying lazily beneath a shade tree quietly chewing their cud. Wyatt, Doc, and a few of the other horses were also beneath a shade tree standing side by side, swishing their tails to keep the biting flies at bay. She could see the pigs enjoying the cool waters of the pond. It amazed her how fast the little piglets had grown in the last month or so.

Not able to find Aren in any of her usual places, Carol headed for the house. She walked in through the propped open back door and was still amazed at the transformation they'd been able to accomplish in just a few days. The house smelled clean and fresh, having lost the musty odor after some good scrubbing. Carol walked into the kitchen, noticing instantly the renewed effort Aren had put into cleaning the blood out of the plywood subfloor. Though for all her effort, the shadows were still visible. She wondered if Aren saw Phyllis's body each time she walked past that section of flooring. She wondered if she felt the stinging tinge of torn skin. Carol had never seen anyone hurt beyond a small cut. She hadn't had to identify her parents after their car crash. Aunt Suzie had done that for her. She'd only seen violence and death on television, and while gruesome, it wasn't someone she'd known personally.

Carol was startled to hear footsteps coming up behind her from the dining room. She was so lost in the visions of Aren's past that she hadn't even heard a door open. Carol smiled when she turned and saw Aren come around the corner with an armload of milled flooring ready to nail in place.

"How'd the interview go?" Aren asked while kneeling to set the large load on the floor.

"It went terrific. I think I'll get the job. They all seemed to like me." Carol pulled her attention away from the speckled floor.

"What's not to like? I bet they find you irresistible and will be begging you to come and work there!" Aren stood and stretched her back. "Come with me, I have something to show you."

Aren took Carol's hand and led her down the hall. The door to the horrifically smelling room was wide open. The room was now void of all the previous contents, including the carpeting. The walls were scrubbed clean and free of cobwebs. The old drapes were gone, allowing sparkling clean windows and screens to let the sunshine in to illuminate the renewed space.

"This is amazing! You did all of this in the few hours I was gone? I can't believe it's even the same space!" Carol exclaimed, twirling around in circles to take it all in. "Oh my God, where did the French doors come from? Were they always there?"

"They were hidden behind the bed with blackout curtains. I opened them up to empty out the room. I think I'll get a lot of use from them, don't you? There's a great view of the pastures from that deck." Aren opened the doors and walked outside. "Do you think it's weird, me taking Phyllis and Ron's bedroom?"

"Aren, it's your house to do whatever you want, and if it's your bedroom then it's no longer Phyllis and Ron's bedroom. You own it now. You can sleep in a different room each night of the week if you want. That said, I don't think your wardrobe will fill a fraction of this closet. It's huge!" Carol walked out of the closet and onto the deck next to Aren. "Oh, you're right, it is a pretty view. Look at that, the porch is covered over here too. I think you should put the loveseat out here. What a great place to sit and enjoy the landscape. It's nice and private." She wrapped her arm around Aren's waist. "So, what are we going to work on now?"

"Well, would you mind if we went back into town? I think we're ready for paint. As soon as that's done, we can start in on the upstairs and then lay the floor."

"I think that I need to go grab my keys and purse!" Carol said, smiling while taking Aren's hand and leading her out of the house.

Carol ran down from the loft just in time to watch Aren put a paper bag in the trunk of the car before climbing into the passenger seat.

"What's in the bag?" Carol asked while starting up the car.

"It's a Wyatt present for my favorite cashier who should be working today." Aren laughed.

She explained her last solo trip into town as Carol drove. Carol was in tears from laughter by the time they pulled into the hardware store. Aren opened the door and pulled the seat forward so Bailey could jump out. She looked through the window and saw a new person at the checkout counter.

"Bummer, I was looking forward to tormenting her," Aren said as they walked into the store. Carol shook her head in response, softly giggling.

"Stop making me laugh! My ribs hurt!" Carol said, poking Aren in the ribs to make her point.

"Hey, Aren, how have you been doing?" Maggie asked as she came from the back office.

"Pretty good, Maggie, how are you?"

"I'm good. I just wanted you to know I fired that cashier later that day. I just couldn't shake how she treated you. I feel I owe you an apology." Maggie's sincerity was clear in her expression.

"It's okay. I didn't blame you. Actually, I'm kinda bummed. I brought her a Wyatt present in a paper bag." Aren winked. "Maggie, I'd like you to meet Carol Matthews. She's been staying with me. Suzie and Frank Cordes were her aunt and uncle."

"It's nice to meet you, Maggie. Aren speaks highly of you," Carol said, stepping forward to shake Maggie's hand.

"It's nice to meet you too, Carol. I'm so sorry for your loss. I knew Suzie and Frank, they were good people." Maggie turned to Aren and asked, "Hey, I noticed that there isn't a horse in the parking lot, where's Wyatt?"

"We came in my car," Carol said.

"You, the famous hermit cowgirl, rode in a car?" Maggie said, acting shocked. "Whatever will the townsfolk think?"

"Yeah, keep it up, old woman, and I'll bring Wyatt inside next time I come a calling." Aren laughed.

"Did she happen to tell you that she worked here during high school and while she was in college? She'd come over after school and work until closing a few days a week for spending money. Then, we'd grab a burger before I dropped her off at home." Maggie smiled at the old memories.

"I didn't know that. So, you were a 'helpful hardware girl' eh?" Carol teased her.

"Don't we have paint to pick out?" Aren replied, blushing.

Maggie tilted her head. "Are you painting the barn?" she asked.

Aren lifted her hat and brushed her hair off her forehead before reseating the hat. She'd known this woman for more than half her life. Maggie had been the one who forced her to admit to herself the love she'd felt for Jennifer. Maggie had been a mentor to her, a role model.

"We're gutting the house and I'm moving in. We've pulled up all the carpet. Peeled all the old crappy wallpaper off the walls and scrubbed every surface of the place. We still need to deal with the upstairs. But all in all, it's coming along nicely. We're going to do the floors in that old oak that Ron had milled." Aren smiled. "You'll have to come out for supper sometime once we get the place finished."

"I'd like that. I can't tell you how often I think of you out there. I should have made it out there over the years. I feel all this guilt, but with all that Ruby was going through—"

Aren put her hand up to stop her. "Maggie, please don't apologize. You were right where you should have been, at Ruby's side. I harbor no ill feelings. I had no expectations. I imagine we've both been dealing with our own demons, and each in our own way. Sometimes we need a little time to heal."

"You're an amazing person. God, you look good. What's up with you two? I heard a lot of 'we' on the housework," Maggie asked.

Aren looked over to Carol who had made her way over to the paint department. She was picking out color chips. What was up with the two of them?

"Like I said, she's been staying with me while they rebuild her aunt and uncle's place, well, it's her place now. She's great. We're taking time to get to know each other. I think we both need it." Aren didn't have a better answer, since she didn't know herself.

"Good for you. It's time, Aren. It's okay for you to be happy, ya know." Maggie always had a way of saying the right thing.

"How about you? How are you doing?" Aren asked.

"I'm doing a little better every day. I still miss her like crazy. This place keeps my mind occupied."

"Well, just remember your own advice. It's okay for you to find happiness too, ya know." Aren smiled as she put her sunglasses back on.

"Yeah, I hear you. Thanks, Aren. Well, you'd better go check on the colors before she has them mixing cans." Maggie nodded toward the paint department.

Aren looked over and saw Carol talking with the clerk. "Roger that. Take care."

"You too." Maggie reached out and squeezed Aren's arm before heading back toward her office.

Aren made her way to the paint department. So much had changed in such a short time, and for the first time in a long time, she felt like this was her home. Carol looked up and smiled as she approached, and she knew full well why she felt that way.

"What do you think of any of these?" Carol asked.

Aren smiled. "Which ones are you expecting me to choose?"

Carol shook her head. "Based on how you did the outside of the house and barn, I'm thinking you'd like this soft beige for a base color, then this sage green for an accent wall or two in the living room, dining room, maybe even the kitchen."

Smiling her agreement, she asked, "And what's the deep red for? Where would I like that color?"

Carol looked up into Aren's eyes, raising her eyebrows mischievously. "You'd like this color behind your bed. The color of passion and heart."

"You know me too well already." Aren's heart leapt at the idea of Carol thinking about her bed.

Aren took the chips and ordered the paint from the young man behind the counter in the small paint center. While they waited for the mechanical shaking machines to blend the dyes to the exact match, she and Carol picked out stain and sealant for the floor, among other items they'd need to restore the lower level of the house. Within a half hour, they were up to the counter with two baskets full of items.

The cashier, glancing up often to sneak a peek at the scars creeping out from behind Aren's sunglasses, added up their order. She was used to it, and she found it didn't make her uncomfortable the way it had before. When she smiled at him, he smiled back, and she wondered how much of people's response to her before had been partly to do with her own insecurities and agitation.

"Thank you, have a nice day," Aren said, accepting the change. She shook her head while pushing the full cart out of the store, Carol walking at her side. Hope and light weren't feelings she was familiar with, but damn if they didn't flow through her now. There was a beautiful woman at her side, for however long that might be, and she was moving away from her past and into the future. She reached for Carol's hand. Change was a good thing.

CHAPTER THIRTY-THREE

The golden walls slowly disappeared beneath the soft, warm beige. It had taken two coats of paint yesterday to completely cover the deep golden color, but once the second coat dried, the house quickly released its grasp on days long gone. Carol still had a touch of paint in her shoulder length brown hair from the day before. Aren couldn't help but stare as Carol carefully stirred the five-gallon bucket of sage green for the long wall that extended from the living room into the dining room. She was stunning, and she looked so relaxed, so at home. She'd become so much a part of Aren's world in such a short time, and she couldn't imagine her not being there.

"What are you staring at?" Carol asked, bashfully smiling. She subconsciously rubbed her nose and now had green paint streaked across her cheek and on the tip of her nose.

"The most beautiful woman in the world," Aren said.

Carol looked at her for a long moment, the air crackling between them, before she grinned and ducked her head, breaking eye contact. She carefully poured paint into two trays before delivering one to Aren. They each took a fine brush and began the daunting task of cutting in the corners and the ceiling before rolling the paint onto the walls. Aren worked on the corner in the living room, while Carol worked on the corner in the dining room.

"What were your mom and dad like?" Carol asked from across the room, not looking away from her detailed task.

Aren was thoughtful for a moment. "I remember my mom being very gentle and sweet. She made the best grilled cheese sandwiches. She loved to read me stories and later loved to help me read stories. She kept a little flower garden in the front of the house that held all the fragrances of summer. She had big hair and was always teasing and spraying it so it would be tall. She wore an apron that was longer than most of her skirts and she loved to run around the backyard with me."

"And your dad? What was he like?"

Aren's back stiffened and her grip on the paintbrush tightened. "My dad was an abusive drunk."

"What happened to them? Were they killed in an accident like my folks?" Carol asked, continuing to prod. "You've just never said how you ended up in foster care."

Aren inhaled deeply. She finished the section she was working on and left to get the ladder from the kitchen. After setting up the ladder and climbing up four steps, she finally decided to answer. "My dad liked to drink whiskey and play cards. I don't know what game he liked best, I was too young to care, but he'd cash his check on Friday and take off until he won or ran out of money. He'd win occasionally, but not often, just enough to keep him hooked. One night when I was eight, he came home after a big loss. Some big men came with him and gutted our house. They took everything, even the fridge, food and all!"

She stepped down from the ladder and moved it over a few feet before continuing. "Anyway, our house was empty except for a couple of lawn chairs and some TV trays. My mom put me back to bed on the floor because they even took all our beds. I tried to go to sleep, but they started fighting. Mom was screaming that she was done, she was fed up with his gambling and drinking and that she'd had enough. She said that she was taking me and going home to her folks. I remember being excited that we were leaving him and hoped that this time it was for real. She'd said it before, but he'd talk her out of it. He'd promise that things would change, promise that he'd be different, and he would be for a while, but then the booze and the cards would always win."

Again, she stepped down from the ladder and again, moved it a few feet down the wall closer to Carol. She was cutting in the green along the ceiling. Aren looked up at the beige cutting crisply to a soft sage green and realized how much she would like the colors once the putrid gold was completely covered up. She stepped up the few steps to reach the ceiling again.

"Did your mom take you away that time?" Carol asked before Aren had a chance to resume the story.

Aren shook her head and took a deep breath. "No, she never got a chance. They kept fighting and pretty soon dishes were crashing in the kitchen and then I heard this loud thwack sound followed by a thud and it went quiet. Somehow, I knew it was bad, that it was worse this time. I snuck down the hallway to check and see if Mom was okay. He'd hit her before, so hard that she was knocked out for a while." Aren took in a deep breath. "Mom was lying on the floor. Her hair was dark and red in the back and blood started pooling on the floor. She was so still, like she was sleeping. Dad was standing above her with a cast iron frying pan clenched in his fist. He dropped the pan on the floor and called for an ambulance, but she was dead when the paramedics arrived. I watched as he picked up the pan and cleaned it up, and he had it back in the cupboard before they arrived. I snuck back to my room and hid. He never knew what I saw that night."

Aren stepped off the ladder and moved it farther down the wall. She noticed Carol had finished the corner and was ready to start on the ceiling from her end.

"Do you want to start rolling the paint while I finish the ceiling line? That way you won't have to try to climb the ladder with your boot." Aren took the break to settle herself here, in her new reality, rather than back then. It was easier to do now, and that brought some comfort.

"That sounds like a deal." Carol refilled her tray of paint and grabbed the roller with the long pole before walking down to the corner that Aren had finished earlier. "Were the police called?"

"Yeah, someone called them in. I guess all the broken dishes were a clue. He was arrested and I was sent off to a foster home until the trial was over. He convinced them that yes, they had been arguing, but that she'd slipped while throwing a plate at him and then she'd hit her head on the counter. They found him not guilty and released me back to him that same day," Aren said, again moving the ladder. "He picked me up in the suit he'd worn to court. He told me that I'd have to do Mommy's work now so that he could go to work. He said he'd try to find me a new mommy but until he could I'd have to step up. Then he had me scrub up my mom's blood off the kitchen floor. How screwed up is that?"

Carol set the roller down and walked over to the ladder where Aren was still perched up against the ceiling. She rubbed Aren's calf and asked her if she was okay. Aren looked down and smiled warmly. She realized at that very moment that she was okay, she was actually healing. The emotional memories remained, but the guilt had subsided. She didn't feel so raw, so intimidated by her father, even in memory, as she had even a few months earlier. Aren nodded that she was doing fine and reached down, gently touching the green paint on Carol's cheek.

"Is that why you have worked so hard to get Phyllis's blood off the floor? Does it bring back memories of your mother lying on the floor?" Carol asked a few minutes later, having returned to her job of rolling the green over the gold. The wall was now almost completely painted.

"I never linked the two, not consciously, anyway. I guess it's possible though." Aren stepped off the ladder and watched Carol for a moment. Their lives were so incredibly different. In the beginning, Carol had said they could help each other heal. Maybe it was working. Carol was the second person she'd ever told about her mom, about her dad, and while her death was still sad, she found she could talk about it. It felt good to be able to share the truth of that night. Release it to the universe so she could have a life she wanted instead of the one she'd had.

CHAPTER THIRTY-FOUR

It didn't take Carol long to finish up the green on the dining room wall. Soon she was in the kitchen with Aren, paintbrush in hand. They'd decided to paint the sage green on the island and the space between the countertop and cupboards to keep the room light. Once they finished that area, they only had the red to do in the bedroom and their painting project would be complete.

"Are you still up for talking?" Carol asked.

"Sure. I imagine your mind is spinning with a thousand more questions." Aren turned and smiled at Carol.

"Did your dad ever remarry?" Carol dipped her brush into the paint and worked at the opposite side of the kitchen.

"No, but he brought plenty of women home. Most of them looked like hookers. They'd smoke and drink right alongside him. I think the nice women, like my mom, could see him for who he really was." Aren shrugged. "Those women didn't come around."

"Well then, did you have to keep being the responsible one? Did you have to keep doing laundry and cooking and all that while going to school?" Carol asked.

"Yep, it was my job and there was no way I'd challenge him. I got up early, made him breakfast and packed his lunch before I went off to school and then hurried home after school to get dinner started and check on laundry. I kept the house clean, did dishes, anything that would keep him from being angry with me. Sometimes nothing made a difference. The house would be spotless and he'd still come home in a foul mood and beat the shit out of me. I remember times that I'd have to wear long sleeves in the summertime just to hide all the bruises."

"So, eventually they took you away from him?" Carol asked while getting started on painting the island.

"A teacher caught sight of my bruises once and called child protective services, but they stopped by right after school, and for whatever reason Dad came home on time that night and was sober. They inspected the house, but I kept it clean, and there was food in the cupboards because I did the grocery shopping. Everything looked like a normal house should. So, they left and so did Dad, in a fit of rage. I didn't want to be home when he got home but I didn't dare be gone either. That was an especially brutal evening."

The painting of the sage green was complete. All they had left to do was paint the wall that would be behind Aren's bed and then they'd be ready to put down the oak planked floor. Aren went outside and washed out the roller and brushes while Carol stirred the brick red. She sat there absorbing this new chapter, the earliest chapter, in Aren's life. Aunt Suzie had always said that God would never give us more than we could handle. Given all that she was learning about Aren's life, she didn't know how that could be the case. Would she have survived if she'd walked Aren's path? Would she have been strong enough to take it and come out the other side? Carol shook her head. She doubted it. How could she ever trust another human being? Why would she want to? Aren walked into the room and handed Carol a brush.

"Are you up for one last wall?"

"I can be up for one more wall. Please tell me we'll tackle the upstairs another day." Carol dramatically flopped backward onto the floor.

"Even I'm not up for tackling the upstairs today. My arms are about spent." Aren laughed.

Carol still had so many questions. She wondered if she was pushing too hard. She tried to ignore the thoughts swirling in her head. She tried to just focus on keeping the paint line crisp and even.

"Ask." Aren's back was to her, in the opposite corner. "You're chewing on your lip. It's your tell when you want to ask a question. So, please, ask."

"I have a tell? Here I thought you've been reading my mind all this time." Carol threw her drip towel at Aren.

"More than one." Aren smiled, tossing the towel back. "And it's probably best that I can't read your mind."

"Well, I still don't understand how you ended up in foster care if you were never pulled from your home by CPS?"

"There's a thug out there somewhere I owe a debt of gratitude to," Aren said, smiling. "One weekend Dad just didn't come home. Monday came and went, still no Dad, the next weekend came, still no Dad. It was such a relief, and I didn't mind at all. I was at school the following Monday looking through the newspapers for current event articles, and on the previous Monday's paper was a picture of this crime scene. I loved crime scenes. I almost became a criminologist instead of a vet, but I realized I might not be impartial to the evidence if I felt like someone was guilty, given what I'd been through. Anyway, I'm looking at this crime scene photo and it looks like my dad. Same clothes he wore to work, same nasty old boots. I sat down and read the article. This man had been beaten to death behind a bar that my dad hung out at a lot. I knew he owed all sorts of people money, and I mean *big* money. We had muscle coming to the house all the time. They were actually very nice to me and would bring me suckers and cheeseburgers. They weren't so nice to Dad, but then he was the one who owed them so much money. My best guess is that they finally got tired of waiting for him to 'strike it big' and just eliminated him to send a message to whoever else might have owed them money."

Aren had finished cutting in the corner she was working on and walked out of the room. She returned with the eight-foot ladder and started on the ceiling while Carol wet the roller in deep red paint. They had a rhythm down now and it made quick work of the wall.

"How did you find out the man behind the bar was your dad?" Carol asked once she was rolling her paint.

"That's actually the funny part of the whole deal. It was maybe another week after I'd read the article and I came home from school to find police in the house. They had a couple of cars out front and some were dressed in suits instead of uniforms. I'm guessing they were detectives. They looked shocked to see me walk in the back door with my key. They asked me who I was, so I told them my name. I asked them if they had found my dad, not that I wanted him home, but it seemed like the appropriate question to ask. They had a lady cop come and talk to me. I guess none of the men knew how to question a young girl. She asked me who my dad was and I told her. She asked me where my mom was and I told her she was dead, and I guess I looked over to the stove. The frying pan was on the stovetop, but I could still see my dad standing there with it in his hand. She asked me to tell her what happened and even though I knew in my heart that he was dead, I didn't have the guts to admit the truth. I told her that I didn't know, that she'd died while I was sleeping." Aren paused to climb down off the ladder. She was finished cutting in the red along the ceiling. She placed her paintbrush in the bucket of water she'd brought in earlier and sat on the floor while Carol finished the last bit of rolling.

"The lady cop took my hand in hers and told me that my dad had been killed. I asked her if he was the guy in the paper that I'd read about a week earlier and she admitted it was him. I tell ya, Carol, I felt so much relief. I felt like doing cartwheels all around the house. I told them thank you and that they could go, but they all just stood there staring at me like I was an alien. I had no concept at the time that I was too young to live on my own. Who knew I couldn't possibly pay the bills and go to school at eleven?" Aren laughed. "The lady cop said I'd have to go to protective services so they could find me a new family to live with. Well shit, based on what I knew of family I didn't want another one. That's when I threw a fit and refused to go. I told them that I cooked and cleaned and did the shopping. I told them that I could do laundry and iron, that I didn't need another family, that I could do it on my own. Obviously, that didn't convince them. The lady cop took me into my room and had me pack a bag of clothes. Again, I refused. I told her that this was my house and I wanted to stay where my mom was. She shoved my stuff into a few paper sacks and picked my ass up! She was a strong woman because I fought her for all it was worth. She tossed me into the back of the cruiser and hauled my little butt off to CPS. I stayed with a family down in Detroit for a little over a year and then they transferred me up here to stay with Phyllis and Ron. So, now you know all about my sordid past, all my skeletons are out in the open. Here's your chance to run for it, though I'm hoping you don't."

Carol dropped her roller into the bucket of water and flopped down on the floor next to Aren. "I'm not going to make that mistake again!" She wrapped her arm around Aren's waist. "So tell me one last thing—"

"I'm almost out of emotional energy," Aren said, "But go for it."

"How'd you turn out so well? I mean, why on earth aren't you a drinking, raging psychotic who, by all rights, should be pissed at the universe for all that you've been through?" Carol asked. "I mean, you have every right to be angry, but how'd you turn out so at peace with the world?"

"Well, my little bookworm, I decided as a kid that I would never be like that as an adult. I checked out every book I could get my hands on about how to heal, how to grow and move on. I was angry and resentful, for a long time, but the books helped with that. I never had an urge to drink, because the smell of booze makes me sick to my stomach. The biggest price I've paid has been in my lack of ability to sleep. Ever since my mom died, I haven't slept well. The demons come out when I close my eyes. They scream at me, I feel the impact of fists, I hear Phyllis's gurgling,"

"Are the nightmares still bad?" Carol asked, pulling Aren closer.

"They still torment me, but I find I'm recovering quicker, and the memories don't hold as much power over me. I attribute a lot of that to you. I've felt more at peace since you've been here than I have ever felt."

Carol lifted her head from Aren's shoulder and looked into her eyes. "Why do you think it's different with me?"

"You took the time to get to know me. Despite the stories you heard, you took a chance on me. You believed in me when you had no reason to do so. I opened up about all the darkness from my life and I can see that you care. It isn't pity, you actually care. Your eyes, your touch, your questions, everything you do and say shows me how much you sincerely care. It's made such a difference for me, helped me face it all. It means the world to me that you know everything and you still care."

Carol reached up and cupped Aren's face in her hands. She leaned forward and tenderly kissed Aren's lips. She pulled her close and held her. To this day, she had no idea what possessed her to duck between those strands of fencing and approach the woman by the campfire, but she was so thankful that she had. She couldn't imagine not having Aren in her life.

CHAPTER THIRTY-FIVE

The next day after morning milking and chores were finished, they walked over to the house to see how the fresh paint looked in the daylight. Aren looked around, impressed at the difference. Even when she'd been here as a teenager it hadn't looked this good. The bad memories seemed to have been scrubbed away. It was her home, in a way it never really had been before, and the thought brought tears to her eyes.

"So, are we ready to get started upstairs, or do you want to start laying the floor?"

"How do you keep this pace up? We painted until all hours of the night last night, got up early and did chores, and we've picked the garden already. Damn, I'm hot and exhausted and you're ready to go and start another full day's work." Carol leaned against the island and stretched her back.

"Maybe it was the four years of doing everything alone, or maybe it's the excitement of seeing this project done and actually moving in. Definitely though, it's the thought of seeing you enjoy this full-sized kitchen, while wearing that spaghetti-strapped sundress again." Aren smirked.

Carol stepped directly in front of Aren. She tilted her head up and leaned in close. Aren could feel her breath on her neck and then at the edge of her ear.

"If I'd known how much you liked that sundress, I would have worn it much more often," she whispered and then kissed Aren's cheek.

Aren's heart skipped a beat. The way it felt to have Carol's lips so close to her ear sent shivers throughout her body.

"The paint fumes are too much, let's go outside." Carol grabbed Aren's hand and led her out to the shade of the back porch. She flopped down on the deck, pulling Aren down next to her. After a few minutes, she sprawled out flat on the deck boards. Aren looked over at Carol. What was she waiting for? Carol was beautiful, sexy, and she had kissed her last night with such tenderness. Aren twisted around to straddle Carol, holding herself up using her hands and knees. She bent down, allowing her lips to brush Carol's ever so slightly. Carol reached up and pulled Aren down on top of her. Her desire was unmistakable when she parted her lips, kissing Aren deeply. Aren moaned, parted her lips, and teased Carol's tongue with her own. She lowered herself on top of Carol pushing herself between Carol's legs. She reached up with her free hand cupping Carol's face. A faint buzzing began to pulse between them. Carol reached down into her pocket and pulled out the vibrating phone.

"Hold that thought, it's the library," Carol said, trying to get her breath.

Aren rolled off and helped Carol up as she answered the phone. Carol walked over to the far edge of the deck while she spoke and Aren looked over at the house across the way. A lot of progress had been made there too. Walls were up, the second story was nearly built, and the truss package was at the ready in the driveway. Would Carol get the job, finish her house, and move out? Once she moved out, would she still want anything to do with her? Or would Aren just be a footnote in a particularly bad time in her life? The thought made her stomach cramp. She didn't want her to go. A loud, excited scream pulled Aren from her thoughts.

"My interview must have gone great. I GOT THE JOB!" She ran across the porch and jumped into Aren's arms. "I'm a librarian! It's all coming together!"

Aren scooped Carol up and carried her over to the double hammock she'd strung out on the back deck. She set Carol in the hammock before carefully climbing into the web next to her.

"Congratulations, my little bookworm. I'm going to miss having you here every minute of the day, but I'm happy for you," Aren said into her ear.

Carol nuzzled up into Aren, wrapping her arm around Aren's waist. "The director said that everyone enjoyed meeting me and they were eager to have me as an addition to their staff!"

"Of course, they liked you. You're irresistible. So, when do you report for duty?" Aren asked, enjoying the view of the farm from her perspective in the hammock, specifically the beautiful woman curled up in her arms. It felt amazing to hold her and she'd enjoy it for as long as it lasted.

"I start work next Monday," Carol answered, her lips against Aren's neck. "I'll work Mondays, Tuesdays, Thursdays, and Fridays from eight in the morning until five at night. I guess that's the good thing about small town libraries, they aren't open all night. And that means I still have the chance to cook for you in that sundress."

Aren felt Carol's lips on her neck, felt her teeth gently graze skin. She shivered with excitement. Aren turned her head, the need to feel Carol's lips on hers suddenly consuming. She was tired of holding back, tired of denying herself because of fear. She wanted to experience, she wanted to share this with Carol. Carol tilted her head back as if she sensed Aren's need. Aren teased Carol's lips with the tip of her tongue and Carol reached behind Aren's head to pull her closer, their kiss instant passion. She felt Carol's hand drop down to her stomach, tugging her shirt free from her jeans. When Carol's fingertips touched the bare skin of Aren's stomach, she moaned, and their kiss intensified.

Carol's hand lifted from Aren's stomach, unbuckling her belt, and then opening her jeans. Her fingers slid beneath Aren's fitted boxers. The touch was electric and stole her breath away. Aren could barely moan in response to the pleasure of Carol's fingertips.

"Oh, Aren, you're so wet," Carol whispered, her hips pushing into Aren's side.

Aren wasn't used to being so out of control. She'd always found pleasure in pleasing the woman she was with, being on top, being in control. This was such a new sensation. She wanted to touch Carol too, see her, feel her. Aren tried to pull up on Carol's shirt but was stopped.

"I want to please you. Let me enjoy your body," Carol whispered into Aren's ear. "Lift up a bit."

Aren lifted herself up and helped push her jeans down around her knees, craving all of Carol's touch. The desire she felt at this moment, so completely open, so exposed, was more than she ever could have dreamed. Aren closed her eyes, pushing her head back into the netting. She felt her shirt being pushed up, felt Carol's delicate touch beneath her bra. Tender kisses caressed her stomach and worked up to her now bare breasts. A gentle summer breeze blew, teasing Aren's wet nipples. She shivered with the feeling of the invisible caress.

Carol explored and savored Aren's body in a way that no one else had ever done. Aren had never known how sensitive the hollow of her throat was and how the delicate touch of Carol's tongue down her neck and to that spot could make her knees feel weak, her hips want to rock. She had no idea that the sides of her breasts were almost as sensitive as her nipples or that she could ever dream of wanting to feel teeth graze the tip of her nipple, but the moment Carol did that, she wanted to feel it again and again. Everywhere Carol touched, she found herself wanting more. Aren's hips lifted into Carol's exploring fingers. She moaned, wanting so much to feel Carol deep inside of her, but Carol teased her by circling her finger just enough inside to make Aren's body quiver with excitement. She lifted into Carol's hand, eager for more, though Carol continued to tease, circling around her clit and then once again barely inside. She leaned down, kissing Aren deeply, pulling away and leaving Aren wanting more. Trailing kisses down Aren's neck, the breeze tickled each spot where Carol's lips had been. Nibbling and teasing Aren's nipples. Aren tangled her fingers into the hammock above her head and lifted her hips into Carol's hand. She felt Carol's fingers slide deep inside. She shuddered, held them there for a second and then pulled her hips back and pushed into Carol again. Aren reached down, holding Carol's hand in place and pushed her hips even harder into Carol's fingers, her clit against Carol's palm. She could barely stand the excitement as her body heated and quivered. Her breath hitched with each thrust.

"Oh, don't stop." Aren moaned, her head arched back as far as it would go into the netting.

Aren held Carol close to her, her hips thrusting into Carol's hand. She was so close to tipping over the edge but didn't want the feeling to end. Their lips were barely touching from a kiss that she couldn't pull away from, but her breaths were so ragged, she couldn't continue either. Carol did something to Aren, something with her fingers that flooded Aren's senses. She quivered and shuddered while consumed with wave after wave of orgasm. Her breath caught in her throat and she pulled Carol close, holding on tightly while she convulsed with pleasure, her body quivering with electrical aftershocks.

"You're incredible, you know that?" Aren managed to say between deep breaths. She kissed Carol deeply, shuddering all over again when Carol pulled her hand away.

Carol fidgeted next to her on the hammock and then something dropped on the deck next to them. Then she heard Velcro followed by a thud. *Ah, the boot.* Before Aren knew what was happening, Carol had pulled herself up and was straddling Aren. She looked down at Aren with seductive eyes, a new look, a sexy look. Aren's heart pounded in her chest, excitement consumed her all over again. Aren traced her hand up the sides of Carol's thighs up to her hips. She expected to feel Carol's shorts but instead found bare skin. She wrapped her hand around Carol, cupping her ass and lifting her hips up into Carol, holding herself there for a moment. She watched Carol tilt her head back, roll her shoulders back and felt her rock her hips into Aren. It felt incredible. Aren brought her hands up beneath her shirt and lifted it over Carol's head. She watched Carol look down and watch her every move and then she looked into Aren's eyes, her tongue curling up, the tip teasing her upper lip. She reached behind her back and released the clasp on her bra, allowing it to slide down her arms and fall to the side. She was completely naked and more beautiful than Aren could have ever imagined. Her full breasts rose and fell with each breath. Aren started at Carol's knees, her fingertips teasing up her legs, around her hips, and up her sides. She cupped Carol's beautiful breasts in her hands, grazing her nipples with the sides of her thumbs. Carol's hands swept up and covered Aren's holding her tightly against her chest, her hips rocking again ever so slightly. She closed her eyes and arched her back. It was the most sensual sight Aren had ever seen.

Aren pulled her hand free and slid it between them. She felt another flood of excitement when she touched Carol for the first time. She tried to tease Carol with the slightest touch, but with Carol on top, she simply took control and pushed into Aren's hand. Aren touched Carol with her fingers and lifted her hips at the same time Carol pushed into her. They both moaned from the sensation. Aren pulled her knees up so she could lift her hips into Carol's, pushing her fingers deeper inside. Carol held onto Aren's other hand, still holding it against her breast. Her hips thrust into Aren faster and harder and Aren could feel her thighs starting to quiver. She pushed her hips up against Carol and held herself there, letting Carol rock against the base of her hand.

"Oh yes, just like that." Carol thrust her hips into Aren.

Aren could feel her tightening around her fingers as Carol pushed with short, forceful thrusts until she shook with orgasm. Carol rolled her hips, shivering and then collapsing on top of Aren, trying to catch her breath.

"That was incredible," she whispered into Aren's ear.

Aren just held her, too taken with emotion to speak just yet. Incredible was not the right word to describe how she felt at that moment. She caressed Carol's back, held her close, and cherished this one moment in time, not wanting it to ever end.

Chapter Thirty-six

The small drought was over, bringing the rains back more often. This created a huge harvest to be picked in the gardens almost every day, much of which was to be canned for winter food storage. Aren was now only attending the farmer's market every other week in order to have enough food for winter. She'd done this each summer for the past three years, having learned the lesson to keep enough aside after that first winter alone. She started a few weeks earlier this year, wanting to have enough for both of them to enjoy all winter long, just in case Carol stayed.

While picking the vast assortment of vegetables, Aren couldn't help but think of all they'd accomplished in the last week or so. The upstairs was completely cleared out. New carpeting had been installed professionally upstairs and the house sparkled with cleanliness. The milled oak flooring had been custom cut to each angle, nook and cranny. Once it was laid, it was so well done it looked like a professional job. Aren and Carol stained the wood to a warm chestnut color and then coated it with two layers of sealant. The new flooring and paint had completely transformed the home. Every time Aren walked into the house, it felt warm and inviting. Their last task was the patience to allow another day for the sealant to dry completely before Aren moved in. She looked over at Carol and wondered how much more time she'd have with her. They still hadn't talked about where Carol would go once her house was done, even though they'd spend their nights tangled in the sheets, taking one another to the edge and over.

Aren picked the vegetables quickly, looking up often as the large thunder clouds rolled in. She noticed that these clouds were especially tall and would likely produce a storm like they'd experienced the night Carol's leg was broken, though she kept this thought to herself.

"Looks like a bad storm is coming. The wind sure is picking up," Aren hollered over to Carol, who was also watching the clouds roll in.

"Should we stop picking? I don't want to be out here in the lightning and thunder," Carol called back. "I know that sounds goofy, but I just got my leg back to normal!"

Aren looked over to the adorable woman standing barefooted in the dirt. She'd been without her walking boot for almost a week and was enjoying her reclaimed mobility. She hardly ever wore shoes.

"We can stop picking if you're nervous. The pigs will thank you," Aren called out, knowing how much Carol was still nervous around big storms.

"Let's keep at it, if lightning starts, I'm calling it!" Carol carried a flat of vegetables to the awaiting wagon. They only had a few rows left, and Aren worked hard to get through them.

Before long, they pulled the wagon all the way into the barn and closed off the long sliding door to keep the wind out. After latching the door closed, Aren released Wyatt from his harness and led him to a box stall that opened out into the pasture.

When she returned to the back of the barn, Carol was already unloading the crates from the wagon into the back area of the barn where the wash basins were located. The space was dark with the door closed. The wind rattled the large door as if to say it too wanted it open.

Aren walked around the large wagon and flipped on the overhead lights.

"And the Lord said 'let there be light' and there was!" Carol quoted while filling the sink with water. Aren shook her head chuckling while stacking the rest of the crates on the far side of the sinks. Bailey jumped into the empty wagon as acting supervisor.

"So, you want to start washing and I'll start canning like we did last time?" Aren asked, setting up the propane burners and pulling down the water bath canners.

"Will we be safe out here, if the storm hits?" Carol asked.

"If it gets dangerous, we'll head to the basement in the house. Okay?"

Sounds good to me," Carol replied, already setting the tomatoes out for blanching.

They worked steadily getting the produce canned. As jars cooled and sealed, Aren would slide them onto the large shelving unit opposite the sinks. The shelves were already almost completely full, and she still had a few more weeks of good harvesting before the cool nights began to diminish the crops. Once the canning was done, they began to blanch other vegetables that would be put into baggies and frozen in the large chest freezer. Aren loved to keep corn, green beans, peas, summer squash, and zucchini in the freezer for winter soups.

Rain began to pound the side of the barn just as they were starting the summer squash. Flashes of lightning snuck through the crevasses between the door and the wall. Thunder rumbled loudly, at times causing the barn to shudder. Aren watched Carol flinch with each clap of thunder.

"We can finish up the squash and zucchini tomorrow. How about we stop here, and get the chores done instead? We'll take care of the animals and get inside."

"I like the sound of that. Can we push the wagon in farther and close these doors as well?" Carol asked, flinching again at the sound of thunder.

"I'm afraid not, I'll need to push the wagon more into this room so I can bring the cows in for milking." Aren extinguished the flames on the propane burners. She dumped the hot water down the drain before storing the two pots on a top shelf. Carol quickly loaded the empty crates into the back of the wagon before loading up the few that remained full.

Working together, they managed to slowly push the wagon into the back room as far as it would go once all was cleaned up and out of the way. Above them came a loud knocking noise when an exceptionally strong gust of wind pounded into the back of the barn.

"I think the wind just knocked the loft door open. Let me run up and check," Aren said, already heading for the loft stairs.

Sure enough, the door had blown open and it continued to flap against the wall in the howling wind. Aren reached for the two-by-four that she'd cut for this very reason during other storms. Using her back and the strength of her legs, she was finally able to fight the wind and get the hinged door closed snuggly against the stops. She slid the long two-by-four into the steel brackets that were bolted to studs on either side of the door.

When she returned to the lower level, she found Carol already milking Ginger. Aren retrieved Cinnamon and set about the task of getting her milked as well.

"Are the thunderstorms always this wicked around here?" Carol asked. "I assumed the storm that hit my aunt and uncle's place was a one-off. I don't remember it being like this when I'd come to visit."

"We have a few good storms each year, but they seem to be getting more intense with climate change. And this one is intense. Usually, it's just distant thunder and good soaking rains. But occasionally, we'll get a good thunder boomer like today."

"How often do you get tornadoes? Do we have a root cellar or some place to go here in the barn if a tornado comes? Or do we have to run to the house?" Carol asked, sounding nervous for the first time that evening.

"I've lived in Michigan most of my life, and while we've had a couple of tornadoes in the state, I've never seen one myself. We've got a basement in the house if we need one, I just hadn't given it any thought." Aren tried to sound reassuring. "Carol, this is just a good thunderstorm, nothing more. It will most likely be done by the time we go to bed tonight."

Aren looked over at Carol, knowing that she'd recently lost the last of her family in a storm like this. She wasn't sure what to do to reassure her beyond spending the evening in the basement. She hoped this storm wouldn't come to that, for Carol's sake. And if Carol thought the storms came around too often, would it make her run? Would she up and leave? Aren pushed the thought away. She'd worry about that later.

CHAPTER THIRTY-SEVEN

Lightning and cracks of thunder continued to accompany the rain well into the early evening. After the chores were finished, Carol and Aren made their way up to the loft. None of the animals seemed eager to venture out into the rain. They all sought refuge in the coziness of their box stalls. Bailey was curled up on her dog bed, as usual unaffected by the world around her. The wind was finally easing up its relentless pounding on the barred loft door. Aren had defrosted steaks for dinner, but knowing the fire pit was likely now a small pond, she stowed them into the refrigerator for the next day. Instead, they had a hearty salad for dinner with a can of tuna sprinkled on top.

By the time they'd finished eating, the rain had stopped, though the lightning and thunder continued. Aren released the two-by-four and opened the loft door. The sky was an eerie color of various hues of green. She stood there looking at the still sky and swirling clouds above. Her stomach sank.

"Carol, I think we should head over to the house," Aren said, looking out across the landscape. "Now."

Carol walked over to see what Aren was looking at. She no sooner stepped next to Aren when large hail began to drop out of the sky as if dumped from a giant bucket. The noise from the roof above them was almost deafening.

"It's raining baseballs of ice!" Carol yelled. "We don't want to be running to the house in this. It will slice us open for sure."

The wind kicked up again, blowing the large balls of ice into the loft door. It took every bit of their strength to push the door closed against the force of the ice and wind. Aren slid the board back in place. She grabbed Carol's hand and pulled her toward the stairs.

"We've got to find cover!" Aren screamed over the sound of the hail beating against the barn roof.

Aren pushed Carol in front of her and followed her closely down the stairs. The cows were bellowing. Doc, Wyatt, and the other horses were all nervously shifting within the box stalls. Still, the hail relentlessly pounded down on the back of the barn and the roof above. Carol turned and looked to Aren for direction. Then, as suddenly as it had started, the hail stopped. Aren peered out the opening of one of the box stalls and watched the green clouds begin to churn. She ran to the back door of the barn and unlocked it.

"What on earth are you doing? Let's get to the house!" Carol cried out from the front of the wagon.

Aren ignored her. Pulling with all her might, she forced the door to break free from the melting ice balls piled up against it. Aren stood there in the four-foot of opening she was able to achieve and stared as the dark clouds above the woods beyond the pasture began to quickly swirl, at times allowing blue sky to peek through.

She turned and ran to the front of the barn, pulling Carol along by her hand as she passed. Once they were at the front of the barn, Aren pushed open the small step-through door. She stepped out into the eerily still air and looked out to the western side of her property.

"Look, do you see it forming?" Aren asked, pointing to the swirling ocean in the sky. "Can you see the clouds swirling out there?"

"We should be heading for the basement, not standing here like idiots!" Carol tugged on Aren's hand.

The winds picked up again, shifting and swirling so that there was no identifiable direction from which they blew. Aren and Carol watched the swirling clouds up above. Aren thought it looked like fluffy icing coming down from the sky as fold upon fold of clouds swirled together. The rain pounded down in large, heavy drops. The impact of the rain felt like small hail with the winds blowing so hard.

Carol pulled Aren toward the house. The rain pelted their skin as they ran across the ice-slick yard, slipping on large patches of hail. They carefully made their way up the back porch steps, kicking clumps of ice out of the way. They stopped and stood beneath the overhang. Aren couldn't take her eyes off the storm. The clouds appeared miles tall and were still swirling around in powerful circles.

"I've never seen anything like this," Aren hollered above the roar of the storm, pointing at the beginnings of a tornado emerging from the clouds high above. The funnel continued to grow, darting for the ground. Before it even touched down, trees at the far edge of the pasture swirled and creaked with the pressure from the wind.

The funnel seemed to touch the ground right at the edge of the woods. Carol tried desperately to pull Aren into the house, but Aren couldn't move. She watched as huge maple and oak trees were sucked up as if they were weeds snapped in half like twigs before being pulled up into the black twister. As it moved forward, it mowed a path into the woods breaking anything apart that happened to be in the way. One especially large tree must have been rejected by the twister because suddenly it was airborne and flying in their direction.

Aren pulled Carol from the porch and dragged her off to the side of the garage as the large tree landed with a wood-splintering boom about a hundred yards from the back porch. Limbs broke free and rained splinters and clumps of leaves down all around them.

"What is it with the trees in this state? Are they all out to get me?" Carol asked, wiping the water from her face.

"Shit, I'm sorry. Come on, let's get you inside."

From their stance next to the garage, they took in the huge maple tree sprawling across the backyard. The storm continued to roar, but the twister slowly moved away from them to the northeast. Though as it moved farther away, it seemed to become even larger and more powerful.

"No need now, it's heading away from us." Carol stood next to Aren.

"Looks like it's headed for town!" Aren watched the funnel rip through the woods where they had ridden the horses just the day before.

"Do you think we should head that way and see if we can help at all?" Carol asked through the howling winds.

"The roads will likely be impassable with debris. If we can calm the horses, we should ride in when it's clear so we can navigate around the roadblocks like that tree there. Let's go see if we can quiet them down enough to get a saddle on their backs. If that thing hits town, it'll be a mess," Aren said. They ran for the barn. In the distance, they could hear the tornado sirens wail out the warning. Hopefully, the folks took it seriously and ran for cover, she thought, now at a dead run.

CHAPTER THIRTY-EIGHT

Once the horses were ready, Aren ran past Carol to a closet in the back of the tack room.

"What are you doing?" Carol asked, standing in the doorway.

"People are likely going to be cut, broken, whatever. I don't know if enough emergency personnel will be able to assist. I'm only a vet, but I've got much of the exact same triage meds and supplies. If we're going into town, I want to go in prepared to help, instead of fumbling around like I did when your leg was broken." Aren quickly stuffed boxes of syringes and many different color tipped needles into a large sack, along with rolls of tape and thick, padded gauze. A bunch more stuff was added before Aren ran from the room, darting sideways by Carol and for the loft stairs. I'll be right back!"

Aren ran up the stairs into the loft. She pulled the door open closest to the stairs and watched the tornado barrel its way toward town. It had become even bigger than before and still it roared loudly. She turned and ran to the refrigerator and then pulled open the small crisper drawer. She tossed the vegetables out of the drawer and reached for the glass bottles of medications in the back. She pulled out every bottle of lidocaine she could find, then ran into the bathroom and found a large bottle of Ibuprofen for pain, a couple of bottles of alcohol and Betadine, along with chemical ice packs, small towels, her stethoscope, suture kits and anything else she could fit into the pack. On her way back to the stairs, she reached for the halogen head lamp she'd used in the winter and stuffed it into the pack just in case. At the staircase, she reached for the last item on her mental list, her trusty chore knife. Running down the stairs, she stuffed her knife into the back of her jeans.

She ran into the tack room and pulled two lead ropes off a peg and also grabbed a few coils of strong rope. She ran out to Wyatt's saddle and tied the rope onto either side using the dangling leather straps. She stuffed the lead ropes and halters into one of the saddle bags on each horse. Carol ran for the flashlights that they kept charged in the tack room and stuffed those into a saddle bag.

"I think that should do it. You should probably put jeans on, I don't want you lanced open by a tree limb before we even get to town."

Aren turned around and looked at Carol. Her hair was drenched and sticking to her face along with a few partial tree leaves. She was soaked to the bone and her teeth were chattering as if she was chilled, but Aren didn't think that was it. The last time Carol looked like that, she was lying in the grass with a broken leg. Carol wrapped her arms around herself and turned away from Aren, heading toward the stairs.

"Hey, wait, look at me. Are you okay? Is this too much? We don't have to go, or I can go and you can stay here and be safe." Aren set the pack down and walked over to cup Carol's face in her hands.

She looked up in Aren's eyes, drew in a deep breath, and exhaled slowly. She leaned in and wrapped her arms around Aren's waist.

"I'll be okay. If one of us is going then we're both going, together. This helps though, being in your arms, even if for a second. Now, let me run up and get changed."

Aren watched Carol run for the stairs while she hoisted the full and heavy pack onto her back, buckling the waist strap tightly. She'd do everything in her power to keep them safe.

Carol returned a few minutes later wearing jeans and boots. She smiled at Aren while mounting up. They guided the horses through the barn door, and once through the back gate, they allowed the horses to open up as they raced for town, watching ahead for debris.

They could hear the storm far in the distance. They could also hear the sirens still wailing out the warning to take cover. Aren prayed that people would have heeded the advice, but she knew that reality would likely be different. Soon the trail through the woods ended and they carefully made their way out onto the forest service road. Wyatt knew this path well, and once on the road, dug in for speed. Somehow, he too sensed the urgency of the moment and ran faster than Aren had ever seen him move.

Aren had no idea how much time had passed since the tornado touched down. It seemed like only seconds had passed, though she knew better, and however long it had been, she felt like they couldn't get to town soon enough. Once out on the main road, the evidence of the storm became all too real. Branches and mailboxes were strewn across the road. The scattered debris became more intense the closer they got to town. The wind was still whipping and swirling the rain in all directions making it hard to see. There were a few cars on the shoulder of the road with their passengers standing up on top of the hood or roof, hoping to get a better look at the storm. Some screamed out warnings that there had been a tornado ahead, though she could no longer see it. Aren remained focused, constantly searching for the safest path as they raced for certain devastation.

Finally, their journey brought them to the edge of town. The sirens had silenced, leaving behind an eerie creaking and popping of wood splintered by the fierce winds. The twister seemed to have finally dissolved as quickly as it had appeared, although the sky was still tinted with an eerie green hue. Aren pulled back on Wyatt's reins, slowing him to an easy walk.

"Watch for electrical wires on the street," she called over to Carol, who had followed her lead and was easily walking Doc down the road.

They looked from side to side at the devastation around them. The twister had cut a huge path right through the center of town. Cars were flipped up on top of houses and slammed into trees that had somehow stayed anchored, though they weren't much more than rooted poles now. A stoplight had blown through the roof of a parked car. They navigated the horses around the splintered remains of someone's roof which was now spread all over the road. People were finally starting to emerge from their cellars here and there, walking out to the street and taking in the destruction as well.

"I want to head over to the hardware store, just to make sure Maggie is okay," Aren said once they were able to work their way around the stranded roof.

It took them some time to work their way a half mile up the road. Cars, furniture, sections of houses, and downed power lines littered the streets and sidewalks. Thankfully, so far, they hadn't found a person lost to the storm. When Aren looked for the hardware store, all she saw were the crumbled remains of brick and glass. Her heart pounded and she nudged Wyatt to speed up racing toward the remnants of the building. Maggie was the closest thing to family she had besides Carol. Parts of the store littered the parking lot and street. Bricks had been thrown in every direction, shattering through car windows, houses, and one even sticking out of a downed telephone pole. Aren pulled back on Wyatt's reins and slid off his back. She tied his reins to the bumper of an upside-down car and ran toward the debris, calling for Maggie.

Chapter Thirty-nine

Carol tied off Doc in a similar fashion and went to the other side of the rubble, also calling out for Maggie. They flipped over a section of shelving unit and found nothing beneath it. Aren turned her attention to another section of shelving and ran toward it. It looked like it was resting on top of something, though she couldn't tell what it was. She called for Carol to help her push up the long run of shelves.

They lifted with all their strength and could barely budge the more than twenty feet of shelving.

"I'm going to pull up on it one section at a time and you tell me if you see anyone trapped beneath it, okay?" Aren explained to Carol.

Carol knelt and looked beneath each section of shelving as Aren lifted it up. The first two sections seemed to be nothing more than rolls of landscaping plastic or mailboxes, but in the third section, Carol caught the movement of a hand.

"This one, someone's under this one!" Carol shouted.

"Would you hand me that section of shelf over there so we can prop this up a bit?" Aren asked. Carol nodded and ran for the metal shelf. They shoved it into the opening and it held the shelf with some stability.

Aren knelt and peered into the opening, "Can you hear me?" She called into the darkness beneath the shelf. The hand made a thumbs-up sign. "Hold on, I'm going to see if we can lift this shelving off of you. Try to move out from under the shelf if we get it high enough, okay?" Another thumbs-up indicated that the person heard her.

Carol followed Aren to the horses. "Leave Doc tied. I think that bit of a wall should help me get some lift on the shelving. I'll need you to stay by the person trapped and help pull them free. Please don't crawl beneath the shelving just in case the rope snaps or something." Aren turned to look at Carol. "Promise me!"

"I promise." Carol ran back to stay with the trapped person.

Aren freed the rope from Wyatt's saddle, then went to the shelving and tied the rope off through holes in the metal at the top of each side. The base of the unit was still bolted into the concrete of the floor. Aren closed her eyes briefly and exhaled a sigh of relief. It would stay in place instead of sliding over the person beneath it. She ran over to Wyatt and untied his reins before she led him over to the rope and quickly secured it to the saddle. After checking for a clear path, she took the reins and asked the large horse to walk forward. The rope grew tight quickly, and Aren could see Wyatt straining to pull the bent metal up to its original upright position. His hooves slid in the wet, muddy ground, but still Aren urged him on. She could hear the metal creaking, beginning to give and rise. Wyatt dug his hooves in and continued to pull, stretching the rope to guitar string tight.

"Okay, stop!" Carol called out. "She's free."

"Is it Maggie?" Aren asked, while backing Wyatt up. She patted him on the shoulder before running around the small base of the building and meeting up with Carol. Carefully, Aren helped Carol pull the person free. Aren sighed with relief to see Maggie crawl from beneath the shelving.

"Maggie, can you talk?" Aren asked, kneeling beside her. Other than a few scrapes, she appeared unharmed. Aren quickly removed her pack and unzipped the main compartment.

"Yeah, I can talk. I had a mouthful of insulation when you called out for me. That's why I couldn't do anything but move my hand. I couldn't open my mouth and risk inhaling it," Maggie said, trying to sit up.

"Just stay down there for a second would ya? Let me take a quick look before you try to move too much," Aren said sternly. As she looked into Maggie's eyes for shards of glass and checked her over, she asked, "Was there anyone else in the store when it hit?"

"Bunch of people, when the sirens went off, I sent them all down to the basement and was just heading for the stairs myself when the building came apart like a damn puzzle tossed in the air," Maggie said.

"Well, as amazing as it is, you appear to be unharmed other than some bumps and bruises," Aren said, hugging Maggie tightly. "Where's the stairway? I imagine everyone down below would like out."

Maggie stood up carefully, holding her lower back and brushed off her clothes. She turned and took in the store. It was completely leveled. She walked carefully over to the location of the stairwell.

"It should be here, beneath this car," she said, pointing to a station wagon balancing on its side.

"Well, let's see if we can move it," Aren said as she worked to untie the rope from the shelving. The knots were pulled too tight with the effort Wyatt had put into moving it. Rather than fight the knot, Aren pulled her knife out of her jeans and cut the rope as close to the knot as she could. "Maggie, do you have a tow strap around here? I want as much distance between the horse and car as possible. I'm afraid he'll spook when the car comes crashing down if it's directly behind him." Aren looked at the angle of the crushed heap of metal and tried to figure out the best way to do it.

The windows had all been blown out. Aren climbed up on top of the vehicle and tied the rope onto the frame of the car. She checked the area for downed power lines and led Wyatt over to the spot.

"Hell, nothing's left! I'm sorry, Aren, but I can't find anything to help you!" Maggie hollered out, kneeling in front of another shelf, pulling out items and tossing them over her shoulder. Carol, too, was searching the rubble for what Aren needed.

"It's okay, I'll just have to use this other coil of rope and hope it's strong enough," Aren called back. She released the rope from Wyatt's saddle and knotted the two splices together. Again, she tied the free end to Wyatt's saddle and urged him forward. One of his rear hooves found a stout tree root deep in the mud and allowed him to thrust forward. The tangled metal box on wheels began to budge a bit.

"Come on, Wyatt, you can do it, boy."

He pulled, frantically seeking out footing. Finally, he managed a few steps of solid purchase and the car fell, bouncing the shocks and springs to their limits.

Aren hugged the huge horse and watched with a smile as those trapped in the basement began to emerge. She caught Carol's eye and gave her a big smile. Even with the destruction all around them, today felt like a win.

CHAPTER FORTY

Almost an hour had passed since the tornado had plowed through the tiny town. Emergency vehicles were stuck outside town, unable to get around the broken roads. Aren could hear chainsaws off in the distance working to clear a way in. She gathered those she'd freed and asked them to mill around town and see if anyone needed help, and then she and Carol mounted up and began to search for anyone wounded or still trapped.

They hadn't gotten more than fifty feet down the street when the calls for help began to sound from all directions.

"Hey, cowgirls, there's people over here that need help!" A large bellied man waved from across the street.

"Over here, too," an older woman called out.

"Try to keep them calm, we'll be over there in just a moment." Aren called to the older woman as she urged Wyatt toward the man waving for help.

Carol and Aren slid from their horses and ran over. They both fixed instantly on the battered family pulling themselves from a storm culvert. The father looked to be the most seriously injured.

"Could you see if you can find me some clean water?" Aren asked the man who'd waved them over as she pulled her pack off.

"That twister hit and we couldn't get over to the storm shelter. I just shoved everyone into this culvert. We could hardly breathe with all the wind and stuff flying around in there," the battered man managed to say while helping his family out of the metal tube. Carol got on the other side and helped them make their way out.

Aren quickly looked the kids over, but they were fine, just scared more than anything. The parents had taken the brunt of the injuries, each having blocked an end of the culvert with their bodies. Most of their injuries were superficial and wouldn't need much more than a good cleaning, but a few were deep enough to need stitches.

"My wife first, Doc," the man asked, holding his wife in his arms.

Aren smiled at the man's love for his family. "I'm a veterinarian, actually. I can numb these cuts and get them stitched for you, or you can wait for emergency services to get into town." Aren gently pulled shards of glass from the woman's arm.

"I know who you are, and I appreciate your help. Please, get her sewn up. It doesn't look like we'll have help anytime soon." The man looked around at the destruction, and his wife nodded in agreement.

Another man ran up wearing an old, weathered John Deere ball cap. "The police station and the fire house are GONE!" He was breathing heavily. "There's a police car buried in what's left of a house, but we haven't been able to find any of the officers. Both of the fire trucks and the ambulance are scattered around. The firehouse is just gone!"

Aren looked up at him. "See if you can find a metal pipe and bang it on the floor. Listen to see if you hear a response. They may be trapped in the basement. If they are, try to move what's trapping them, and then come and get us if you can't." She knew the best way to keep people from panicking was to give them something worthwhile to do. The big-bellied man ran up carrying two gallons of water.

"I found these and some more over at the convenience store. How they survived I'll never know, but there's a few cases of them still boxed up neat as could be in what I'm guessin' was the storeroom. The store's gone, but the water was just a' sitting there." He handed the bottled water to Carol.

"Thank you. Carol, would you open one of them for me? It'll sting a lot less than this alcohol." Aren smiled at the man, who knelt to watch Aren work.

She flushed out the wounds with a five-to-one mix of water and Betadine solution before drawing a bit of lidocaine into a syringe.

"Are you allergic to any medications?" Aren asked the woman. She shook her head. "This will numb your cuts so I can stitch them. It's lidocaine, just like they use in the hospitals, okay?" Aren explained.

The woman nodded, wincing a bit as Aren injected the solution into the few cuts that needed stitches.

"Okay, let's give that a second to numb up before I clean out those cuts with a disinfectant. Then we'll have you sewn up like new." Aren pulled out a suture needle. As she stitched the woman's forehead, she explained, "These sutures will dissolve in about ten days. Just keep it clean and covered. Once things are cleared out around here a bit, I'd have your doctor take a look just to make sure there's no infection. Conditions like this don't make for a sterile working environment."

"Thank you. I know none of us around here have been too kind to you, yet here you are helping." The husband looked suitably embarrassed.

"I recognize you two from the farmer's market. You're out there all the time buying goodies." Aren smiled.

Aren's heart hammered in her chest. It was the first time she'd sutured since Kentucky. She kept the supplies up to date, but hadn't used her skills since that fateful night four years ago. She found herself praying her hand stayed steady and she was able to see in the dimming light.

CHAPTER FORTY-ONE

Darkness quickly swept across the small town. Someone brought a generator to the street. Several men worked together to clear off a section of road to be used as a triage unit until emergency service vehicles could get into town. People started to appear with halogen lights from their garages or lanterns from their root cellars to hang for lighting. A few showed up with cots and set them up out in the open area. Those with injuries sat on the curb waiting for their turn. Maggie had walked Wyatt and Doc over to a hand pump well in the park to get some much-needed water and grass.

"Ok, we'll need to see that lady next. We have limited time to suture so all the deep wounds are first priority unless someone passes out or has a broken bone, though I have yet to see any injuries that bad." Aren naturally took charge of her area.

The man wearing the John Deere ball cap came into the tent helping a police officer stay steady on his feet. The officer gladly took a cot offered to him. Aren rushed over to the man in the cap.

"Did you free everyone trapped in the station house?" she asked.

"Yeah, I think we got 'em all. Some of the other fellas are helping more folks over here. The guys stuck in the firehouse are headed over too," he said, taking his cap off and scratching the sweaty, stubbly hair on his head.

"Do you think you can take a couple of people and find me some more sterile gauze or maxi pads still sealed in the wrappers, really anything sterile that I can use to cover up some of these wounds? I'm running low on supplies. I'd also like more syringes and twenty-gauge needles if you can find them and something to use for sutures. Who knew we had so much glass in this town!" Aren ran her hand through her hair, wiping away the sweat.

"You got it, need anything else, Doc?" he asked, returning his ball cap to his head.

"If you can find me a couple of cups of coffee, I'll be forever grateful! One with cream and sugar if at all possible," she said, smiling.

The man hollered for a couple of his buddies and left to find Aren's list of supplies. She looked down at the police officer, who looked back at her with eyes that weren't quite right.

"Carol, could you bring me a pen light?" Aren asked, kneeling beside the officer as more uniformed men hobbled in.

Aren lifted each of his eyelids and used a pen light to check the retraction of his pupils. They were dilated and slow to respond to the light. His skin color was especially pale, and his hand was cold and clammy.

"Were you trapped, Officer?" Aren asked him.

"I, I don't know." He continued to look at her, dazed.

Aren took her pen light and traced the outline of his body. He had all the signs of having lost a lot of blood. His pulse was weak.

"I'm going to have you turn onto your side a bit, okay? Do you feel pain anywhere?" Aren asked.

"What about my stitches?" the lady sitting next to the officer asked.

"He's in shock and could die if I don't figure out where he's bleeding from. Your stitches will wait a few more minutes!" Aren had no time for prima donnas.

She ran her hand over the officer and found blood. His right thigh was sticky and wet.

"I'm going to have to roll you over."

Carol helped Aren roll him over on his stomach. The back of his pant leg was soaked with blood. Using her knife, she cut the pants open to reveal a deep gash from his inner thigh, just above his knee. Carol had the water ready but Aren held up her hand to stop her. She dug into the backpack and pulled out a roll of Coflex. She unwound a good portion of it and rolled it between her palms until it was more like a shoestring than a flat bandage. Aren wrapped it around the officer's leg and tied it snugly. Next, she reached for a stout branch lying on the concrete beside her. She placed the branch beneath the tied bandage and began to twist, cutting off the circulation in his leg. The man screamed in pain and Aren found herself wishing county help would arrive quickly. She wasn't prepared to help this man in dim lighting with one weak eye, nor could she handle another death on her conscience.

"At the bottom of my bag there's a bag of saline wrapped in a hand towel," Aren said to Carol, trying to hide the fear she felt.

Carol handed her the bag of saline.

"Can you help me roll him onto his back again? I need to start an IV."

Aren and Carol worked together to get the man on his back again.

"Carol, could you hold this while I get the line started? His pulse isn't good." Aren rubbed her eye and tried to focus on his arm in the dim lighting. She struggled to locate a vein even with the pressure band. She closed her eyes, adjusting to total darkness and then opened them hoping to see something. *Found one!* She inserted a needle into the man's arm and affixed the tubing to the plastic on the back of the needle after it was taped into place. She broke the seal in the tubing allowing the saline to flow and then adjusted the drip to an appropriate volume.

"Can anyone check to see if help is arriving? This man needs more than I can do for him." Aren looked down at the officer. His pulse was becoming stronger.

"What's your name, Officer?" Aren asked.

"Murph, Thomas Murphy," the officer mumbled.

"You hang in there, Murph. Stay with me until help arrives, okay?" Aren brushed back his sweat soaked hair.

"Emergency services are coming! I see the lights," someone called out.

"Hang on, Murph. Help is coming, okay?" Aren held his hand.

Aren reached for Carol with her free hand and was grateful when Carol squeezed back and sat at her side. It had been a long evening. Her medical training had kicked in, and she was grateful for that, but she couldn't deny the relief she felt when the professionals arrived.

CHAPTER FORTY-TWO

The rain finally began to let up well into the night. More of the town's population gathered in the makeshift medical center. Most wanted nothing more than to be with people they knew. A few barrels were brought out into the street and filled with wood for warmth and light. Children of all ages were out there with sticks from the trees roasting marshmallows and talking about what they were doing when the tornado hit.

Aren and Carol continued to work through the night, helping where they could. Once everyone's wounds were tended to, they checked on their pain and inspected the wounds for any sign of infection. At some point in the night, a woman approach Aren and Carol offering them something to eat. Hunger hadn't crossed Carol's mind until she smelled the hot soup and biscuits. They graciously accepted, sitting down on the concrete to enjoy the snack.

Many of the uninjured in town began to scour up cans of soup, stew, and chili. Pretty soon everyone was snacking heartily on food in a surreal community picnic. Some of the kids brought out Bluetooth speakers, streaming music and then entertained everyone for some time with dancing and goofing around.

Carol accepted a cup of coffee from a lady she recognized from the library. She found a quiet spot on a sidewalk bench that somehow survived the storm and watched the flames dance in the barrels. The adrenaline from the evening was wearing off, leaving her tired and sore. She looked around to see that everyone had come together to help one another, all differences set aside, even Aren, especially Aren, but then, that was who she was. Carol knew that about her now.

"Mind if I join you?" Maggie's voice pulled Carol from her thoughts.

"Please." Carol skootched over and patted the bench seat.

"I wanted to thank you. You two sure saved my bacon tonight."

"It was all Aren. I have yet to find something she can't excel at. She's amazing." Carol watched Aren talking to the medical team.

"Oh, you have a lot more to do with it than you give yourself credit for. She has her weaknesses, you know it as well as I do. She'd long ago given up, shut down. I saw it happening and could do nothing to stop it. She needed you in her life. You brought her back."

"I needed her too, Maggie. I was so lost when I came out here to visit. My life was turned completely upside down after that storm and she was right there, in every sense of the word, she was there." Carol sipped her coffee.

"Are you still just visiting or are you here to stay?" Maggie asked.

"This is home. I can't imagine my life without her." Carol smiled when she saw Aren headed in their direction.

"I can't tell you how happy that makes me." Maggie squeezed Carol's hand.

"Oh, where'd you find coffee?" Aren asked, standing in front of the bench.

"Don't worry, I managed to snag one for you too, minus the cream and sugar." Carol held up a small insulated cup. "It might be cold."

"You spoil me." Aren accepted the cup and tipped it back, downing the contents in one gulp.

"Aren, here, take my seat." Maggie stood and pulled Aren into a tight hug. "Thank you for checking on me and pulling me out. I love you, kiddo."

"I love you too, Maggie. Would you like to stay out at the farm while the store's rebuilt?" Aren asked.

"Thank you for the offer, but Deb beat you to it." Maggie stepped back looking from Carol to Aren. "We've been spending a little time together lately. I will take you gals up on that dinner that you promised me though. I'm excited to see the changes you've made to the house."

"Deb, huh? Is she—" Aren raised her eyebrows.

"Who knows? We shall see." Maggie smiled.

The sun was peeking above the tree line in the eastern sky. Carol looked around. "Where's Wyatt and Doc? They didn't bolt, did they?"

"No, no, not a bit. I used your rope and made them a small corral in the park over there. They have grass to munch on and a big ol' bucket of water. Their tack is on a picnic table next to their new pen, covered with some plastic I found." Maggie smiled.

"Well, we should get going. I swear I hear the cows bellowing from here." Aren hoisted her pack up.

"I'll walk you two over," Maggie said.

Wyatt and Doc were lying quietly in the moist morning grass. Wyatt stood when he noticed them approaching. His ears perked up and he nickered loudly, walking to the rope closest to Aren.

"Hey, big fella, you did a good job last night," Aren said, hugging the massive horse.

"Girls! Girls!"

Carol turned, looking for the source of the voice.

The man with the John Deere cap made his way across the grass. "I'm glad you gals are still here, I wanted to say thank you for all your help last night. I swear you were sent by the angels!"

"That's nice of you to say," Aren said. "My name is Aren Jacobs and this is Carol Matthews, what's yours? I'd hate to keep calling you 'the guy with the John Deere cap.'"

The man laughed before sticking his hand out toward Aren. "Doug McMichael, I'm the mayor of our little town."

"Mayor? I thought Kirk—"

"He retired, moved to Florida a few years ago. I was elected his replacement." Doug smiled.

"Well, congratulations. I'm sorry, I don't get off the farm much," Aren said.

"We're all sure glad you came in last night. Thanks again for all your help. I don't think ol' Murph would have made it without you two. From what I hear, he should make a full recovery. They have him at the hospital working on that leg."

Doug looked at Carol. "It was your aunt and uncle who died in that last storm, wasn't it? Damn shame, they were good folks. I see it runs in the family. You no sooner heal from that and then chase this storm in to help us. Glad to hear you accepted the job over at the library."

"Thank you. It's kind of you to say," Carol said.

Doug turned to Aren. "Thank you for helping out the community. I know you've had a tough go if it over the years. I just wanted you to know how much we appreciate you helping out." Doug turned and looked at the sun, then looked back at Aren, "Don't know that I've ever seen you without your sunglasses on. Bet that sun's bright in your good eye." He reached into his shirt pocket and pulled out a pair of aviator sunglasses, handing them to Aren. "You can use these if you'd like."

Aren slid the sunglasses on. "Thanks, that helps more than you know."

"Happy to do something to show our appreciation." Doug smiled sweetly. "Well, anyway, thank you both. Have a safe ride home."

Maggie turned to face Carol and Aren. "Look at you two, schmoozing with the mayor. Cowgirl, your image is blown," she said, wrapping her arms around their shoulders.

"Keep it up, old woman." Aren pulled the plastic off the tack and reached for the halters.

Carol took a second to look around. Aren and Maggie laughing, people still milling around, arm in arm. This was home. She was part of a community.

CHAPTER FORTY-THREE

Carol rode home in silence, completely exhausted. She wasn't entirely sure she hadn't fallen asleep for a bit on Doc's back. They turned the horses out to pasture and made quick work of the morning chores, eager to get out of their sweaty and mud-soaked clothes. Carol took Aren's hand and led her up to the loft. There was something she had to do first, before a shower and before sleep. There was so much she wanted to say, so much she was ready to say.

"Aren, did you want to try to get a few hours of sleep?" Carol asked.

"I'd love to, but if I do, I'll never sleep tonight, and besides, I'm too keyed up. I'm thinking coffee and a shower." Aren picked up the coffee pot.

"Could we talk for a minute first?" Carol asked, taking the coffee pot out of Aren's hands and setting it back on the counter. She tugged at Aren's hand. "Come sit with me."

Carol pulled Aren over to the Adirondack loveseat. Aren sat down and looked up at Carol, her eyes full of concern.

"Are you leaving? Is it all too much?" Aren's voice barely a whisper.

Carol knelt in front of Aren and touched her cheek. "God, you're adorable, even with mud all over your face and chunks stuck in your hair, you're sexy as hell." Carol reached for Aren's hands.

"You didn't answer the question. Are you leaving, Carol? Please, just tell me." Aren's voice cracked with emotion.

"No, I'm not leaving. It's not too much, but it's not enough, either."

"I don't understand. What do you mean?" Aren sat forward.

"Down at the pool, you asked me to tell you when I've decided what I want, where I want to call home. We've taken the time and have gotten to know each other, and the more I learn about you the more I know exactly what I want." She brushed hair away from Aren's eyes. "What I want is you, Aren. You're home. The storm last night brought everything into focus for me. I trust you. I worry about you, your safety, every emotion you have. I care about you, but more than that, I love you. I have fallen completely head over heels in love with you. I don't care where we live, the loft, the house or somewhere entirely different. I just want to be with you. I'm hoping it's something you want too." A tear trickled down Aren's cheek and Carol reached up and brushed it away with her thumb. "Aren't you going to say anything?"

"You love me? I'm home? You choose me? I've never wanted to hear something as much as I've wanted to hear those words from your lips. I've been so scared that our time was almost up, that they'd finish your house and you'd move on. Oh, Carol, I love you too. I want a life with you. I'm so completely in love with you. I catch myself daydreaming about the future, about what comes next, and you're right there, such a part of everything I imagine. I love who you are, absolutely everything about who you are. I love your sense of humor and the way you look at life. I love how you want to know everything about everything. I love how you can say so much with just a look, just an expression. I can't remember ever feeling so happy, so excited."

Carol leaned forward, gently touching Aren's lips with her own. She wrapped her arms around Aren's shoulders and pulled her in close. Their lips parted, and when their tongues touched, Carol wasn't sure which one of them moaned, maybe they both had. Either way, their kiss instantly intensified. Aren stood and suddenly Carol was cradled in her arms, and their lips never lost contact. Carol heard a door close and she pulled away from the kiss. They were in the bathroom. She blinked as if coming out of a spell and looked at Aren.

"I want to take you to bed, but we need a shower first." Aren lowered Carol to her feet.

She knelt down, unlaced Carol's boots, and slipped them off one at a time and then her socks. Carol closed her eyes and enjoyed the feeling of Aren's hands unbuttoning her jeans and lowering the zipper. Her breath was hot on Carol's skin and then her lips were even hotter, kissing her just above the panty line. Aren traced a path of kisses across her stomach all the while her hands worked on sliding Carol's jeans and panties to the floor and then her lips were on Carol's inner thigh.

"Shower." Carol's voice caught. Aren's tongue barely touched her clit. "Before I can't stop." Carol's legs were becoming weak.

Aren stood and their eyes met briefly before her shirt was lifted up between them. Carol had heard of smoldering eyes though she never experienced anything like what she just saw in Aren's eyes. The desire in her gaze sent shivers throughout Carol's body. Yes, she felt it too, that same insatiable need. There were still far too many clothes between them. She reached behind herself and unclasped her bra, allowing it to fall to the floor.

Standing in front of Aren completely naked, Carol reached for the button of her jeans and pulled it free. She put her hands on Aren's hips and slowly ran her fingers up the sides of Aren's stomach before lifting her shirt over her head. She lifted the sports bra over Aren's breasts and up her extended arms. She left it at her elbows, bending down to take Aren's nipple into her mouth. Aren moaned and the bra flew somewhere in the bathroom before her fingers dug into Carol's hair. Carol put her hands on Aren's hips again and slid the jeans and underwear down as far as she could while still paying attention to Aren's nipple with her tongue. She worked her way down Aren's stomach pushing the jeans farther down as she explored and then reached for one of Aren's boots, but ran her hands up the inside of Aren's legs instead. She knew how wet Aren would be and she wanted to feel her with her tongue. She slid her fingers between Aren's thighs, and the moment Aren spread her legs apart slightly, Carol teased her with the tip of her tongue.

"Boots off...shower." Aren's words weren't much more than gulps of air.

Carol had to force herself to stop. She wanted to bring Aren to the edge right there against the wall with her legs tangled up in a pair of jeans. She pulled Aren's boots off and helped her out of her socks before following Aren into the shower.

The water was hot and their kiss was hotter. They lathered each other up, all the while kissing. Carol let Aren pivot her around beneath the running water. She leaned her head back beneath the spray and closed her eyes, letting the soap and water wash away the previous day. She felt Aren's hand in her hair and then felt Aren's lips on her neck, teasing her with kisses and nibbles. It all felt so good. Aren's touch moved lower, her hands cupping Carol's breasts, her thumbs teasing Carol's nipples, and then she pulled away.

Aren turned Carol around again, the water spraying her neck, her breasts. She kissed the back of her neck and down her spine. Aren crouched down behind Carol and pulled on Carol's hips until she was sitting on Aren's thighs. She felt Aren's lips on her neck, her hands exploring her sides, exploring her breasts, and then both hands wrapping around her and dropping down between her legs. Carol leaned back into Aren and spread her legs open wide. She craved Aren's touch and needed to feel Aren inside her. Carol leaned her head back and closed her eyes. The hot water spraying all over her body along with Aren's touch created a sensory overload where everything tingled. She could feel Aren's breath in her ear and felt her fingers explore between her legs. Carol pushed her hips into Aren's fingers and moaned loudly when Aren held her hand firm and pushed her fingers deep inside. It was exactly what she craved. She felt Aren's teeth graze her shoulder and then her breath was hot on Carol's neck. Carol's pace picked up, as her need became almost unbearable. Fireworks built up inside, the kind of orgasm that leaves you with no dignity. Carol rocked and thrust herself into Aren's hands, and she moaned and cried out as an orgasm consumed her. She clamped her legs shut, trapping Aren's fingers in place. She convulsed and quivered with the aftershocks, her hand tightly gripping Aren's thighs.

"Holy fuck," Carol whispered, releasing her hold on Aren's hands with her legs.

Aren wrapped her arms around Carol and just held her in her lap for a moment.

"Ah, shit. The water's getting cold." Carol stood up quickly and helped pull Aren to her feet.

"Go, grab a towel, warm up. I have to rinse really quick." Aren stepped into the cold spray. "Whoa, that's freezing!"

Carol stood on the bathmat, an oversized bath towel wrapped around her. She opened her arms and invited Aren to share her warmth when she stepped out of the shower.

"Oh, that's more like it." Aren wrapped her arms around Carol inside the towel.

"Bed. I'm not done with you yet." Carol backed out of the bathroom, holding Aren tightly in her arms. She walked Aren backward toward the bed.

She playfully pushed Aren down onto the bed and then threw the towel to the side before climbing on top of her. She worked her way down the bed until Aren was lying naked before her. She bent over and kissed Aren's shins, her knees, urging her legs apart. Carol moved up her body, kissing her inner thigh, her hips, and then her stomach. She crawled up Aren's body, pushing her hips between Aren's legs. She moved her hips in tiny circles until Aren moaned and dug her fingernails into Carol's ass, pulling her tightly against her.

Carol leaned down and kissed Aren with such passion that her body was responding again before she'd fully recovered. She worked her way back down Aren's body, kissing her neck and then taking a nipple in her mouth. Aren buried her fingers in Carol's hair when she flicked her nipple with the tip of her tongue before sucking it back into her mouth. She looked up in time to see Aren throw her head back into the pillow and let out a long moan. Carol worked her way down Aren's body, kissing her stomach and her hips. She moved down and kissed Aren's inner thigh and received another moan. Carol could no longer resist. She lowered herself just as Aren pushed up into her. Carol swirled her tongue around Aren's clit and then sucked it into her mouth and stroked it with her tongue.

Aren's fingers buried in her hair, holding Carol close. Her moans grew louder with each breath and faster with each flick of Carol's tongue. Carol trailed her fingers up Aren's leg, teasing her with her touch.

"Yes." Aren lifted into her and rocked her hips.

Carol slipped two fingers inside and flicked Aren's clit with her tongue. Aren rocked her hips faster, and Carol could feel her tightening, feel her legs begin to quiver. All of a sudden, Aren called out and reached for Carol while moving her hips in tiny circles. Her legs closing around Carol's head, holding her in place. Carol flicked her tongue once more, holding it there and circling.

"Oh, Carol," Aren called out and then pulled Carol up her body, wrapping her legs around Carol's hips and holding her close. Carol laid her head on Aren's chest, listening to her ragged breaths and pounding heart.

"I love you, Aren."

"I will never get tired of hearing that." Aren kissed Carol's forehead. "I love you too."

Chapter Forty-four

Aren caught herself singing along with the music drifting in from the kitchen. She looked at herself in the mirror and nodded her approval. Her white button-down shirt was crisply ironed and tucked neatly into black jeans and secured with a black belt. The dark gray wool vest matched her dress boots perfectly. Not half bad, if she did say so herself. She clicked the light off and made her way toward the kitchen.

Carol was dancing her way around the dining room table, adjusting each place setting until it was perfect. She looked absolutely stunning in her dark green corduroy dress. Her hair was tucked back behind her ears just like it had been that first night that she'd cooked dinner for Aren. The diamond earrings caught the light from the candles in the center of the table. The sight of her swaying to the music took Aren's breath away.

She walked up behind Carol just as a slow song started to play. "Excuse me, beautiful, may I have this dance?"

Carol spun around, her eyes sparkling, and accepted Aren's hand. She stepped in close and draped her arms over Aren's shoulders. Aren inhaled deeply, enjoying the sweet floral scent that was Carol's perfume of choice. She loved the way she'd catch a hint of the fragrance whenever she walked into the house. She dropped her hands low on Carol's back, enjoying how her body felt as she swayed to the music.

"You look sexy as hell. How long do we have before everyone arrives?" Carol leaned forward a bit and tugged on Aren's earlobe gently with her teeth.

Aren felt a shiver course throughout her body. "Not long enough, I'm afraid."

The doorbell sounded just as Aren spun Carol away from her. She spun her back in close and kissed her passionately. "That will have to hold you over for a couple of hours." Aren winked and then turned toward the front door.

"Tease!" Carol playfully pushed on Aren's shoulder.

"Happy Thanksgiving!" Maggie and Deb said simultaneously.

"Happy Thanksgiving, come on inside. Let me take your coats." Aren stepped back and opened the door wide.

"I know you said not to bring anything, but I also know you know better, so here's an apple pie, a cherry pie, and some apple cider from the orchard. It's the last of the season, and I can't get enough of that stuff." Maggie offered Aren the boxes before slipping out of her coat.

"I couldn't stop her, sorry, Aren." Deb laughed.

"That's okay, it just means you two will have to stay all week in order to help us eat all of this food." Carol stepped into the foyer with outreached arms. "Happy Thanksgiving, you two." She hugged each of them.

The doorbell chimed again just as Aren was hanging up the coats.

"That will be Gail and Valerie from the library." Carol made her way to the door.

More Thanksgiving greetings erupted in the foyer where Aren accepted coats and Carol accepted a couple more additions to the menu.

"Thank you both for inviting us. The holidays can be so lonely," Valerie said.

"Come on inside, everything is ready. We're happy you're here." Aren followed the group into the kitchen.

"Hi, Maggie, hi, Deb. Maggie, how's the hardware store coming along?" Gail asked.

"It's almost ready to reopen. The crew has been amazing. They expect I can open sometime next week."

"That's great news," Aren said, looking up from her task of carving the ham.

"Hey, Carol, I didn't see a sign across the street when we pulled in. Did you sell the house?" Deb picked an olive off the tray and popped it in her mouth.

"Yes, we did. It closed a couple of weeks ago. The new owners seem nice enough." Carol pulled a casserole dish from the oven.

"She and Aren made a substantial donation to the library. Valerie's been ordering like crazy. We'll be able to fill the two new stacks with all of the books that are arriving," Gail said.

"I supported the idea, but the donation was all Carol. She deserves the credit." Aren enjoyed being part of the conversation. The game night they had hosted a few weeks earlier had much the same feel. Light, honest, and carefree conversations. Aren found herself looking forward to the get-togethers.

"New furniture and donations to the library, it's like you're rolling in the dough." Maggie pulled up a stool and joined the conversation.

"We needed some furniture that was ours and Aren has done so much. It felt good to be able to contribute to our home. The same with the library, some of those books were falling apart. I loved being able to contribute to the community. I think Aunt Suzie and Uncle Frank would have approved."

"I think it's wonderful. Your home is so beautiful! Game night last week was a blast. You two are the best hostesses," Valerie said.

"The table is set if you lovely ladies would migrate to the dining room." Aren carried the platter of ham and turkey.

Aren watched the group settle at the table. It was the first holiday in years where she felt surrounded by love and friendship. So much had changed in the past six months and she was so grateful to Carol for turning her world upside down and making all of this possible. Somewhere, in those six months, she found peace, happiness, and an unbelievable love.

"I'd like to say something." Aren stood up, holding her glass of cider in the air. "This year, it feels like Thanksgiving is special again. I have an amazing woman at my side who I love with all of my heart, and a table full of friends to share new experiences with. I treasure each of you, thank you all for being in our life. It means the world to me. Happy Thanksgiving." She swallowed against the lump of sweet emotions that rose with the sentiment. She'd never dreamed life could be so beautiful.

"Thank *you*, for being in our lives. Happy Thanksgiving!" Maggie raised her glass.

"Happy Thanksgiving!" Everyone around the table raised their glass.

The rest of the night was full of love and laughter, and as she held Carol in the early hours of the morning, she knew life was finally exactly what it should be.

About the Author

A vivid imagination spurred Nance Sparks's desire to write lesbian romance. People watching evolves into a storyline. Taking in the flailing arms of two strangers on the far side of the street creates two characters with personalities full of dimension. Observe as another person walks by, spinning in a circle to take it all in, and there's the plot twist. Life is full of stories waiting to be told. Nance enjoys bringing these stories to life.

Nance lives in south central Wisconsin with her spouse. Her passion for photography, homesteading, hiking, gardening, and most anything outdoors comes through in her stories. When the sun is out and the sky is blue, especially during the golden hour, Nance can be found on the Wisconsin River with a camera in hand, capturing shots of large birds in flight.

Books Available from Bold Strokes Books

A Woman to Treasure by Ali Vali. An ancient scroll isn't the only treasure Levi Montbard finds as she starts her hunt for the truth—all she has to do is prove to Yasmine Hassani that there's more to her than an adventurous soul. (978-1-63555-890-6)

Before. After. Always. by Morgan Lee Miller. Still reeling from her tragic past, Eliza Walsh has sworn off taking risks, until Blake Navarro turns her world right-side up, making her question if falling in love again is worth it. (978-1-63555-845-6)

Bet the Farm by Fiona Riley. Lauren Calloway's luxury real estate sale of the century comes to a screeching halt when dairy farm heiress, and one-night stand, Thea Boudreaux calls her bluff. (978-1-63555-731-2)

Cowgirl by Nance Sparks. The last thing Aren expects is to fall for Carol. Sharing her home is one thing, but sharing her heart means sharing the demons in her past and risking everything to keep Carol safe. (978-1-63555-877-7)

Give In to Me by Elle Spencer. Gabriela Talbot never expected to sleep with her favorite author—certainly not after the scathing review she'd given Whitney Ainsworth's latest book. (978-1-63555-910-1)

Hidden Dreams by Shelley Thrasher. A lethal virus and its resulting vision send Texan Barbara Allan and her lovely guide, Dara, on a journey up Cambodia's Mekong River in search of Barbara's mother's mystifying past. (978-1-63555-856-2)

In the Spotlight by Lesley Davis. For actresses Cole Calder and Eris Whyte, their chance at love runs out fast when a fan's adoration turns to obsession. (978-1-63555-926-2)

Origins by Jen Jensen. Jamis Bachman is pulled into a dangerous mystery that becomes personal when she learns the truth of her origins as a ghost hunter. (978-1-63555-837-1)

Pursuit: A Victorian Entertainment by Felice Picano. An intelligent, handsome, ruthlessly ambitious young man who rose from the slums to become the right-hand man of the Lord Exchequer of England will stop at nothing as he pursues his Lord's vanished wife across Continental Europe. (978-1-63555-870-8)

Unrivaled by Radclyffe. Zoey Cohen will never accept second place in matters of the heart, even when her rival is a career, and Declan Black has nothing left to give of herself or her heart. (978-1-63679-013-8)

A Fae Tale by Genevieve McCluer. Dovana comes to terms with her changing feelings for her lifelong best friend and fae, Roze. (978-1-63555-918-7)

Accidental Desperados by Lee Lynch. Life is clobbering Berry, Jaudon, and their long romance. The arrival of directionless baby dyke MJ doesn't help. Can they find their passion again—and keep it? (978-1-63555-482-3)

Always Believe by Aimée. Greyson Walsden is pursuing ordination as an Anglican priest. Angela Arlingham doesn't believe in God. Do they follow their vocation or their hearts? (978-1-63555-912-5)

Best of the Wrong Reasons by Sander Santiago. For Fin Ness and Orion Starr, it takes a funeral to remind them that love is worth living for. (978-1-63555-867-8)

Courage by Jesse J. Thoma. No matter how often Natasha Parsons and Tommy Finch clash on the job, an undeniable attraction simmers just beneath the surface. Can they find the courage to change so love has room to grow? (978-1-63555-802-9)

I Am Chris by R Kent. There's one saving grace to losing everything and moving away. Nobody knows her as Chrissy Taylor. Now Chris can live who he truly is. (978-1-63555-904-0)

The Princess and the Odium by Sam Ledel. Jastyn and Princess Aurelia return to Venostes and join their families in a battle against the dark force to take back their homeland for a chance at a better tomorrow. (978-1-63555-894-4)

The Queen Has a Cold by Jane Kolven. What happens when the heir to the throne isn't a prince or a princess? (978-1-63555-878-4)

The Secret Poet by Georgia Beers. Agreeing to help her brother woo Zoe Blake seemed like a good idea to Morgan Thompson at first...until she realizes she's actually wooing Zoe for herself... (978-1-63555-858-6)

You Again by Aurora Rey. For high school sweethearts Kate Cormier and Sutton Guidry, the second chance might be the only one that matters. (978-1-63555-791-6)

Coming to Life on South High by Lee Patton. Twenty-one-year-old gay virgin Gabe Rafferty's first adult decade unfolds as an unpredictable journey into sex, love, and livelihood. (978-1-63555-906-4)

Love's Falling Star by B.D. Grayson. For country music megastar Lochlan Paige, can love conquer her fear of losing the one thing she's worked so hard to protect? (978-1-63555-873-9)

Love's Truth by C.A. Popovich. Can Lynette and Barb make love work when unhealed wounds of betrayed trust and a secret could change everything? (978-1-63555-755-8)

Next Exit Home by Dena Blake. Home may be where the heart is, but for Harper Sims and Addison Foster, is the journey back worth the pain? (978-1-63555-727-5)

Not Broken by Lyn Hemphill. Falling in love is hard enough—even more so for Rose who's carrying her ex's baby. (978-1-63555-869-2)

The Noble and the Nightingale by Barbara Ann Wright. Two women on opposite sides of empires at war risk all for a chance at love. (978-1-63555-812-8)

What a Tangled Web by Melissa Brayden. Clementine Monroe has the chance to buy the café she's managed for years, but Madison LeGrange swoops in and buys it first. Now Clementine is forced to work for the enemy and ignore her former crush. (978-1-63555-749-7)

A Far Better Thing by JD Wilburn. When needs of her family and wants of her heart clash, Cass Halliburton is faced with the ultimate sacrifice. (978-1-63555-834-0)

Body Language by Renee Roman. When Mika offers to provide Jen erotic tutoring, will sex drive them into a deeper relationship or tear them apart? (978-1-63555-800-5)

Carrie and Hope by Joy Argento. For Carrie and Hope loss brings them together but secrets and fear may tear them apart. (978-1-63555-827-2)

Death's Prelude by David S. Pederson. In this prequel to the Detective Heath Barrington Mystery series, Heath discovers that first love changes you forever and drives you to become the person you're destined to be. (978-1-63555-786-2)

Ice Queen by Gun Brooke. School counselor Aislin Kennedy wants to help standoffish CEO Susanna Durr and her troubled teenage daughter become closer—even if it means risking her own heart in the process. (978-1-63555-721-3)

Masquerade by Anne Shade. In 1925 Harlem, New York, a notorious gangster sets her sights on seducing Celine, and new lovers Dinah and Celine are forced to risk their hearts, and lives, for love. (978-1-63555-831-9)

Royal Family by Jenny Frame. Loss has defined both Clay's and Katya's lives, but guarding their hearts may prove to be the biggest heartbreak of all. (978-1-63555-745-9)

Share the Moon by Toni Logan. Three best friends, an inherited vineyard and a resident ghost come together for fun, romance and a touch of magic. (978-1-63555-844-9)

Spirit of the Law by Carsen Taite. Attorney Owen Lassiter will do almost anything to put a murderer behind bars, but can she get past her reluctance to rely on unconventional help from the alluring Summer Byrne and keep from falling in love in the process? (978-1-63555-766-4)

The Devil Incarnate by Ali Vali. Cain Casey has so much to live for, but enemies who lurk in the shadows threaten to unravel it all. (978-1-63555-534-9)

His Brother's Viscount by Stephanie Lake. Hector Somerville wants to rekindle his illicit love affair with Viscount Wentworth, but he must overcome one problem: Wentworth still loves Hector's brother. (978-1-63555-805-0)

Journey to Cash by Ashley Bartlett. Cash Braddock thought everything was great, but it looks like her history is about to become her right now. Which is a real bummer. (978-1-63555-464-9)

Liberty Bay by Karis Walsh. Wren Lindley's life is mired in tradition and untouched by trends until social media star Gina Strickland introduces an irresistible electricity into her off-the-grid world. (978-1-63555-816-6)

Scent by Kris Bryant. Nico Marshall has been burned by women in the past wanting her for her money. This time, she's determined to win Sophia Sweet over with her charm. (978-1-63555-780-0)

Shadows of Steel by Suzie Clarke. As their worlds collide and their choices come back to haunt them, Rachel and Claire must figure out how to stay together and most of all, stay alive. (978-1-63555-810-4)

The Clinch by Nicole Disney. Eden Bauer overcame a difficult past to become a world champion mixed martial artist, but now rising star and dreamy bad girl Brooklyn Shaw is a threat both to Eden's title and her heart. (978-1-63555-820-3)

The Last First Kiss by Julie Cannon. Kelly Newsome is so ready for a tropical island vacation, but she never expects to meet the woman who could give her her last first kiss. (978-1-63555-768-8)

The Mandolin Lunch by Missouri Vaun. Despite their immediate attraction, everything about Garet Allen says short-term, and Tess Hill refuses to consider anything less than forever. (978-1-63555-566-0)

Thor: Daughter of Asgard by Genevieve McCluer. When Hannah Olsen finds out she's the reincarnation of Thor, she's thrown into a world of magic and intrigue, unexpected attraction, and a mystery she's got to unravel. (978-1-63555-814-2)

Veterinary Technician by Nancy Wheelton. When a stable of horses is threatened Val and Ronnie must work together against the odds to save them, and maybe even themselves along the way. (978-1-63555-839-5)

BOLDSTROKESBOOKS.COM

Looking for your next great read?

Visit BOLDSTROKESBOOKS.COM
to browse our entire catalog of paperbacks, ebooks,
and audiobooks.

Want the first word on what's new?
Visit our website for event info,
author interviews, and blogs.

Subscribe to our free newsletter for sneak peeks,
new releases, plus first notice of promos
and daily bargains.

SIGN UP AT
BOLDSTROKESBOOKS.COM/signup

Bold Strokes Books
Quality and Diversity in LGBTQ Literature

Bold Strokes Books is an award-winning publisher
committed to quality and diversity in LGBTQ fiction.